D0063225

Dream Girl

Awakened

Dear Reader:

Sometimes you always want what you can't have, and for some, like the characters in *Dream Girl Awakened*, you can't have whom you desire. Such is the case of Aruba Dixon, who feens her best friend Victoria's husband, Winston. Aruba, married to a man who can't seem to hold down a job, constantly dreams of an ideal relationship with Winston, a wealthy prospect. Meanwhile, she is unaware that her own husband, James, whom she has put on the back burner, is actually being pursued by Tawatha, a single mother of four. No one is satisfied with what's waiting at home.

Imagine a novel where everyone is entangled in hopes to fulfill their own dreams. Stacy Campbell's debut project is complete with twists and turns and surprises. But like everything you do in the dark, you cannot hide it forever. Find out what her characters face as their eyes are opened to what's going on behind closed doors.

As always, thanks for supporting Strebor Books, where we strive to bring you the most groundbreaking, out-of-the-box literature in today's market. If you would like to contact me directly, feel free to email me at Zane@eroticanoir.com. You can also find me on Facebook @ AuthorZane and on Twitter @planetzane.

Blessings,

Zane

Zane
Publisher
Strebor Books International
www.simonandschuster.com/streborbooks

ZANE PRESENTS

Dream Girl
Awakened

A NOVEL

STACY CAMPBELL

SBI

STREBOR BOOKS
NEW YORK LONDON TORONTO SYDNEY

Strebor Books
P.O. Box 6505
Largo, MD 20792
http://www.streborbooks.com

ISBN 978-1-59309-457-7
ISBN 978-1-4516-9654-7 (ebook)
LCCN 2012951344

First Strebor Books trade paperback edition February 2013

Cover design: www.mariondesigns.com
Cover photograph: © Keith Saunders/Marion Designs

10 9 8 7 6 5 4 3 2

Manufactured in the United States of America

For information regarding special discounts for bulk purchases, please contact Simon & Schuster Special Sales at 1-866-506-1949 or business@simonandschuster.com

The Simon & Schuster Speakers Bureau can bring authors to your live event. For more information or to book an event, contact the Simon & Schuster Speakers Bureau at 1-866-248-3049 or visit our website at www.simonspeakers.com.

Acknowledgments

This book is dedicated to the four people who knew I had wings and could fly before I did:

Mattie Lawrence-4/19/1929-11/19/1997 (Mother)
Anthony Bernard Gilbert-10/12/1967-2/25/2002 (Cousin)
Brenda Hillard-8/5/1967-8/29/2003 (Cousin)
Roy Lawrence-3/19/1926-11/2/2012-(Father)

Putting finger to keyboard or pen to paper takes courage. Thank you God for everything and especially giving me the courage to use the gift of writing.

Mom, you didn't get a chance to see my writing dream come true, but you always chided me to stop wasting my time and my talents. This is to let you know I was listening. Thanks for being such a wonderful mother and virtuous woman. I miss you dearly.

To my dad, Mr. Roy Lawrence. I am writing this on the morning of your funeral. You will always be the King, the Emperor, the Man, and the best father a woman could ever have. Thanks for being my first male cheerleader, date, encourager, buddy, Chevy Truck shotgun partner, and all-around stand-up guy. Your eyes lit up when I told you I'd written a book. When I told you the writing game was now a game of sales, you grinned wider and said, "Baby, you 'gon sell them books." Your desire for all of your children to receive an education is why I read and write. And write. And write.

To my agent, Sara Camilli, Stephen Camilli, Zane, Charmaine Parker, Strebor Books, and the entire Dream Girl team. Without you, these acknowledgements wouldn't be possible. Thanks for taking a chance on an unknown writer. I appreciate the opportunity you've given me and plan to do my best to honor that chance.

To my husband, Hulian, daughter, Ylana, and son, Malik. I appreciate your love and support. The three of you make me feel I can achieve anything. How did I get blessed with the three of you?

My rock star siblings: Curtis Lawrence, Barbara Mapp, William Lawrence, Becky Lawrence, David Lawrence, and Lillie Lawrence. You have made every day on earth magical through our blood connection and so much more. I love each and every one of you more than words can express. To my nieces and nephews, Mark Anthony Adams, Vernon Lundy, Markina Mapp, Surece Mapp-Nunnally, Joy Mapp, Jerine Reynolds, Ronrico Woodard, Andrea Allen, Crystal Woodard, Antario Wilson, and Jason Lawrence. It's been amazing to grow up with each of you and see how strong and independent you all are. I love you. Cousin Amy Stanton, you complete the tribe. To my sisters-in-law, Darlene Lawrence, Lorraine Lawrence, Veronica Lawrence, and Latumba Campbell, I'm so glad we got to know each other through the gift of marriage.

To my extended family members and in-laws, the Stantons, Lawrences, and Campbells. Without you, I'd have no history, memories, or family.

The Indianapolis Crew: Rhonda Morgan Dix, Nikisha Mundy, Kimberly Wize, Jenice Myers, Mary Lee McClendon, Lisa Coffman, Maria Spicer-Walker, Anita Lauderdale-Woodson, Kara Batts, and Patricia Diawara. Thanks so much for your love, support, and all those nights at dinner that you introduced me as "our friend, the writer."

The Georgia Crew: Detrell Hawkins, Vickie Shorts, Antonio Bernard Lawrence, Victor Carroll, and Lillian Latrealle Smith. Your friendship throughout the years has been phenomenal. I'm glad we crossed paths. A special, come-on-over-here and gimme a big hug to Devetrice Conyers-Hinton. Not only are you a friend and a sister to me, you are a wonderful example of what it means to be an encourager. This book was written in one of the MANY beautiful, leather-bound journals you've gifted me over the years.

To my New Beginnings Fellowship Church family. Spiritual growth is achieved through teaching and the Word. No one does it better than Dr. James Anthony Jackson, Sr. My, how I've grown under your leadership, Dr. Jackson. I thank God for you and First Lady, Tara Cox Jackson. You have reminded me what it means to fellowship with others and I am so thankful that you continue to coax me out of my shell. I extend big hugs to the Multimedia Ministry team. Angela Collins-Cooper, Nicole Norwood, Anita Jones, Sandra Loyd, Tammi Kinchlow, Paulette Spicer, and Anthony Moore. You make ministry a joy and I love co-laboring with you.

To my UPS Family: Sheila Brown, Shayla Gardner, John Woodall, Katie Chapman, Cliff Laswell, Candice Brewer, Connie Mottram, Jeanine Walker, Jajuana Batts, and Andrea Johnson. You make coming to work easy. Not a day goes by that I don't appreciate your wisdom, guidance, and the teamwork we display. To my Trends International Publishing Family: All a girl needs to write a book is two fifteen-minute breaks and a thirty-minute lunch break. Thank you Sherry Gardiner, Carla Briggs, Karl Riley, Aurora Carillo, and Meegail Roberts for unwittingly giving me space and inspiration to write. A special thanks goes out to Mrs. Barbara Twyman-Gibson for all the prayers, pep talks and big sister support.

To the Hancock Central High School Class of 1987. We spent our formative years together and are still growing strong. I appreciate and love all of you and I pray we continue to grow in love and wisdom.

To all the writers along the way who've encouraged me, shared nuggets of wisdom, or simply said, "Stacy, shut up and write," I thank you. I can't name each of you, but I want to give a shout-out to Trisha R. Thomas, Cheri Paris Edwards (let's write that book together for real), Victoria Christopher Murray, Sonsyrea Tate-Montgomery, Parry Brown, Terry McMillan, Margaret Johnson-Hodge, Josette Dixon-Hall, Electa Rome Parks, Adrienne Thompson, Kimberla Lawson-Roby, Dee Stewart, Lolita Files, Bernice McFadden, Marissa Monteilh, Pamela Rice, Kuwana Haulsey, Dijorn Moss, Darryl Wimberly, Lutishia Lovely, Sandra Gould, Gigi Levangie-Grazer, Walter Mosley, and Richard Dry. Marita Golden, thank you for your excellent instruction. I have taken the lessons to heart.

To my fellow aspiring authors, keep writing and keep believing. It can happen for you, too. To all the boys and girls who lost friendships and possible lifelong connections due to grown folks' tomfoolery, this one's for you. If I've missed someone, please, please, please charge it to my head and not my heart.

Stacy

[1]
Owed to Myself

May 21, 2008

Aruba propped up the girls in a Miracle C-cup, checked the smooth, waxed bikini line in her thong, and released her shoulder-length hair from a barrette, proud she'd made an appointment at Aveda Fredericks to iron out her leonine mane of curls earlier in the day. Just as she slipped on her dress, Jeremiah called from the door, "Mommy, you smell good."

As she turned, she stopped mid-smile at the sight of Jeremiah perched atop James's shoulders.

"Yeah, Mah-mee, I haven't seen you this beautiful since—well, you're always beautiful. Are you trying to make me jealous?" asked James, hoping to elicit a smile. "Where you going looking so good?" James was careful not to offend her. He needed to get back in her corner, back into her accommodating thighs.

"Just a company function. Won't be out too late. One of us has to work in the morning. May I have five more minutes to get dressed? *Please.*"

James walked out the door with Jeremiah blowing kisses at Aruba. She balled her fists at James's back. *Ten years and this is the best I can do. Ten years of hanging my hopes on this man's dreams. Ten years of supporting him and he won't even keep a decent job. Was I that dumb in 1998 thinking James was the best I could do? It all ends tonight.*

Definitely! I have one year to accomplish my goal, to make things better for myself and my son. Mind-blowing sex can't make up for all I've endured with this man.

She shook her head in disgust as her mind drifted back two weeks. That Wednesday, James ambled into the great room, parked himself on the sectional, and sprinted into his usual discourse on the job market, the Edomites—his term for the oppressors—and how he never got a chance to shine. He grabbed a 40-ounce from the fridge and proclaimed, "Edomites always tryna keep a brotha down!"

She glared at him as he jumped up, then paced back and forth in the living room, his steel-toed boots leaving small tracks in the carpet.

"I'm glad I walked off that fucking site. Ain't no way in hell I'ma settle for fifteen dollars an hour under those conditions."

"You did what?" she shouted. She counted the cost of his latest job loss, then grew angrier. She knew she'd have some explaining to do since her Uncle Walstine had put in a good word for James at Hinton and Conyers Construction.

"You know how those Edomites do. Segregating *us* to the high, roofing positions while they let the young bloods, the young *white* bloods do the painting and drywalling."

She counted to ten, then remembered Jeremiah was still at Angels in Halos, near Indianapolis. "Maybe I'll discuss this when I get *our child* from day care!"

"Aruba, baby, I forgot about Jerry. Lemme go—"

"Forget it, James! I'll deal with you when I get back."

Aruba grabbed her keys, stormed out the house, and rushed to the center. As she weaved in and out of traffic on I-465, she tallied the twenty-five-dollar-per-minute late fee steadily accruing. Just as she approached the Allisonville Road exit, Mrs. Timmons, the day care director, rang her cell.

"Is everything okay, Aruba? Big meeting today?"

"Yes," she lied, hoping to stay in Mrs. Timmons's good graces. "I've been traveling my region, training for State Farm nonstop. Things have been hectic at the office."

"Not to worry, Aruba. I'm here with Jeremiah and he's playing with Lyric Austin. They're having a blast."

Aruba sighed, unsure of how she'd atone for yet another lie told to cover for James. Before she could exhale with relief, Uncle Walstine's name and number flashed on her caller ID. "Mrs. Timmons, I'm around the corner. See you soon." *Better get this over now.* She swapped from Mrs. Timmons to her uncle.

"Unk, how's it going?"

"You know damn well how it's going! Works-when-he-feels-like-it James just ruined my good name at Hinton and Conyers. I had two more *good* prospects lined up and he goes in there ranting and raving about the Edomites—and Hinton and Conyers are black folks!"

"Unk, I had no idea—"

"Save it. We told you that boy was no good when you brought him around. 'Bout the best thing you got outta that union was Jeremiah!"

"That's not fair, Uncle Walstine. I've been try—"

"Trying. Working like a dog to take care of that…" Walstine paused. "I'm just saying, baby girl, I'm tired of seeing you work so hard. You need to be in a relationship where you complement, not supplement."

"Thank you. I understand how you feel and I'm so sorry about what happened. I'll talk to James about it. I promise."

With that, they said good-byes. Aruba retrieved Jeremiah, went home, and chose to say only hello and good-bye to James for the next two weeks. His romantic overtures; yellow, long-stemmed roses; and candlelight, homemade dinners were met with no enthusiasm. The more she looked at James, the more she thought of Winston. She knew she couldn't give James the silent treatment tonight. She had to weave her web, lay a foundation for the new life she and Jeremiah would soon come to know.

Aruba decided tonight was perfect to take what she deserved—her friend Victoria's husband. After all, Victoria whined about Winston morning, noon, and night. Aruba mimicked Victoria's complaints as she applied makeup to her soft cheeks, compliments of an organic honey-almond facial.

"Aruba, Winston's never home."

"We've moved three times in four years with his practice and I'm tired."

"He only gives me a three-thousand-dollar allowance each month."

"You wouldn't understand unless you've walked a mile in my Manolos, Rube."

Aruba grunted at *that* statement and double-checked the night's game plan sprawled across the bed: MapQuest directions to the conference center where Winston would conduct a presentation on cardiovascular breakthroughs; Winston's favorite CDs—Glenn Jones's *Forever: Timeless R&B Classics*, Boney James's *Shine*, and Charles Hilton Brown's *Owed To Myself*—she had heard wafting from his home office; the last pay stub from James's fifth job in seven months; Winston's favorite perfume, Flowerbomb; photos of her son, Jeremiah, and Winston's daughter, Nicolette, at a Mocha Moms outing. Tonight she had bigger salmon to marinate and pan sear. In one swoop she tossed the plan in her oversized bag and threw on a trench coat. She exhaled deeply when James and Jeremiah reentered the room.

"I wanna come, Mommy," said Jeremiah. Aruba marveled at her three-year-old's obsession with following her.

"Mommy and Daddy will take you to Great Times this weekend. Okay?"

Jeremiah wiggled from James's shoulders as he reached for Aruba's arms. "Mommy and Daddy gonna talk this weekend?"

Embarrassed that her child had noticed the distance between them, Aruba hugged him, and said, "Yes, we're gonna have lots of fun. Pinkie promise."

Jeremiah wrapped his left pinkie finger with Aruba's, and said, "I'm happy. Daddy said you were in an itchy mood." Jeremiah's tendency to drop beginning letters saved yet another fight brewing between his parents.

James, sheepish and remorseful, chimed in, "You know how I get when I'm mad. I'm sorry."

Aruba waved him off without acknowledgment and headed to the garage. James and Jeremiah followed her, giggling and singing "Sesame Street."

Aruba faced James before she entered her SUV. "How 'bout this tune, James. Happy Birthday to me. Happy Birthday to me," Aruba sang and poked her chest.

James thwacked his forehead, embarrassed he'd forgotten her birthday.

"I was gonna get you a gift, but you know I'm a little light right now. I'll get you something soon. I promise."

James tried to lighten the mood as she started her vehicle. "Baby, I'm gonna get another job. I promise," he said, his eyes pleading, sincere.

She backed out of the garage into the driveway, waving to them both. She blew Jeremiah a quick kiss. *Yeah, you'll need a job when I'm done with you. I owe this to myself.*

[2]
Ready or Not, Here I Come

Aruba circled the Marten Hotel parking lot until she spotted Winston's Range Rover. According to Victoria, Winston wrapped up his speeches like clockwork. The Lilly Conference Center, housed within Marten, was the spot of many lectures and speeches Winston facilitated. He didn't mingle too long with colleagues and headed home when he wrapped up his talks because he wanted to respect his wife and marriage. Since his scheduled speaking time was seven-fifteen, Aruba anticipated he'd walk out the front door at approximately eight-twenty-two. That gave her enough time to swing around to the Half Price Books entrance, turn on her hazard lights, and wait for Winston to cruise by since she "accidentally" ran out of gas. She'd even taken care to leave her gas can home. No need to make his job easier. She had inroads to make. As she waited in the hotel parking lot, she received a nod from the heavens: raindrops. A few sprinkles multiplied, fell heavier, and relaxed her. *I couldn't have planned this any better.*

She leaned back, queued Glenn Jones in the CD player, and pondered her circumstances. She thought of Jeremiah and how much better off he'd be with Winston as his father. Vacations. A bigger house. Private school. Legitimate playdates and outings with Mocha Moms and the women she'd charmed in Victoria's neighborhood. As Glenn Jones gave Toni Braxton a run for her money belting out "Another Sad Love Song," she superimposed herself in Victoria's role. Aruba whipped out a note pad, scribbling out house rules for her new life: Greet Winston with a hug and a kiss each morning. Treat Alva, our nanny, with the utmost respect. Give Winston head and sex whenever he wants it, not just for procreation. Be frugal with our finances, so we can retire and travel. She continued scribbling, this time pronouncing her new name. Mrs. Winston Faulk. Mrs. Aruba Faulk. Aruba Aneece Faulk. She rolled the titles off her tongue respectively, settling on the first name. Mrs. Winston Faulk sounded sexier, glamorous. A hell of a lot better than Aruba Dixon.

"Mrs. James Dixon." She shuddered at the pronunciation of her married name, her pathetic reality. Not that she always felt that way. She still glowed at the memory of meeting James ten years ago. She'd just slit open a box of Cuisinart toasters in JCPenney's housewares department. She gazed at the towering display rack lacking Foreman Grills, quesadilla makers, and pizza stones. She dragged a stepladder from the corner, climbing up to make room for the just-arrived stock. As she descended the ladder, a rich, baritone voice below called out, "Excuse me, are you Kenya Moore?"

Aruba sighed at the tired line she received from men and women. It was true. She could be Kenya's twin. Same banging body. Same hazel-green eyes. Same smile that made men whip out their wallets and spend cash or swipe credit cards after Aruba convinced them their wife, girlfriend, significant other, or boyfriend just *had* to have the latest gadget in their kitchen. The same smile either stopped women in their tracks while spitting out the refrain *bitch*, or made them sidle next to her, and say, "My son in the military will be home on leave next week. Can I bring him in to meet you?"

Aruba steeled herself to face what she knew was an older gentleman. She formed the image in her mind: Dark. Short and stocky. Horn-rimmed glasses. Balding head. Hoodwinked, she turned to find a totally opposite vision: A dreadlocked god who stood at least six feet seven inches tall. He beckoned her to descend the ladder. He was a little too light for her taste, but handsome just the same. As she climbed down, she eyed the blue Nike warm-up suit that hinted of days spent at Gold's Gym. The white muscle shirt he wore accented six-pack abs. She got lost in those perfect white teeth, those blue-green eyes that danced. *Our kids would have gorgeous eyes.*

"What would a former Miss USA be doing in Penney's?" she asked, unable to mask her attraction to him.

"I was serious. You look—"

"Just like Kenya Moore. I get that often."

Not one to allow lapses in conversations, James continued, "I'd love to get my hands in your hair sometimes."

"Excuse me?"

"Everyone wants a stalker, right?" James smiled and handed Aruba a business card. "I'm a barber and stylist and I'm looking for new clients."

She eyed the card. "Wow, do you go around hitting on every woman in South Dekalb Mall?"

"Only the beautiful ones."

"Gee, thanks." Aruba turned to walk away as James grabbed her arm.

"Just kidding. Let's try this again. Hi, I'm James Dixon. And you are?"

She hesitated as he extended his hand. Something about his spirit made her smile. "Aruba Stanton."

"Really, I'm here because my moms sent me to get," he pulled a slip of paper from his pocket, "a Black and Decker Steamer. Ever since Mom's sugar was diagnosed, she's been steaming food, watching her weight and whatnot."

"Good for her. Several of my family members have diabetes and it's no joke."

Aruba moved the ladder aside and directed James toward the steamers. They chatted, exchanged pleasantries, life tidbits. James shared that he was from Atlanta, grew up in the Bankhead area, and had a younger brother, Marvin; an older sister, Teresa; and dreamed of owning a string of beauty salons one day. He knew he'd succeed because black men and women liked to look good. Aruba sweetened the conversation by adding she was from Harlem, Georgia, a junior at Clark-Atlanta University majoring in mathematics, and an only child. The pleasantries continued until a little old lady called out, "Miss, will you help me find a Wilton cake decorating kit?"

"So may I call you sometimes, Miss Aruba?"

"How 'bout you give me your number and I'll call you?"

"You gonna brush me off like that?" he joked. He asked for the business card again and scribbled a number on the back. "This is my home number and my cell. The number on the front of the card is the shop I work out of."

"Leaving no stone unturned, heh? I promise, I'll call," said Aruba, holding up the peace sign.

He watched her guide the older woman leaning on a cane to a different section of the department. Aruba waved one last time.

The thought of that wave lulled her back to the present. *I should have never called him.* Glenn Jones crooned, "Where is the Love?" She eyed her watch. Eight seventeen. She crept out of the hotel parking lot, drove down to the entrance of Half Price Books, stopping as she pressed on the hazard lights. She waited. Hoped. Wondered if the positioning was right. Whether he'd know it was her. Just as she thought she'd lost her mind, that her life with James had in fact created this lunacy attack, she noticed a shiny black Range Rover pass by, slow up, then cruise backward in her direction.

Showtime!

[3]
Cappuccino, Latte, or Me

Winston recognized the Honda Pilot and the neon bumper sticker immediately: *LOVE CONQUERS ALL*. A staunch advocate of marriage, he admired Aruba's long-suffering stance with James. As he backed up to be of assistance, his mind drifted to Victoria's pillow-talk about Aruba and James. He thought of those conversations as he wondered why Aruba was out in the rain alone. Thought of James's chronic unemployment, his quick temper, his disdain for the Edomites. Remembered the night Aruba and Jeremiah showed up at their doorstep, Aruba holding her bottom lip as blood trickled onto Jeremiah's face and their Travertine flooring, and how Victoria stopped Aruba in her tracks, running to and fro for towels, so the floor wouldn't be ruined. Aruba and Jeremiah slept in the basement that night as the family listened to Jeremiah cry for his daddy. Nicolette sauntered downstairs, gave Jeremiah a pillow and blanket, and they slept arm in arm. Winston, convinced Aruba and Jeremiah deserved a better life, offered financial assistance. Victoria snipped, "How's he ever going to be responsible if we bail him out?"

Victoria hesitated when Winston suggested she take Jeremiah along with Nicolette to Mocha Moms outings. She rolled her eyes and refused sex for two months when he suggested she get Aruba's recipe for Aruba's by the Sea, a mean dish of baked tilapia, shrimp, rice, and a splash of other unknown but hearty flavors.

She drew the line when Winston offered the basement during the month Aruba anticipated divorcing James. "Winston, we have a home, not a hotel. That's the end of it."

"But she's your friend, Tori."

"We all have to live with the choices we make."

Now, approaching Aruba's vehicle, umbrella in tow, Winston tapped on the window. As the window opened, he was pleasantly surprised by the music, the sight of her, her scent.

"What happened?"

"Winston, I wasn't sure it was you. I was headed to an insurance meet-and-greet on Keystone when I ran out of gas. I know I'm too late for the function now. May I get a ride down the street to the gas station?"

"Need you ask?"

Winston opened her door, allowing Aruba to join him under his umbrella. Maybe it was the lack of sex, the long hours, the arguments with Victoria, but he noticed Aruba's stunning beauty for the first time. He offered his suit jacket. As she slid it over her fitted black dress, he was amazed by the hourglass figure before him. He'd always seen her in sweats, her curly ringlets piled atop her head. He'd never seen her hair straightened and would remember to compliment her as they headed to the gas station.

"Oh, I forgot my gas can. Do you happen to have one?"

"Sure. We can go to BP."

They jumped in his ride, Winston taking in the Flowerbomb perfume, trying to contain himself as they drove to BP.

"So what's this meet-and-greet you're headed to? Or should I ask *were* headed to?"

"Just trying to drum up new customers. You know the routine: champagne, finger foods, lies, laughs. I hate being late to functions."

Winston chuckled at the thought of office parties for the sake of the company. That was one of the reasons he had started his own cardiology practice. He believed in doing his own thing, calling his own shots.

"I remember those days." Shifting the conversation, he asked, "What perfume are you wearing? You smell divine."

"Oh, it's Flowerbomb. Victoria gave it to me. She said it makes her smell like something crawled up in her and died. You like it?"

"I do. It smells good on you." He tried to hide his disappointment, but he never understood why Victoria was so unappreciative. He went out of his way to buy her trinkets and tokens of affection, but enough was never enough.

"I asked James to come along, but he didn't want to mingle tonight."

"Too many Edomites," they said in unison.

They laughed at that, their banter continuing as they headed to BP. He filled the gas can and they headed back to Aruba's car. Winston stood outside as Aruba returned to her vehicle. He noticed her nervous smile as he poured gas in her tank. *I bet James has taken every dime. She probably doesn't have gas money.*

He tapped on the driver's side window. "Follow me back to BP. I'd like to fill your tank."

"I can't ask you to do that."

"You didn't ask me. I offered."

"Okay. But you have to promise to let me pay you back."

"You can pay me back with one of your great recipes."

Aruba blushed. She followed him to BP, amazed at how smoothly things were going. She knew she had to take it slow, to approach the matter delicately. No slips. One day at a time.

She pulled alongside pump eight, waited for Winston to get out and fill her tank. She eyed him from her side mirror, admiring his chivalry, his drive. He was one of the most beautiful men she'd ever seen next to James. Winston's boast of being from the City of Brotherly Love was always followed by Aruba muttering the phrase, "city of *sexy*, black brotherly love," under her breath. Winston's rich dark skin, shaved head, muscular frame, and towering six-four stature underscored what really turned Aruba on about him: deep-set dimples. Whenever he smiled, she wanted to stick her tongue in the center of his dimples, kiss him there as a start, and work her way down. She often told jokes in his presence just to make him laugh. Now, as he pumped her gas, she thought of what it would be like to kiss him as a thank-you. She thought of how she'd maneuver that feat.

When he was done, he tapped her window again. "If I'm out of line, you can say so. I'll understand. Since you don't want to go to the function, would you like to join me for a cup of coffee at Starbucks?"

"Winston, I'd love to."

[4]
Lies Have Short Legs

"Yeah, James, that's what I'm talking about. Fuck me harder, James. Damn, this shit is da bomb!"

James caressed Tawatha's breasts as she bounced up and down on him. She was a little noisier than he liked, but a good screw nonetheless. He'd met Tawatha Gipson, the secretary at Hinton and Conyers Construction, his first day on the site. She made a point of showcasing her double-D headlights as she pointed out the breakroom, showed him how to clock in and out of the automated time system, and where the steel-toed boots and goggles were located. She tried to present herself as the girl-next-door, but he knew what she was all about when she got up to make copies of his hiring documents and I-9 form, twisting her massive ass, giggling every five words about how handsome he was and how he looked like a pro baller. Even asked, "You ever played with the Pacers?"

He ignored her that first day, trying to keep his New Year's resolution of doing right by Aruba. His resolve waned the next day when Tawatha stepped into the office wearing a short, wraparound print skirt; a low-cut, V-neck blouse; and no bra. He figured she placed Band-Aids on her nipples as not to expose them. All the guys on the site made a bet as to which one would sleep with her first. They stood around the cooler or dangled from skyscrapers, chatting about "State Fair." That was the name Marcus Fullerton had given Tawatha while munching a double-decker ham and roast beef sandwich his wife had prepared for him. "Man, ass like that oughta have its own exhibit at the State Fair. Damn, I wanna get with her."

Rodney Lansky added, "Man, I wouldn't tap that with somebody else's dick. I heard she got four kids."

"Hell, that turns me on even more." This from Abie Fortner. "I know women with just one child that don't look that good. Her stomach is as flat as an ironing board. State Fair is a bad bitch!"

Tawatha ignored their advances. She only had eyes for James. She took special care to greet him every day with a cup of coffee in hand, prepared for him just the way he said he liked it. He pretended he didn't notice the way her natural, shoulder-length fishbone braids, highlighted with auburn streaks, were twisted in intricate perfection. Or the way her cocoa brown skin always smelled of shea butter or lavender. Or the way her slanted eyes lit up when he was near. She wasn't as tall as Aruba, which made him fantasize all the more about having a shorter woman to tousle around in bed. She was forever running her fingers through his dreads, telling him she had a closet fantasy of learning to do hair. She honed in on his Samsonesque glory, slipping him a card with the name and number of her cousin who oiled locks at a shop on the eastside. James slid the card in his pocket, determined not to let yet another woman distract him from being a better husband.

Then Aruba started in on him again. Bitched about him finding and *keeping* a job. Asked when he'd help with the utility bill, the truck notes, the gas bill. After he'd quit H&C, he knew he had to be on his best behavior. He'd worn out his welcome from siblings Teresa and Marvin. James could only do one thing at that point: housecleaning. He kept things spotless when he was unemployed. He made sure dinner was ready when Aruba came home, the laundry was fluffed and folded, and the smell of lavender and vanilla wafted throughout their home. It was during a laundry session he fished Tawatha's number from his pocket. Didn't realize Tawatha had scribbled her office line on the card until he'd dialed.

"I can't lose this job," she said after they chatted a few minutes. "Hell, Mr. Hinton be listening to conversations like he the FBI and shit."

They continued that way for a week. Got better acquainted via text messages, online chats through AOL, and during late-night cell calls when Aruba was asleep. Their first encounter at Motel Six on the Southside left James wanting more. It wasn't until Aruba told him about the insurance meeting that he decided he'd have a quickie in the house. He called Tawatha, found out where she lived, and picked her up at the Phoenix apartments as Jeremiah nursed hot milk and crackers and fell asleep. He tucked Jeremiah in bed upstairs when they returned and allowed her to do a lap dance before the festivities began.

Now, as she humped up and down on his Johnson on the sectional, screaming and grunting like this would be the last time she'd get some, he knew he'd made a mistake. He hoped she wouldn't awaken Jeremiah.

"Come on, damnit, don't stop now!!"

James looked past her flopping headlights at the wall clock, trying to time Aruba's arrival. He had to get Tawatha off of him and out of the house.

"Smack my ass, James. Smack me!"

Tawatha pulled James's dreadlocks, tightened her muscles around him. She quickened her pace, oblivious to his presence.

"Damn, I'm coming!"

Tawatha leaned forward, sweating over James's chest, the headlights heaving up and down now.

"Shit, you can fuck," Tawatha shrieked, rolling off James and covering up with the sheet he'd given her earlier. She breathed heavily, exhausted from the workout. She surveyed her surroundings for the first time since she'd gotten there.

She checked out the flat-screen, the elegant family photos lining the mantel above the fireplace, the furniture appointed just-so, the five-star-hotel cleanliness of the home. *Me and my kids can rest real nice up in this place.* "I'ma go get some orange juice out the fridge before we start on round two."

Wrapped in the sheet, Tawatha scooted to the refrigerator like a mermaid as James wiped himself down with a wet towel.

"James, I'ma wash up in the half-bath. You mind?"

"No, T. Go right ahead. I'ma take a quick shower."

"Not without me!"

"You might try some more of your moves and wake up Jeremiah. Just stay put. I'll be back."

James darted upstairs to the bathroom. He could kick himself for bringing Tawatha home. The only reason he'd planned the tryst at the house and not a hotel was because all bets were off when he picked Tawatha up at her place. No way was he having sex in her apartment. His first clue was the smell that slapped him when she cracked open the door. He wasn't sure what it was, but he told her he'd wait outside until she was ready. She insisted he come inside, and he tried, but the pile of shoes behind the front door made it difficult for him to squeeze through. He looked at the full and twin mattresses propped against the living room wall and wondered if she had beds for herself and her children. Ants marching in single file crawled atop piles of clothes on the floor and KFC, Home Depot, and Walmart circulars were strewn about the coffee table. The sight made him retreat to the bathroom. After tripping over towels, lingerie, and more clothes, he decided to hold his urine 'til he got home. He wouldn't piss in that toilet for a reality TV series. It looked as if it hadn't been cleaned in two years.

The condition of Tawatha's apartment and his maxed-out Visa made it impossible to get a hotel room. He could strangle Aruba for not paying the bill for him. She claimed she couldn't do it because she had to take care of the "essentials," but he knew she was lying. He'd grown sick of her poor-mouthing about how his sporadic employment was getting them further behind and deeper in debt. What really pissed him the fuck off was when she suggested stupid shit like getting rid of one car to save money, turning off lights to conserve energy, washing clothes in cold water, turning off water as he brushed his teeth or washed his face. The way she carried on you'd think *she* was an Edomite.

He showered, went back downstairs, and jumped when Tawatha snuck behind him and planted a kiss on his back. As she circled him and knelt to the floor, he pushed her head away from his penis.

"Come on, daddy, let me suck it right. You know you like this."

"Look, Tawatha, I gotta take you back home."

"James, my momma's keeping my kids all night. I thought I could stay with you. You got me all hot and bothered now. I gotta have some more of this dick. You know you got the magic stick, right? That's what I'ma name you. Magic." Tawatha caressed his penis, baby-talked to it. "That's a good boy, Magic." She planted light kisses on it.

James moved her hands. "Tawatha, I never said you could stay the night."

Tawatha stood to face James, disappointment clouding her face. "Bullshit. You said you and your wife were separated. Sounds like an open invitation to me."

Damn. James sat down on the sectional, leaned back. He'd forgotten he'd told her Aruba had stormed out a week ago, leaving him and Jeremiah to fend for themselves. He had to think of something, anything. Nine o'clock was fast approaching and he'd planned to have Tawatha fed, polished off, and back home by nine-forty-five. He expected Aruba home by at least ten-fifteen, and the last thing he needed was another round of ultimatums or a fistfight between his wife and his jump off.

"Look T, umm, my wife left. But she came back two days ago."

"Thought you told me that bitch was old news. Good as you've been to her, providing for her and your kid, and she gon' leave like that. Why you let her come back?"

"T, she has breast cancer."

"For real?"

"Yeah. We found out at St. Vincent's over a week ago."

Tawatha put her head on James's chest. "I'm sorry to hear that. Man, that's too damn sad."

Pleased with the direction of the conversation, James continued, "We're starting an aggressive round of chemotherapy within the next two weeks. I know I said it was over, but what kind of man would I be if I didn't stand by her? You understand, right?" James placed his arms around Tawatha's shoulders to soften the blow.

Tawatha's enthusiasm deflated. "So where is she now?"

"She went to a support group meeting. Her girlfriend was taking her to a wig store after that. I couldn't bear the thought of going with her."

"So *that's* why you needed this distraction. I'm so sorry."

"I don't want you to think I used you. I really like you."

"Naw, I don't feel like that. But hell, you better take me on home."

Tawatha gathered her clothes. She dressed hurriedly, miffed she wouldn't wake up to a refrigerator full of food, a clean house, a bed with a cozy mattress and at least six-hundred thread-count sheets. She thought of the mattresses in her living room and wondered how she'd replace them since her youngest daughter's bedwetting had ruined them. She looked around James's house once more, ashamed four kids by four different men hadn't yielded this kind of life for her. *I gotta plan this stuff better.*

"James, you got a few dollars I can hold? My EBT card is empty and I need to get some groceries."

"What? H and C stiffing you?"

"Naw. I had to choose between summer camp for my kids and food."

"Wait here, I'll be back."

James remembered Aruba stashed extra cash in the bedroom media center, tucked between *Norbit* and *Mona Lisa Smile*. He went upstairs to the bedroom, peeled off five twenties from the wad, putting the rest back just as Aruba kept it. He looked in on Jeremiah, smiling at his son. He didn't want to awaken him. Taking Tawatha back to the Phoenix would take twenty minutes tops. No need to wake up little man. James went downstairs, rejoined Tawatha on the sofa.

"I got a hundred. That enough for you?"

"Thank you, James. I appreciate it!" She hugged him and reluctantly grabbed her purse. She stuffed the money in her bra, still trying to concoct an alibi, so she could spend the night. The instant James turned his back, she tossed her thong under the sofa. She sat back, then noticed he was missing something important.

"Ain't you gonna take your son with us?"

"I'll be right back. I'm just dropping you off."

"It'll only take a minute to get him."

"Trust me, I'm coming back home," said James.

Tawatha glanced up the stairs. She knew she wouldn't win a mother of the year award, but she felt uncomfortable about James leaving

Jeremiah alone. She thought about the short drive it would take to get back to her apartment, then bit her lip and muttered a short prayer under her breath. "Please let him stay asleep until James gets back home."

He grabbed his keys and headed across town to take Tawatha home. Tawatha fished through the CDs and popped in Musiq. She sang now, throwing her hands up, feeling the fierce thump of the sound system.

"So what kinda truck is this? I've been looking for something different 'cause that hoopty of mine is giving me all kinda trouble."

"Toyota Sequoia. I love how it rides."

James cruised down the street, simmering again over Aruba's words. "We need to sell that truck. We can get by with one vehicle for now." She always thought she knew so much about money, about finances. Just cause she had a mathematics degree. So what if the creditors were calling night and day? So what if he had to hide the truck around the corner at their neighbor's house a few nights a week just to stay two steps ahead of the finance company? Shit, you wade in the water till it calms down, right?

"James, did you hear me?"

James decreased the volume of the music. "What? T, I didn't hear you. I was thinking about my wife's chemotherapy."

Tawatha sidled next to James after hearing this. She knew his wife would be too tired in the days to come to take care of his needs. If she couldn't be number one, she'd at least relieve him of tension, make the days ahead easier. He'd told her the reason he'd left Hinton and Conyers was to explore entrepreneurial opportunities. James had big dreams and needed a woman like her to see them come to fruition. He never told her she would be that woman, but how long would his wife be around to help him? If she couldn't start with his stomach—like she planned to do the next morning by preparing a big breakfast—she'd start between his legs. She cocked one leg over his and kissed his right ear.

"Stop, T. I'm trying to drive."

"I'm not stopping you, baby. Keep going."

Tawatha made small circles around James's ear. She nibbled his lobes as she reached beneath his T-shirt, massaging his nipples. She visualized the chipping paint and buckled flooring in her apartment. No matter how much she tried, she couldn't shake the desperation of her surroundings. As she worked her way down, unzipping his pants, licking his inner thighs, Tawatha hoped this time she'd perform a trick well enough to hold on to a decent man.

"T, come on now. Stop, girl."

"Tell me you don't like it, James."

James tilted back as Tawatha leaned over, jimmying his penis from his briefs.

She removed strawberry-flavored lube from her pocket and smeared it on his penis. She started slow at first, making small circles around the tip, listening to him moan in ecstasy. She licked him softly, increasing her rhythm and speed, taking her lips farther down the shaft. She loved hearing him call her name, loved the fact he was losing control. They were both so caught up in the moment, they didn't hear the screams of the onlookers as a blue Cutlass Supreme crossed the center lane and sideswiped James.

[5]
Old School, New School

"I didn't know you were a Glenn Jones fan," said Winston, cutting a raspberry crumb bar in quarters and gazing into Aruba's mesmerizing eyes. He stirred his caramel latte and marveled at the coincidence of running into her. It had been a long time since he'd chatted with someone who could relate to his musical jones. Most women never entertained his love for music. As if all he cared about was surgery and being glued to his practice.

"Who wouldn't be? He's fabulous!" Aruba raised her voice two octaves, stopping short of rah-rah-ing like a cheerleader. She combed her memory for Googled details.

"I've been a fan of his since high school. He's a real singer with incredible range, not like the young'uns that lean on samples and misogynistic lyrics. How can women allow themselves to be called bitches and hoes?" asked Winston.

"Wait a minute, some of the new school can sing. Kem, John Legend, Urban Mystic, Anthony Hamilton, Chrisette Michele have old-school soul."

"Never heard of them. Maybe you can introduce them to me sometime."

"You've never heard of Urban Mystic?"

"Honestly, the name makes me think of a drink."

"He redid a phenomenal version of Bobby Womack's—"

"You're telling me someone had the nerve to sing a rendition of

The Poet's song and live to tell the story?" Winston leaned forward as if sharing a secret. "That's why I've never listened to track ten of Glenn Jones's *Forever Timeless* CD because he redid 'I Wish He Didn't Trust Me So Much.'"

"Urb, excuse my slang, put his spit on 'Woman's Gotta Have It' and tore it up. He also sang the hell out of Sam Cooke's 'A Change is Gonna Come' on his second CD. He has that Sunday meeting, juke-joint, brown rot-gut liquor singing pouring from his soul. Think James Cleveland merged with Otis Redding meets Luther and K-Ci."

"Let me guess. You were a soprano at Mount Nebo Missionary Baptist Church in someone's Southern town?"

"Guess again. I can't hold a tune in a bucket. But I love good music." She sipped her cappuccino. "Why had I never heard of Charles Hilton Brown until I met you?"

"You're kidding, right?"

"Of course, I had to check him out and discovered like so many musicians, he didn't get his just due back in the day."

"And no one has heard anything from him since his one and only album," Winston lamented.

"He's in hiding, so you won't bother him." Aruba winked at Winston.

A toddler two tables over yelled to her mom, "I want a lemon bar, not a blueberry muffin." The girl pouted, then tossed the muffin at her mom. Before her mom could retaliate, the little girl made haste and scooted under three tables, charging the display wall of mugs, teas, and coffees. Several of them tumbled down as she screamed, "Lemon, lemon, lemon!"

"Paula, come back here this instant!" her mother shouted as she tried to get Paula under control.

"No!" Paula crossed her arms, stroked her mane of red curls, and watched as her mother and a barista cleaned up the mess she'd made. Winston, Aruba, and other members of the captive audience anticipated the mom's next move.

"Twenty-dollar bet she spanks her," said Winston, removing his wallet from his suit jacket.

"Twenty-five she gets the lemon bar," said Aruba.

Paula traced circles on the display case with her fingers, leaned into it, and pressed her nose near the lemon bars. Her mother, flustered and embarrassed, pulled a ten-dollar bill from her purse and quietly ordered a lemon bar and a tall hot chocolate. A chorus of no-she-didn'ts and sighs sailed through the room. Students looked up from their laptops and shook their heads.

"I'd never let Jeremiah get away with that."

"Your son is so well-behaved, I don't think he'd try it," Winston complimented.

"Nicolette wouldn't do that, either. She's a good girl."

"That's no thanks to Tori. That's all on Alva." Winston surprised himself making the stark admission. He'd prided himself on presenting a united front in public, to colleagues, to family, and friends. Now, in the midst of whirring cappuccino machines, Motown oldies drifting through Bose speakers, and a toddler who needed the look and a firm tap on her backside, he was letting his guard down. *Get a grip, Winston, get a grip!*

"I think you owe me twenty-five dollars." Aruba smiled and unzipped her purse.

"Guess I do, huh?"

As Winston opened his wallet, Aruba's purse dropped, the contents spilling on the floor.

"Paula's made me all thumbs," said Aruba.

As she knelt down to gather her things, Winston was by her side. "Let me help," he said.

Aruba lightly placed the belongings in her purse, picked up her phone, scrolled through the five missed calls, then dismissed the unfamiliar number as one of James's women. She placed the phone on the table. She retrieved the letter from the construction company, offering Winston a pensive look.

"Aruba, what's wrong?"

"Nothing you'd want to hear about. What goes on in the family, stays in the family."

"You take twenty-five bucks from me, subject me to Toddlers Gone Wild, and now you can't talk?" said Winston, hoping to lighten her disposition.

"I'm not stupid, Winston. I know Victoria has shared things about me and James with you," said Aruba, feeling out Winston to see just how much Victoria had blabbed.

"I probably know more than I should, but that's inconsequential. Just talk. I'm here."

On cue, the first tear dropped. Aruba had practiced this scene about fourteen times in various places: the office bathroom stall between coffee breaks and lunch; in traffic on her way to work as she played her favorite slow jams; watching chick-flicks in the family room on Friday nights.

"I'm so overwhelmed, Winston. Some days I feel things will be okay. I pray that if I'm a good wife, James will come around. But other days…" Aruba dabbed her eyes with a napkin. "I guess I wish things were normal. Whatever that means. It's my birthday and my husband didn't even remember. Do you know how that makes me feel?"

Do I ever? Winston couldn't remember the last time he had received a birthday gift from Victoria. Winston also recalled his pastor saying that marriage was a sacred bond between two people. No matter how disastrous, how chaotic, one should never speak against the union. He wanted to tell her she was wasting her time, that there were other single, available men out there searching for someone of her caliber, but he decided to stay the course of appropriateness.

"Have you thought about going to counseling, Aruba? I know a few excellent family therapists and an awesome psychologist you guys could call."

"Oh, I guess I'll go in between finding a part-time job, since James finds it so difficult to stay employed." Aruba slid the envelope containing separation notices and the last pay stub from Hinton and Conyers to Winston.

She watched Winston eye the stub, his eyes registering concern. *How does a man not work to take care of his family? This paycheck wouldn't cover one of Victoria's purses.* He slid the envelope back to Aruba and took her hand. He took in a deep breath, waited a few seconds, then gazed into her eyes.

"I'm being inappropriate again, but I need you to do me a favor. Promise this stays between the two of us."

"What are you talking about, Winston?"

Winston released her hand and reached for his checkbook again. He spoke as he completed the task. "This is just a little something to help you out. Please don't tell anyone about this, Aruba. This is from my mad money account Victoria doesn't know about."

When he was done writing, Winston handed Aruba the check. She glanced and did a double-take at the amount.

"Winston, this is ten thousand dollars. I can't take this from you." She slid the check toward him, her fingers trembling.

"You can and *you will* under the condition you use it to catch up on a few bills and save some for a rainy day." He slid it back to her.

"I...I don't know what to say." Aruba cried sincerely this time, floored by Winston's largess. She planned how she'd divvy the money. The recession had been the perfect cover for the financial breakthrough plan she had concocted three months ago. She had lied to James and said State Farm had slashed her sixty-five-thousand-dollar income in half. She had deposited half of her salary in their joint account; the other half went to a fund she dubbed TWT/TIN: that was then; this is now. Each time she scanned her bank statement that went to her rented post office box, the guilt she felt disappeared. She wondered why she hadn't separated her funds years ago. She would deposit eight thousand in the fund for future use, spend a grand on a Fourth of July bash, and treat herself to something nice. She stood to hug him, then stopped after the phone rang again. She knew she had to answer this time. She held up one finger to Winston in a *shhh* gesture as she snapped open the phone.

"Hello. Yes, this is she." She waited, held her head for a moment. "Oh, my God. Where?"

Aruba quickly gathered her things as Winston stood to help her.

"Aruba, talk to me. What happened?"

"James was in an accident. He's at Methodist Hospital."

"Come on. I'll drive you there."

[6]
The Doctor Will See You Now

Aruba and Winston approached the nurse's station as Winston held her close. He wanted to assure her everything would be fine, even if he wasn't sure himself.

"Hi, I need to know…"

"Dr. Faulk, is everything all right?" The nurse, Susan Bills, perked up. She adjusted her stethoscope and stood, leaning close to him.

"A patient, James Dixon, was brought here earlier. We need—"

"The accident. Oh yes," said Susan, interrupting him again. She skittered from the desk to the chagrin of waiting patients, motioned for Winston and Aruba to follow her, then punched her passcode to admit them to the ER.

They stepped in stride with Susan and listened to her prattling a mile a minute. "Talk about lucky, Dr. Faulk. Somebody upstairs was dishing out a double dose of grace and mercy tonight. James and that lady, Taniqua or something, were so blessed they didn't sustain any life-threatening injuries. I mean, with what she was doing and all, she's—"

"What lady?" Aruba stiffened.

"Oh, I guess it was his girlfriend or something."

"What about the baby? Where's Jeremiah?"

"It was just the two of them." Susan, now aware of how she'd thrown standard procedures by the wayside at the sight of Winston Faulk asked, "Is he a relative or patient, Dr. Faulk?"

"He—"

"He's my husband," Aruba said, interrupting Winston and steaming with each breath she took.

Susan conferred with another nurse about James's whereabouts, unaware he'd been admitted to a room shortly before Winston and Aruba's arrival.

"Susan, it's okay. Just take us to the room," said Winston.

Embarrassed, Susan pressed the button for the elevator. They rode to the third floor in silence. When they entered room 312, James's legs were elevated and he crouched forward to rub the bandages wrapped around his head. Susan exited the room without a word or a backward glance.

"James, where the hell is Jeremiah?" Aruba hissed. "And who were you riding with?"

"Why are you here with Winston? Did you have to call *him* to come with you?"

"Answer the question!"

James fell back on the pillow. "See, I just ran out for a minute to take Donnie's sister home, and there was an accident. I just left him alone for a little while."

"You mean to tell me our son is home alone, right now, and you—"

"Aruba, go home. I'll stick around and talk to James. Just get to Jeremiah now." Winston rubbed her shoulder before she turned to leave.

Aruba mouthed thanks to Winston and stormed out of the room. Now a twinge of guilt hit her as she thought of how James had left Jeremiah alone. What if he'd fallen down the steps? What if he'd eaten something he shouldn't have? What if big-mouth Susan had blabbed that a child was involved? And who the hell is Donnie? She calmed herself, tried to breathe. It made no sense for her to lose it now. Not when she was so close to escaping the hell she called a marriage.

"Look, Doc, me and my family don't need your help." James grew angrier as he took in Winston's dapper appearance from head to toe.

"Oh, is that right? Your wife runs out of gas, hears from a nurse you're with another woman, and your son is home alone. But you don't need anyone?"

"Look, nig—" James paused. "I mean, Winston, you don't know what you're talking about. This is a big misunderstanding."

"Is your unemployment a misunderstanding? Is your inability to take care of your family a misunderstanding?"

Unaccustomed to hitting below the belt, Winston stopped. He knew he'd revealed too much and hoped Aruba wouldn't pay for his concern with James's heavy-handed love.

"What I do with my family is my business. I takes care of mine, dawg."

Winston's fists balled at this statement. James reminded him so much of his Uncle Sheldon. Before him was a man like his uncle. One with promise, intellect, someone who could make a positive contribution to society. If only he had direction and guidance. Uncle Sheldon proved to be the family tragedy. Got a law degree, but never practiced. Received a Ph.D., but got dizzy at the thought of sticking around to gain tenure. Concocted, invented, and sought patents for at least two thingamajigs, but didn't have the heart to see them through. He even had committed suicide in grand fashion by leaping to his death during the Macy's Thanksgiving parade, falling near the NBC commentators. The family's three words about Sheldon were always, *What a waste*.

"Look, man, I'm not judging you. I just think you have a beautiful family and they need you, James."

"Yeah, whatever. Just 'cause I can't give my family what you can, doesn't mean I don't love 'em."

"I apologize for being rude. I barged in here making accusations and I was way out of line. I've got to get home to my family. Call me if you need anything."

Winston placed his business card on the table near a pitcher of water and exited the room. He wasn't sure what had happened earlier, but he had to strengthen his resolve. Aruba had awakened feelings he didn't know he had. It was best to let them rest.

Aruba's heart raced as she climbed the stairs. The house was silent. She held her breath as she opened the door to Jeremiah's room. He was asleep. The soothing sounds of Baby Mozart's sleep rhythms lulled him. The track had been cued to repeat the tune. As much as she hated James's behavior, he'd do something small that calmed her nerves from time to time. Jeremiah could sleep through a train wreck with those sounds. Still, she knew it was time for them to move on with their lives.

[7]
Glamour Doll

Victoria sat in the media room upstairs, leafing through *Heywood-Wakefield Blond: Depression to '50's*. Summer was upon her and it was time to redecorate the Brown County cabin. Each year, Victoria found it necessary to decorate it for the tourists who frequented the cabin. She made a note to contact the web administrator at Brown County Log Cabins to feature the new items she planned to purchase. She wanted to please travelers paying five hundred dollars per night. After watching TCM's tribute to Dorothy Dandridge, she thought this year would be great to add pieces from Heywood-Wakefield's Trophy and Dakar lines. She visualized Dorothy and Harry Belafonte sitting out back on the deck, grilling corn and steaks while singing their nights and days away. *Beautiful and classic. Just like me*, she thought as she circled the items she'd purchase and jotted the prices on a small pad on the coffee table. Victoria paused, gazed at herself in the mirror, and smiled. She was ten years Winston's junior and basked in the compliment that she actually looked twenty years younger. Thanks to a personal trainer, Pilates, and an aversion for the fat-back, collard greens, and meaty pork chops her aunt had rescued her from when she was six, she kept her petite, size-4 frame, a perfect 36-24-36. At thirty-three, she was the spitting image of her aunt, Marguerite Mason, an actress whose claim to fame was a familiar face in lots of eighties movies as well as a video dancer and primary performer with the Isley Brothers. Victoria weighed herself daily, made Alva, her nanny, stock the refrigerator with blueberries, yogurt, and fish, and kept photos of herself throughout the house as a reminder of how beautiful God made her. The stretch marks from Nicolette were the only hiccup in her life, and she'd arranged a visit with a cosmetic surgeon to alleviate that nonsense.

"Shopping for the cabin, I see," said Winston. He sat next to her on the sofa, undid his tie, and leaned over to kiss her. Victoria pulled away.

She didn't hear Winston pull into the garage or climb the steps off the kitchen. She pursed her lips at the sight of him. "Hey, I'm deep in thought here. Announce yourself the next time." Victoria flipped a few more pages, then turned to Winston. "There goes my concentration. I'll have to get back to this later." She tossed the book aside, her brows knitted in a see-what-you-made-me-do "V."

"I can make it better if you let me." Winston winked, hoping Victoria was more frisky than frigid tonight.

"Is sex all you think about? Is that all I am to you?"

Winston chose not to respond to that one. If that were the case, the ink wouldn't have dried on their marriage certificate before he bedded one of the halo-effect cuties that invented illnesses to get next to him. "Tori, I wasn't talking about—"

"Well, what did you mean?" she snapped.

"Tori, I love you. I had an experience tonight that reminded me how blessed we are."

"Oh, did some dropout from Haughville decide he or she would go back to school because they see how accomplished you are?"

Victoria thought Winston's community involvement was cute at the beginning of their marriage, but now she was tired of it.

The calls from high schools around Indianapolis for him to speak, the luncheons where he served as guest of honor, always bringing home trophies and awards, and the donations he rained on every civic organization known to mankind wearied her. Why couldn't they just be alone, enjoy his success and his money on a smaller scale? Why did she have to share him with everyone? She was content being home with Alva, Nicolette, and shopping. Now he was gearing up to tell another story about some downtrodden soul who would struggle to get a GED in hopes of being like him.

"Where's your sensitivity, babe? This is about someone we know." Winston rubbed her leg, hoping she'd soften and get over herself. "James was in an accident tonight. I was with Aruba at the hospital."

"Are you serious? What happened?" Engaged in his words, she moved closer to Winston.

"Luckily, it was a sideswipe. He was with someone else and left Jeremiah at home. I think you should call Aruba and find out how they're doing."

"Well, that's typical. I told her a long time ago to get rid of him, but noooo, she's holding on for dear life to a marriage that's not worth saving." She reared back on the couch and continued her ranting. "She's a pretty enough woman to get a better man than James. I mean, she probably couldn't get someone like you, but she doesn't have to struggle the way she does. There's no way I'd be with a man that broke and out of touch with reality."

"Is that so, Tori?"

Victoria's damage control efforts kicked in. "What I meant was she's a hardworking person who deserves more. Do you understand what I mean?"

"What I understand is that you've been staring at Heywood-Wakefield items too long. Go call your friend, Tori."

"Okay, Winston. I'll call in a few minutes."

"Nicolette knocked out? Did Alva have a hard time getting her down tonight?"

"She's tired. We went shopping today and she had the quaintest bear constructed at Build-A-Bear. She's been asleep for an hour."

Winston left the media room and entered Nicolette's room, exhausted. He kissed Nicolette's forehead, acknowledging her as his center, his sanity. The love he had for her surpassed the craziness of life with Victoria. Tori couldn't be satisfied and he didn't know how to appease her anymore. She complained about everything. Lately, the nagging took on a life of its own. The house was too small. *"I deserve more than seven-thousand square feet."* The cars weren't new enough. *"Every Kobe, 50 Cent, and Shaq can get a Range Rover and a Mercedes. I want a Bentley."* She whined about a new ring. *"I know you're not Kobe, but can I at least have four carats? Harry Winston is calling my name."* His practice wasn't visible enough. *"If Ian Smith can host a show, why don't you?"* Seeing Nicolette made it all worthwhile, reminded him of why he chose to work hard so his family wouldn't need or want for anything. He watched her napping, her chest rising and falling with soft breaths. He touched her hands and smiled. "Rest, daddy's girl. I love you."

Winston dragged to their bedroom, removed his clothes, and jumped in the shower. He wanted to wash away Victoria's voice, his discontentment of late, his thoughts of Aruba. He wondered how Aruba was doing, if things had turned out okay with James and their situation. He wondered how he could be there for her more, and what he needed to do to concentrate on his own union.

[8]
It's Generational

"**M**omma, I'm just asking you to come get me in the morning! I've been in an accident. I'm at Methodist." Tawatha steadied her cell phone in one hand as she turned to secure the ties on the back of her hospital gown.

"Honey, it'll have to be after the kids leave for school. Plus the 'E' and the needle on my gas meter are close enough to make a baby."

"Is Mr. J.B. there? Can he give you some gas money? Maybe I can sneak outta here tonight."

"He's pulling a double at the foundry. I thought you were out with Lasheera and Jamilah. They can't bring you home?"

Tawatha shifted in the small ER bed and fiddled with the admission bracelet on her arm. The night wasn't supposed to go down like this. She was doleful about not convincing James that she and the kids should move in. She didn't try to find him in the hospital, but figured he'd been admitted to a room since his business was so successful. *His wife is probably in his room rubbing on him and kissing those sexy lips. If only we were married. I know things would be better for me and the kids.* She pretended she wasn't in pain and the aches were nonexistent as not to be admitted to the hospital. No health insurance. She'd been meaning to fill out the paperwork at Hinton and Conyers for insurance, but knew the bimonthly payments of $180 would suck the life out of her anemic paycheck. Her life had become a maze of shuffling her pitiful paycheck, food stamps, and under-the-table jobs that left her un-fulfilled and tired. No child support, no contact with her children's fathers, and no prospects for a new apartment. She still had to think of a lie to tell her mom.

"Well, I got in the accident after we left Olive Garden. Sheer and Milah went to Club 7 after we ate to get their dance on, so I bet their phones are either on vibrate or shut off. I'll just try and get a cab or something."

Roberta paused a moment. She had enough time, gas, and money to pick up Tawatha, but she was tired of enabling her. *Bet she's out with somebody's man or husband. Humph. Letting her stay at the hospital oughta teach her a lesson.* Roberta felt guilty for her thoughts because she realized Tawatha was a branch from her whorish tree. Only dumber. Roberta Gipson remembered all the men in Riverside, California that marched in and out of Tawatha's and Teresa's lives when they were small. She also rued the fact that prior to the twins, she was hopeful about moving to L.A. and owning a clothing shop, meeting a man with whom she could build a future, and providing a stable and nurturing environment for the children they would have. As one of few black students in her business classes at U.C. Berkeley, she was shunned by whites who resented her intelligence and the ease with which she grasped concepts; she was ostracized by blacks for being too white in her thinking. Whoever heard of a sista wanting to have a productive future, land, a stable life, and spouting that stupid scripture about leaving a legacy for her children and her children's children? Her life appeared to be moving smoothly until that breezy afternoon in May as she prepared for her ad-vanced economics final. She was seated outside in the quad near the library, wearing Levi's bellbottoms, a floral peasant top, and leather sandals. She wasn't afraid of basking her dark skin in the sunlight because her color accented the sheen of her Afro that was meticulously picked out and oiled each day. She fondled her wooden hoop earrings as she read. As her eyes drifted off the page, the sight of a drop-top, cranberry Cadillac convertible with white leather interior and sparkling spoke wheels arrested her. More striking than the car was the butterscotch-complexioned man who emerged from the car and strode across the walkway into the library behind her. Roberta normally associated such cars with hoods and pimps, not ones passing through the portals of a campus library on a Saturday afternoon. Roberta gathered up her books to go back to her apartment. As she grabbed the last book, she dropped two folders, the contents strewn about by the wind. As she hastened to pick up the papers, a polished, shiny pair of Stacy Adams approached her hands, startling her. She stifled a gasp as Mr. Cadillac stooped next to her, hands held out, with a sheath of papers.

"I believe these belong to you, Miss," he said.

Roberta could not contain the grin spreading across her face. Flustered, she tried to say thank you, but was silent.

"I'm Shirley Gipson. What's your name?"

"A man named Shirley?" was the best response she could muster. Embarrassed, she extended her hand to him. "Roberta. Roberta Lawrence."

"Nice to meet you, Roberta. Yes, my mother wanted a girl so badly she named me Shirley. I get a lot of attention and mistaken identity with it."

She spied the book *Business Policies, Text, and Cases* in his hand. "Are you a student here?"

"I've been discharged from the Marines, I'm a part-time student, and next fall I'll be full-time. This is required reading for September. Never too early to start, right?" Not wanting the moment to end, he added, "Would you like to join me for ice cream?"

Damn, a fine brother, driving a Caddy, enrolled in school, and reading to prepare himself for the days ahead? Why wouldn't I say yes?

"I'm there! Just let me get the rest of my things."

They sped away to Farrell's for vanilla sundaes with chocolate syrup and strawberries. As they swapped stories—his about serving in Vietnam, hers about owning a business—Denise Williams and Johnny Mathis chided them both with the words, "Too Much, Too Little, Too Late." Roberta would appreciate that omen later.

Theirs was a whirlwind relationship. Shortly after finishing her finals and graduating, Roberta took time off before starting the job search. They traveled up and down the scenic California coast: San Pedro, Marina, Monterey, Yosemite, Big Sur, and Lake Tahoe. They picnicked at the Presidio; they made love at Half Moon Bay; they visited the wine groves of Napa Valley, and went sailing in the Berkeley Marine. September had come and gone, no job search, no job, no mention of school on Shirley's part, and the undeniable ache of Roberta's breasts and two months of missed periods. This couldn't be happening to her. However, unlike the women in her family who'd gotten pregnant, deferred dreams, and abandoned them, she knew Shirley would right this wrong and marry her. As she dressed to go to Shirley's apartment to share the news, a knock at the door halted her.

"Who is it?"

"Carol Gipson."

Roberta scanned her memory for Shirley's relatives she had heard him speak of during their time together. A Carol didn't register. Roberta would postpone chit-chatting with her because she was on her way to see the Gipson she knew. Shirley.

Keeping the chain secure, she opened the door. "May I help you, ma'am?"

"You've been seeing my husband, Shirley, and we need to talk."

Roberta paused. Her fingers trembled as she unhooked the chain and stepped aside. Carol waltzed into her apartment, the smell of Opium permeating the room as she took a seat in Roberta's favorite tawny La-Z-Boy. Even in casual attire, Roberta knew Carol was a classy, sophisticated lady. Her hair, swept in a dramatic updo with curls cascading her delicate face, was as perfect as the red crinkled frock she donned. She leaned back in the chair, opened her purse, and pulled out a pack of Viceroys. She smoothed out the full-shape cotton dress, her silver and red bangles jingling as a rhinestone-crusted lighter emerged from her purse. This woman could have easily been headed to a Con Funk Shun concert or a supper club. Carol was someone she would have loved meeting under different circumstances. Instead, she sat in her own apartment, wondering whether to run, call the police, or pray like her grandmother in North Carolina used to do when fierce rains tapped on the tin roof of their family home.

"Mind if I smoke? I don't normally do so inside. We can step out on your balcony."

Carol's cool demeanor frightened Roberta. What did she want? Roberta would have pegged Carol as Shirley's sister or a cousin, since they resembled each other so much. She sat across from Carol on the loveseat and crossed her arms over her stomach. "Why are you here?"

"Beloved, I'll cut to the chase. I've been following you and Shirley up and down the coast for months now. I'm not going anywhere, so I suggest you leave Shirley alone."

Roberta stammered, "I don't under…Shirley loves me."

"You and every other Berkeley student he's bedded over the years. I guess I should be grateful he finally found someone black to pass the time with, heh?"

"He's a stu—"

Carol rattled off Shirley's story as she'd done in other women's apartments and houses over the years: "Student. Part-time, but starting full-time in the fall, right?" She let out a bitter chuckle. "You'd think he would have changed the story after all this time." Carol shook her head, dragged on her Viceroy, and blew perfect smoke rings. She leaned forward near Roberta's face. "Roberta, right? How old are you?"

"Twenty-one."

"Shirley and I are both thirty-nine, have three children, and aren't getting divorced anytime soon." Carol pulled out her wallet and flipped through photos of the children. She passed the photos, proud of her angels. "These are the triplets, Candace, Connie, and Carson."

Roberta took the photos and eyed the kids. Same butterscotch skin. Beautiful smiles. Wide-eyed innocence. She passed the snapshots back to Carol. "He told me he was twenty-nine."

"More facts for you, Doll. He *was* discharged from the Marines. He *did* serve in Vietnam, and at the core of his being, he's decent. But you've been riding in *my* daddy's Cadillac, enjoying *my* family's money, and have been wearing a lot of *my* clothes."

Carol was confusing her more and more.

Carol cut to the chase, answered the question she saw on Roberta's face. "Why do I stay, right? Well, in my case, it's cheaper to keep him for now. But as soon as the kids are gone, our union is a done deal. You're young and attractive enough to get a man of your own. I suggest you stop seeing Shirley while there's still time to keep your dignity in check. I'd hate for something to happen to you."

Carol snubbed out the Viceroy in an ashtray, placed the photos back in her purse, and sauntered out the apartment as elegantly as she'd entered. Roberta, cemented to the loveseat, waited an hour, then called Shirley. When he answered on the first ring, she managed, "Thanks for telling me about Carol. Don't ever call me again," before gently placing the phone in its cradle.

Ashamed she'd been so easily duped, Roberta packed her things and moved seven hours away to Riverside. She found a job at a local funeral home, handling the books. Shocked to learn she was carrying twins in the second trimester, she fed and nurtured the babies in her womb. She gave birth to the girls, both darker versions of Candace, Connie, and Carson. The last of the fight inside of her came with the final push that was Tawatha. Her lips swore off men. Her hips said otherwise. In less than a year, she found herself knee-deep in men wanting to help her take care of the kids and have a place in her heart. Rich ones. Poor ones. Married ones. Professors. Mechanics. All promising the same thing: "Roberta, a woman as fine as you needs to be loved and protected." The men, with their sugary promises, transformed her. She opened her legs a bit wider, faked orgasms longer, and stroked their egos to the point of nauseating herself long after the sheets were cool. In exchange for the theatrics, they paid her rent, kept her and the girls' hair dolled up and her nails pristine. Shirley and Carol had taken her down and she vowed not to be Cupid's victim again. Roberta acquired property, supported her siblings and cousins in North Carolina, and always, always blessed those she loved at Christmastime with stuffed boxes of mink stoles, Sunnyland Farm orange-frosted pecans, Japanese pears, and checks ranging from $100 to $500.

The girls thought of her as a goddess, a queen. She too felt invincible until pneumonia kidnapped Teresa at age eight and released her in death. That was hard to bear. Shirley never knew about the girls, so what need was there to invite him to the funeral? She'd forged his signature on their birth certificates and took on his last name as a reminder that a brief meeting can alter the course of one's life forever. After the funeral, she made Tawatha close her eyes and point to a new state and city to start anew. Tawatha pointed to Indiana and read I-N-D-I-A-N-A-P-O-L-I-S aloud.

"That's where we're going, baby. That's our new home."

A new home. That memory, painful and stabbing as it was, reminded Roberta of the importance of self-control. How could she leave Tawatha at the hospital when she knew she was responsible for a great deal of her daughter's foolishness?

"Tawatha, we'll be there in the morning."

Roberta looked in on her grandchildren, Aunjanue, Sims, Grant, and S'n'c'r'ty. She'd send them off to school in the morning and figure out how to help Tawatha secure a new place to live.

[9]
Palm Saturday

Victoria's biggest pet peeve was Winston's knack for RSVPing them for events without her consent. Particularly on holidays. Why couldn't they just enjoy the Fourth of July at *their* house, on *their* deck, flipping brats, jumbo burgers, and marinated steaks on *their* Weber grill with friends from the neighborhood? But no, he had to tell Aruba they'd join them to celebrate James's return to mobility after the accident. She rolled her eyes at Winston behind her shades and continued playing with Nicolette as they drove to Aruba's. She didn't know what had gotten into Winston, but after the cookout, she planned to have a long chitchat about his behavior.

First, it was the music. She knew he enjoyed old-school, but lately he'd been thumping the sounds of Anthony Hamilton, Urban Mystic, and John Legend throughout the house in heavy rotation. Add that to the silly mantras he'd been spewing out—accept the good; let's give thanks for what we already have; Victoria, when was the last time you counted your blessings and focused on someone other than yourself—and she was sure she'd lose it. Maybe he'd been working too many hours. The final insult was when she didn't get *the* Bentley last month for her birthday. He said it was too gaudy and that her Mercedes S600 would have to do for now. Her only consolation was the Harry Winston band she received. At least it was an upgrade from her Tiffany ring. Since he'd held out on the Bentley, she'd decided to hold out on sex a little longer. That would teach him a lesson.

"Babe, what's wrong?" Winston stroked Victoria's face. She ignored the question and colored the poppy fields in one of Nicolette's *Wizard of Oz* activity books. Nicolette did the same thing in the backseat.

"Mommy, Daddy's talking to you."

"Honey, I don't hear anything. Since no one hears me, why should I listen?"

Nicolette tapped Winston's shoulder from her booster seat. "Mommy's being a bad girl."

"Yes, she is, Nicolette. What do you suppose we should do to her?"

Nicolette shrugged her shoulders and continued coloring.

"You still sulking over the car? Why is that so important to you, Tori?"

"Winston, I've had my car two years now. What happened to getting me a new car every two years?"

Winston tapped his fingers on the steering wheel. "There's nothing wrong with your car."

"Next, you'll tell me to drive it until it's paid for."

"Victoria, when was the last time you—"

"Counted my blessings and focused on someone else other than myself. *I get it!*"

She turned her attention to the window and watched the gas prices at each service station they passed. Why was everyone complaining about the prices? Who coined the phrase, "pain at the pump"? Doesn't every woman's husband keep the tank filled like Winston? He never allowed her gas hand to go below half full. More importantly, why didn't she get her dream car? It wasn't as if they couldn't afford a Bentley. She didn't want a yacht, a private jet, or her own hangar at the airport. What was so wrong with wanting to drive a classic car that matched her beauty? She stared at her reflection in the mirror and hoped others at the cookout would find her stunning. The only reason she got excited about the party was the '80s theme. The invitation, emblazoned with painted red roses and a replica of the My-T-Sharp barbershop, blasted the song "Soul Glow." The song brought back memories of living in L.A. with her aunt and all those auditions and rounds they made together. Marguerite had snagged the role of Lisa in *Coming to America*, but had come down with tuberculosis two weeks before shooting began. Too weak to work and quarantined by her doctor, she had bowed out of filming. Marguerite's agent's words popped in her mind again as he'd tried to make Marguerite feel better, his East Coast timbre filling their living room via speaker phone: "I know Eddie Murphy is headlining the film, but who's gonna take him seriously as an African prince? I bet the movie probably won't make big box-office sales anyway." Victoria remembered Shari Headley coming by their rented apartment in Queens with chicken soup, Tylenol, and steamy gossip from the movie set. That's how Marguerite rolled in Hollywood and the Big Apple, acquaintance to all, friend to few. She taught Victoria that women were to be tolerated, not trusted. Victoria half listened to her aunt's rationale, though, because she knew there was no woman in the world who could wrest Winston from her grasp. He'd be a fool to leave someone so beautiful. Who else could spend his money, look good on his arm, and ride the ups and downs of his career as she had?

"Mommy, do you smell that food?" Nicolette asked. She scooted up in her booster seat and leaned forward to catch the sights and sounds emanating from Aruba's house.

"I love eating here," Winston added.

"Mommy, promise me you'll eat a plate with me and Daddy. Meat this time. Not all the vegetables."

"I'll think about it, Nicolette. I promise."

Winston parked on the curb because cars crowded the driveway. They headed toward the front door. Winston felt silly wearing the Michael Jackson *Thriller* jacket and jeans, but he didn't want to disobey the invite. He passed on the Jheri Curl wig Victoria suggested. Victoria spied the license plates as she smoothed the carbon copy dress worn by singer Pebbles in the video *Mercedes Boy* and took note of how many friends and relatives had joined the party. They'd traveled from Georgia, Louisiana, California, Kentucky, North Carolina, and Maryland. Morris Day and the Time's "Jungle Love" floated from the backyard with a rousing "Oh-eee-Oh-eee-Oh" being yelled out by the crowd. Nicolette snapped her fingers, wondering if Jeremiah was eating a hot dog or playing his Wii.

Winston rang the doorbell, anticipating James. When the door swung open, Aruba took his breath away. Aruba, donning a V-cut dashiki that accented her sun-kissed skin, bopped her head to the music. She beamed when she saw Winston, then remembered he wasn't alone.

"Come on in!" She hugged them and stepped aside for them to enter.

"Miss Aruba, where's Jeremiah?" Nicolette asked.

Aruba motioned the Faulks to follow her to the kitchen. She peered around Winston.

"Where's Alva? I thought she'd get out the house today."

"Rube, you know she doesn't get out that often."

"Hey, it's not like we didn't offer," Winston added. "She said she had reading to catch up on." He continued to smile at her as if they were the only ones in the room.

They were interrupted by a clearing throat. "I have a name, too."

Aruba looked at her mom, Darnella, who'd stopped dicing onions and bell peppers for the potato salad. "Mom, these are my friends, Winston, Victoria, and Nicolette."

"You know I know Victoria from the last time I was here. Don't you dare ask for my cobbler recipe this time, either," Darnella joked with Victoria. She hugged each of them, then sat back down at the island. "I'm almost done with this potato salad. I hope you all enjoy it."

"I promise I'll try it this time," said Victoria.

Aruba gathered Nicolette in her arms, kissed her. "May I offer you guys something to drink? James is manning the grill. We'll be eating in thirty minutes or less. Everybody else is out back. Come on."

"I'll have some of your lemonade if you whipped up some." Victoria couldn't deny that Aruba knew her way around the kitchen. She could take the simplest items and make a feast. In Aruba's presence, she wished she'd learned to cook when she was younger. Marguerite insisted she not learn to cook because she might burn her hands or ruin her back bending up and down near an oven. During those moments they hung out together, Aruba regaled her with tales of learning to cook when she was nine years old. The last time Darnella was in town, they'd tried in vain to show her how to prepare a soul food feast. Victoria cut her finger slicing tomatoes and got tired separating collard greens from the stems. She felt dizzy right now at the thought of cooking, taking care of a child, satisfying a husband, and staying sane. *Thank God for hired help.*

The four of them stepped through the patio door, onto the deck, and into the backyard where three white tents were set up. Most of the crowd danced as others sat at tables decorated for the occasion. Instead of traditional red, white and blue Fourth of July adornment, each table held a remnant of the movie *Coming to America*.

"Everyone, these are my friends Winston, Victoria, and lady Nicolette."

"Hey," the crowd sang in unison, returning to D.J. Cheese's spinning and scratching grooves.

A man rocking a Reverend Ike finger-waved 'do shouted to Victoria, "Marry me and come back to North Carolina! I'll take real good care of ya!"

The crowd laughed and his wife, Ida, seated next to him, jerked her neck around. "Shut up, Herbert!"

James slathered barbecue sauce on the ribs as he sized up Winston in his jacket and jeans. He still didn't understand why Aruba had invited them. It's one thing for a man to make a mistake in the heat of passion, it's another thing to be exposed. By someone like Winston no less. Now he had to step up his game, so he wouldn't look like the unemployed villain to this bourgeois muthafucka. Luckily for him, he'd been under doctor's care for the last two months. That was at least enough time for Aruba to stop riding him about finding work. She even had stopped talking divorce the last two months since the accident. Hell, she was almost like the woman he'd married. Running around, changing the gauze on his injuries, not bitching about the bills, at least letting a brother see her curves in those sexy negligees. His leg injury prevented him from being intimate, but he knew she wanted him just as much as he wanted her. Her new attitude even made him forget about Tawatha for the time being. Maybe, just maybe this was what he needed to be faithful. He was even pleased that Aruba wasn't so uptight about money these days since the company salary cuts. Last year this time, she wouldn't have dreamed of throwing a party for everyone, but this year, she must have seen the light and realized how good she had it at home.

"Hey, need some help with those ribs?" Winston interrupted James's thoughts.

"I got it. What's up, man?"

"It's good to see you up and about, James. I was a little worried about you at the hospital."

Yeah, right. "Staying off my feet has been good for me. I think this is what I needed. Spending time with Jerry and Aruba has been good for us."

"I meant what I said at the hospital, James. If you need anything, just let me know."

Like I'd fucking ask. "Thanks, man. Good looking out."

Victoria nursed lemonade spiked with vodka and wondered what James and Winston were talking about at the grill. Her slumped shoulders were not lost on the older women at the tables. They gossiped about their husbands, the presidential election, and why such a pretty girl was shrouded in that ugly don't-bother-me countenance. Victoria offered to help Aruba and Darnella in the kitchen, but she'd been shooed away, told to go mix and mingle with the crowd. She knew Aruba's friends Bria and Renae would be arriving later with their husbands. Since marrying and disappearing into Winston's world, she felt rusty and out of place in social settings. She shook off those thoughts, scanning the crowd for a familiar face, someone with whom she could trade barbs. When she turned right, a woman one table over looked up from a half-eaten tangerine and winked. She spat seeds in her hands and tossed them in the tangerine peels. She pointed a finger at Victoria. "Come here."

"Me?" Victoria asked, touching her chest.

"Yeah, you, sugar."

She joined the woman, hesitant and simultaneously amazed someone noticed her over the raucous card games, prattling, and dancing.

"I'm Maxine, Aruba's grandmother." She patted the seat next to her.

"It's good to finally meet you. I've heard so much about everyone. Actually, Aruba talks about her family all the time. I'm her friend Victoria."

Victoria remembered Aruba saying her grandmother was grown and sexy, but wasn't that every granddaughter's claim? Maxine's flawless skin, lightly dusted with powder and the color of teak wood, glowed. The warmest smile Victoria had ever seen set off Maxine's high cheekbones. Maxine wasn't trying to hide her age; her salt-and-pepper hair flowed past her shoulders in spiral curls. The smell of The One body oil drifted from her skin. Victoria's quick head-to-toe glance of Maxine's outfit yielded a well put-together summer outfit: diamond hoops, a flowing, peach-colored silk blouse, painted-on jeans, and peach stilettos. She ran peach-colored nails through her curls, and yelled to James, "Bring me one of those ribs. I'm starving! I need more than this fruit."

Maxine had the body of a thirty-year-old and Victoria guessed she was at least sixty-five. *Damn good genes!*

Maxine turned her attention back to Victoria. "That's good to know Aruba talks about us. We sure do miss her and that baby."

"Don't you all miss James, too?"

Maxine discarded the tangerine peels in a plastic plate, ignoring the question and continuing,

"So, how many of our people do you know at this party?"

"Only a few," said Victoria.

"You see the woman over there in the red halter top and jeans?

The one talking a mile a minute and probably won't come up for air?"

"Yes. She's quite the social butterfly."

"That's James's sister, Teresa. She's probably drumming up business. They live down in Atlanta and, honey, she can plan weddings out of this world. She's the go-to person if you want an elegant affair."

"Does she do only weddings?"

"That's her specialty, but she does it all. Even decorates cakes. Remember Toni Braxton's wedding? Teresa did most of it."

"What about the guy who stood up when I walked in and asked me to marry him?"

"That's my brother, Herbert. Ida's been putting up with his roving eyes for years. But if she likes it, I love it. He lives in North Carolina, but my brother Walstine lives here in Indy. You can't get away from the Stantons, baby."

Victoria chuckled at Maxine's wit. "I'm sure the guy near the grill is James's brother."

"Yes, Lord. No one in that family will admit it, but those boys have a rift between them. I can sense it. Marvin, that's his brother's name, runs his mouth as much as Teresa. He has his own garage business. He said he's putting Overhead Garage Doors out of business or will die trying. I thought he was talking trash until our last family trip, but he's well respected in Atlanta. I think it riles James that Marvin, who's his baby brother, is so successful."

"James's brother and sister are both business owners?"

"Girl, yes. But don't get me to lying about why they won't help him." Maxine turned her attention to the patio. "The fox that just stepped off the deck with the bowl of potato salad is my daughter, Darnella. That's Aruba's momma. Have you met her?"

"I have. I love her peach cobbler. I begged her for the recipe the last time they were in town, but she wouldn't budge."

"It's really my recipe. I'll give it to you before we leave. I don't believe in hoarding recipes from people. Even if I give it to you, ours won't taste the same because each person puts their own love into cooking. Know what I mean?"

"I would be forever grateful."

"So if you know Darnella, you know my son-in-law, Lance?"

"Yes, ma'am. He insisted on washing my car last year. I think he just wanted to take my Mercedes for a spin."

"I've got a good son-in-law. They've been married thirty-five years and are still going strong. I think that's why Aruba stays with James. She wants what her parents have. I want to tell her so badly to give up the ghost, but I know that's not my place."

"You know a lot about both sides of the families. What gives?"

"Victoria, the Stantons and the Dixons are fellowshipping people! Every year, we all go on a trip together. James's people and our folks pick out a location and spend a weekend together. The last time we went to Tom Joyner's Black Family Reunion. I want to do the Fantastic Voyage cruise, but the older folks swear they can't spare a week off to hang out. Like they're doing so doggone much in retirement. I've got at least two bikinis I need to try out."

"Miss Maxine, you do not have bikinis!"

"Don't you?"

"You're something else."

Maxine eased into the next subject. "I couldn't help noticing you look lonely. You okay?"

"Yes, Miss Maxine…I'm fine."

"Call me Maxie. Why are you so sad?"

Victoria clutched her cup. "Miss, Maxie, I'm wonderful, really. I have a good husband, a beautiful home, a lovely daughter, good friends…"

James slipped a plate of ribs to Maxine, kissed her cheek. "Let me know if the sauce is too hot."

"You know I will."

"You want something, Victoria?" James asked.

"I'll probably grab some vegetables a little later. Thanks for asking."

James pimp strolled toward the grill, hoping Maxine didn't devour Victoria.

"There I go again, getting in grown folks' business. Ole Maxie didn't mean no harm. I guess it just seemed like something was missing, that's all."

"Missing?"

"Well, for a woman who has this great life, I wouldn't have put you and your husband together."

"Ma'am?"

"When you came in. I would have pegged that fine man as your brother. Not your husband."

"Oh?"

"Sugar, don't mind me. You get this age and you feel you can speak your mind to anybody."

"I'm not the least bit offended. I've heard that before."

"He seems like a nice man."

Maxine retrieved her purse, dug inside, and pulled out a set of Tarot cards. Willadean, her sister, looked up from her Tonk game two tables over, and shouted, "Maxie, put that mess back in your purse. We didn't come up here for that."

"Did I ask you anything?"

Maxine glared at Willadean. She knew her family was embarrassed by the gift she possessed. Was it her fault she was granted sight? It's not as if she asked to see into the future, to be forewarned of events to come. From the time she predicted her father's death right down to the second at twelve years old, Maxine was haunted by that feeling she'd get when someone near her seemed empty, misguided. She would have left well enough alone with Victoria, but there was something about her walk, the sadness in those eyes, the anxiety she displayed among all that laughter and fun. Maxine saw it in the spirit. The cards enhanced her gift, so she carried them for moments like these. She was careful, though, to ask if a person wanted a reading. She never forced her gift on others, nor did she make light of the information revealed. Seldom were the cards off beam.

"You mind if I read for you?"

"Read?"

"You know, with the cards. Interested in knowing what the future holds for you?"

Victoria glanced around to see if others were watching their exchange. She remembered going to readings with Marguerite in L.A. Obsessed Marguerite. Always inquiring about when she'd be an A-Lister. Kept saying she wanted fame like Roberts, Streep, and Hawn. The L.A. reader, Sister Audrey Wilcox, told Marguerite an Oscar wasn't in the cards, but service to mankind was in her future. She finally gave up the red carpet fixation and started a community theater for Carmel, California youth.

"What harm could it do?" asked Victoria. She swigged on her lemonade and watched Winston laugh and throw his head back at a joke thrown out by Aruba's uncle Herbert.

"Let's go inside. It's a little noisy out here and I can't concentrate or give a good reading. Too many distractions."

Victoria and Maxine snuck past Aruba and the children playing Wii and settled down in Aruba's home office. Maxine meditated briefly, opened her eyes, and pushed the deck toward Victoria on the desk.

"Shuffle them for me. When you're done, select seven."

Victoria shuffled the cards, then laid them in a seven-card spread. Maxine breathed, flipped over the first card.

"The fool," said Victoria. "What does that mean, Maxie?"

Maxine's specificity made her popular throughout the South. She made sure, based on the temperament of her clients, not to reveal more than they could handle.

"Who is Lillith?"

"My mother." Victoria leaned closer.

"The fool stands for new beginnings. She put you in the hands of someone else to pursue a new beginning with a man. Clifford was his name, correct?"

"My God. Mr. Cliff. Clifford Rutland. That's him. Was him."

"Your mother thought he was perfect for her. He got her out to Texas and left her high and dry. That's how you came to live with Marguerite, right?" Maxie felt she was frightening Victoria. "Honey, you all right?"

"Yes, I just wondered how my mom was doing. I think of her so much."

"She's fine. Embarrassed is all. Don't give up on her yet. You'll be reunited with her in less than three years. Pick another card."

Victoria flipped over the next card and registered a quizzical look. "The Wheel of Fortune."

"Aaah, fate and destiny. Try if you might, you just can't stop it. Change is coming in your life and soon, so be prepared."

"What kind of change?"

"I see you helping others."

Victoria chuckled. "Maxie, I help myself to good sales. That's about it."

"Oh, you've been on top of the world for a long time now. Storm's gonna hit you soon. You'll be forced to rethink all that's important. Pick another card."

"The Lovers."

"The Lovers aren't always sexual in nature, but most times are. Why do you withhold sex from your husband?"

"I…"

"Did I startle you? Anytime I'm too personal, you can ask me to back down."

Victoria wasn't sure how to proceed. How could she tell Maxie that while she enjoyed the perks of her lifestyle, sex was the only thing she felt she had control of in the marriage. He made the money, built the houses, bought the cars, stashed cash for Nicolette's college fund. Couldn't she have control of something? "I guess I'm tired a lot."

"Honey, love is a flame that must not be left unattended; it must be fueled and allowed to burn for as long as possible. Your husband is under pressure at his job. He craves and needs your attention now more than ever. As you enter the coming months, light a candle each night—" Maxine stopped midsentence.

"Maxie, what's wrong? What do you see?"

Maxine swooped the cards from the table, reassembled the deck, and clutched her chest. "I'm done for the day, Victoria. I hope I was able to help you in some way. Please, please look well to the ways of your household." With that, Maxine fanned her face with papers from the desk and went back to join the party.

Victoria sighed and wondered what she'd do now. There was always something legitimate in the cards.

[10]
Let's Start Fresh

"Watha, what's up with you? What's this all about?" Jamilah grinned from ear to ear. She entered the two-story home, carrying a bottle of wine and her famous sweet and spicy ribs.

"Yeah, who died and left you an inheritance?" Lasheera joked.

Tawatha waited to invite Jamilah and Lasheera over to her new place. Waited until everything was just so. They were her girls and she wanted them to be proud of her, the new digs, the new furniture, the new man who would soon be her husband, her new lease on life. The Fourth of July was the perfect holiday to debut the newness, her independence.

"Sheer, why somebody gotta die to live better? Can't I be sick and tired of being sick and tired like Fannie Lou Hamer?"

"Milah, did PBS re-air *Eyes on the Prize*? She only talks about the movement when the show airs."

Lasheera playfully stuck her finger down her throat, pretending to gag at Tawatha's words.

"I know, Sheer. Somebody's done put some sticknotic on our girl. Touch her forehead. I hadn't seen you this happy since you were with Grant's father." Jamilah placed the ribs and wine on the gathering table in the kitchen next to a killer spread. "Who's all this food for? Where are my babies?" Jamilah looked outside toward the backyard for Tawatha's children.

"Momma and Mr. J.B. took them to White River Park. This is all for you two. Kind of a thank-you for being there for me since the accident. Heck, for always being there."

"Wait, that's one thank-you, a heck, no cussing, and a conservative outfit. Oh yeah, Jamilah, she's sticknotized."

"Sit down in the living room and shut up. I'll bring you guys some drinks."

Lasheera and Jamilah settled on a chocolate leather sofa. Floored they didn't have to swim through piles of clothes, a maze of newspapers and clutter, or the rancid odor of rotting Chinese take-out seeping through a trash bag, they took in the everything-in-its-place order of Tawatha's place. So many questions ran through their minds. How could she afford this house? Who was the new man—because Lasheera and Jamilah knew metamorphoses in Tawatha's life were always tied to a man—and what did he do for a living to give her this kind of hookup? Jamilah fell in love with the open floor plan of the home. The photos in the dining room warmed her heart because Tawatha symmetrically had arranged eight photos of family and friends in black frames above a stylish banquet table. The best photo was of Lasheera, Tawatha, and Jamilah on the playground during fifth-grade recess. Jamilah had forgotten about that photo and the wonderful times they shared in school.

"Where did you find that old photo of us?" Jamilah asked.

"Girl, Momma dug it out of the attic. Nice, huh?" Tawatha milled around the kitchen, pulling juices and liquors down on the counter for drinks. "I wonder whatever happened to Mrs. Hopkins?"

"Watha, why'd you have to bring up that old coot?" Lasheera sucked her teeth and rolled her eyes at Tawatha.

"Come on, Sheer. If it hadn't been for Mrs. Hopkins, we wouldn't be friends."

"Yeah, Watha's right. You just won't let it go. Thought you were learning to forgive and forget in church."

"No, I won't let it go. That woman segregated us because of our names. Had the nerve on the first day of that school year to ask Principal Thornton, 'Whatever became of the Paulas, Anthonys, Tiffanys, and Gregorys of the world?'" Lasheera mimicked Mrs. Hopkins's proper, clipped tone. "'If one more Raheem, Laniqua, or Quedawntay shows up, I'll die and rip up my teaching license!' Then she had the audacity to make the three of us sit in the back of the room so she didn't have to call on us."

"Weren't we the smartest girls in the room, though?" Jamilah reasoned.

"You got that right," Tawatha chimed in.

While Tawatha mixed drinks, Jamilah and Lasheera recalled the good old days, brought up old classmates, shook their heads at the crazy turns their lives had taken.

"Milah, here's a peach martini for you, and, Sheer, here's a strawberry daiquiri for you," said Tawatha, removing the drinks from a gorgeous crystal tray and placing them on matching coasters on the coffee table.

"And where's your drink?" asked Jamilah.

"The pineapple juice is mine. I've got to watch my girlish figure."

"I can't take it anymore. What's going on and who is he?" Lasheera demanded as she swiped the cherry from her drink.

"First things first," Tawatha said, joining her friends in the living room. "I'm in this place on a lease-to-own basis. Mr. J.B., my momma's boyfriend, owns properties all over Indy. For once, Aunjanue's big mouth came to our rescue. When she let it slip that a cockroach crawled across S'n'c'r'ty's mouth while they were playing on the floor, Momma almost passed out. She asked J.B. if I could live in one of his places for a trial period. If I maintain the place, pay my rent on time, and enroll at Momentive Credit, they'll help me with ownership."

"That's wonderful! I'll have somewhere new to stay when I'm driving back and forth to Bloomington," Jamilah announced.

"Bloomington?" Lasheera and Tawatha said in unison.

"You're not the only one with a surprise. I've been accepted at IU! I start next month. I'll be majoring in pre-law."

"Shut up! That's great. How long was you gonna keep it a secret?"

"Lasheera, as big as your mouth is, I know you would have told someone," said Jamilah.

"I'm proud of you, Milah. No one deserves this more than you. You practically gave up your life after high school to help your dad take care of your mom. Then no sooner than she died, you had to nurse your dad. Feels like he suffered forever until he died last year. Girl, you've been through it." Tawatha reminisced about Jamilah's hard times.

"Yeah, but I'll be a twenty-nine-year-old freshman. Make that thirty since my birthday is next month."

"Well, if forty is the new thirty, then thirty is the new eighteen. You're gonna do well in Bloomington. Just don't act like you don't know us when you get that big-time job," said Tawatha.

"I know. I guess I'm just scared. I feel like I waited so long."

"Better late than never," Lasheera chimed in.

Jamilah spat out the next question while she had the nerve to ask. "How's Zion, Sheer?"

Lasheera winced at the sound of her son's name. She encouraged Jamilah and Tawatha to mention him, keep his existence real to her. Two years had passed since the custody battle, but the wound was still open, fresh. The only thing worse than losing Zion was *how* she'd lost him. Lasheera knew drugs were a no-no, but six years prior to giving birth, she became a crack addict. Lasheera, Jamilah, and Tawatha created a no-judgment zone in eighth grade. The girls felt the sting of teasing as each one bore the cross of their nicknames: Big Booty Tawatha; Jamilah, the Indianapolis Zebra, so named for her biracial heritage; and Old Refrigerator Lasheera, tagged for being a tattletale and unable to keep secrets. The constant playground refrain for Lasheera was, "You're just like an old refrigerator. You can't hold nothing!"

The no-judgment zone they'd created kept her alive when she foolishly decided to smoke crack with Marvin Anderson, a married bouncer who was the love of her life at the time. Tawatha and Jamilah didn't hesitate to get out of bed at two in the morning to pick her up when she phoned. Her hangout was downtown near New Jersey and Washington Streets, donning little more than daisy dukes, neon tank tops, and sandals. She marched around the streets, soliciting men for money, tricks, food, or a warm place to rest during the winter months. Marvin kicked the habit but continued to sleep with her, producing Zion. Once his wife discovered a crackhead created what she couldn't after eighteen years of marriage, she insisted Marvin sue Lasheera for custody. Her girls were there for her as she struggled to get the monkey off her back. Cried with her when the police retrieved Zion from the middle of busy, late-night traffic while Lasheera gave Lean On Me, the New Jersey Street wino, a blowjob. Nursed her to health as she went through detox. Asked what they could do to help after Marvin and his knife, his nickname for his wife, carried Zion from the courthouse. She wanted a new start and would stop at nothing to get it and her son back.

"Zion's doing pretty good. Linda calls him things like 'bastard' or 'out-of-wedlock mistake' when Marvin isn't around."

"She says things like that?" Jamilah asked.

"I may be suffering, but Marvin ain't exactly walking in the park, either. Every chance Linda gets, she throws the affair up in his face. I'm scared she's gonna lash out at Zion. That's why I want him back."

"What's the next step for you?" asked Tawatha.

"Well, my attorney, Mike Requeno, has been helping me find a job. I have to provide a stable place for Zion. I can't blame my parents for being leery about letting me move back in their place. I've put in applications everywhere and Mike said he has some contacts at a few places. I need some clothes for my search, too."

"Try Dress for Success. They provide suits and business attire for women like you getting back on your feet. I think they're down on Meridian," Jamilah offered.

"Mike also told me to make inroads within the community. Volunteer doing community service, join a church. I've been attending New Beginnings Fellowship Church. I really like it."

"With Dr. James Anthony Jackson? AKA Jack? Girl, I listen to him on the radio. I like the messages he puts out there. I might have to join you one Sunday," said Jamilah.

"You deserve a chance to raise your kid," Tawatha added, gulping more of her pineapple juice.

"I'm glad Marvin is decent enough to share pictures and updates with me."

"Ummm, Watha, don't think I'm through with my questions," Jamilah chimed in to lighten the mood. "Who is this man who has you acting strange?"

"I gotta keep this one under wraps. He's the best man I've met in a long time."

"Sounds serious," said Lasheera.

Tired of riding shotgun with misery, Tawatha chewed on a pineapple chunk from her drink, sat back on the sofa, and exclaimed, "You heifers better be in shape by next summer for your bridesmaid dresses."

[11]
Flirting in September

Winston swiveled in his leather office chair and twirled his favorite fountain pen. So many thoughts invaded his mind lately, he felt as if he'd suffocate. How could he have allowed another woman to capture his heart? He'd thought it impossible to desire another woman. Particularly his wife's friend. Definitely not another man's wife. But there she was, occupying his mind with the memory of her dancing eyes, the way she tossed her hair when she laughed, the way her smile melted him. He felt shame when he thought back on the barbecue two months ago. He truly forgot Victoria and Nicolette were standing next to him as he gazed at Aruba. He wanted to run his fingers through her hair and give her a deep passionate kiss.

If that wasn't enough, Cedars-Sinai dangled a tempting carrot to join their research team. Victoria would explode at the thought of moving again. No, she'd divorce him if they moved again.

As he looked back over his life, he marveled at the blessings showered upon him. His parents, Dr. and Mrs. Adam and Margaret Faulk, planned his life detail by detail. When Winston was born, a trust was opened in his name. Private school was a necessity, not an option. He blossomed in school, acing all his classes and garnering a perfect score on his SATs. The only thing his parents couldn't control was his awkwardness. Not sure from which side of the family his clumsiness sprouted, they watched their tall, gangly son trip over chairs, fall down steps, and slide down hills during summer and winter vacations. At bridge parties in their summer home on Martha's Vineyard, Winston listened to his mother's friends boast about their beautiful children and of him stated, "Margaret, Winston is so intelligent, bless his heart. And those dimples will get him far." Margaret laughed it off while sipping scotch and soda.

Adam, confident his son would grow into himself, told him no man should have one profession, so Winston set his sights on becoming a doctor, lawyer, and CPA, choosing to utilize medicine as his primary career. Not until medical school did the Faulks' smart but different son flourish. Gone was the acne, lithe frame, the thick glasses. Winston beefed up, and standing at six-four, quietly gained attention from women. The newness of women smiling at him, passing their numbers, or offering first dibs at developing his bedside manner flattered him, but dissipated when he met Victoria, a UCLA undergraduate student. She caught his attention as she skated by bopping her head to music booming from a bass-thumping stereo on Venice Beach. Equally attracted to him, she skated toward him, looked in his eyes, pointed to an ice cream cart, and asked, "Chocolate Crunch or Cherry Vanilla?"

Ice Cream at Sal's Ice Cream and Confectionary Dreams mobile cart morphed into movies, high phone bills during his residency, and a year-long engagement that culminated in a lavish wedding reviewed in *The New York Times*. Victoria's beauty captivated Winston so much so he ignored her incessant chatter about wanting the finer things in life, about making sure her husband and marriage had to be better or else. Now, he wanted so much more. Intimacy, communication, someone that had his back. As Victoria shared Aruba's plight and James's misdeeds, he wondered how Victoria would react if that type of adversity plagued them. He knew the outcome: She'd be gone.

"Dr. Faulk, there's someone here to see you," Janice buzzed over the intercom, snapping Winston back to the present.

"Did I have any appointments today?"

After a brief pause, Janice responded, "It's a Mrs. Aruba Dixon here to see you."

"Send her in."

Winston hurried to greet her, welcoming the unannounced visit. As he opened the door to say hello, he got excited watching her work her mojo.

Aruba sashayed into the office, picnic basket in one hand, gift bag in the other. The cream-and-aqua wrap dress that hugged her voluptuous body couldn't be hidden beneath the cream linen jacket she wore. Aruba took advantage of the unseasonably warm weather by ditching the stockings and sporting aqua stilettos. A French mani and pedi told Winston just how much she cared about pampering herself.

"Let me help you with that," Winston offered. He placed the picnic basket and gift bag on a nearby table. "What did I do to deserve this visit?"

Aruba removed her jacket as well as the basket from the table. She stood closer to him, allowing him time to take in the scent of Flowerbomb. "Well, I haven't had a chance to adequately thank you for the generous gift, the ER visit, and your encouragement. No one has ever been that kind to me, so it's payback time."

"This isn't necessary, but I'm not complaining."

Aruba stopped counting the lines she'd crossed two hours ago. If Victoria wasn't going to take care of Winston's needs, she would. Too much time had passed since she'd put her snag-him-in-a-year plan in action. While James went to a dental appointment, she took the morning off to prepare all the foods she knew Winston loved. She packed a change of clothing for the office. Victoria had shared Winston's schedule several times. He only saw clients after eleven on Wednesdays, so the timing couldn't have been better.

"Tell me you didn't prepare Aruba's by the Sea."

"I won't then."

Aruba beamed as she spread a checkered blue-and-white table-cloth on the floor. Winston watched her bend down to remove Pyrex dishes of food from zippered containers.

Down, boy, down.

She removed a matching set of plates, glasses, and silverware. Aruba prepared Winston's plate, piling lots of shrimp and extra seafood sauce on his rice. She placed two garlic sticks on a separate saucer. Winston's mouth watered at the food sitting before him.

"Before you touch a morsel, let me spread a napkin on your lap."

Winston sat Indian style and took in the aroma of everything. Save his mother and Alva, no woman had ever served him to this degree. Aruba took care to make sure he had enough to eat, that he would savor the meal, even down to the dessert. She'd baked banana rum cake, his favorite.

"Say grace for us?" she asked.

"Father, thank you for the marvelous food before us. Bless the hands that prepared it and let it provide nourishment for our bodies. In Jesus' name, Amen."

Winston dug in, relishing his good fortune.

"I want to get a few things off my chest. I've been so mortified since the night of the accident. I feel awful about the gas, the money, the fact you even had to come to my aid. I think I'm most ashamed of the fact I'm not where I want to be. Please let me know how I can repay you for helping me out."

"A few more lunches like this and we might be even."

"I'm serious. This is hard for me. Oh wait, you've got a little sauce on your chin." Aruba leaned into him, her breasts rubbing against Winston's arm. She wiped his mouth off, then took her seat across from him again.

Thank God for the napkin. Winston's manhood rose again. He fought hard to concentrate, to keep the conversation decent. "Since you're serious, why the shame?"

"Look at you and Victoria. I look around and see so many couples working together, doing their thing. I just wish I had what it took to inspire James a little more. I see so much in him. I love him and I believe in him. I'm just not sure how to pull out all the good I see."

Winston's jaw tightened. That wasn't exactly what he wanted to hear and he wasn't sure why. He wanted to offer encouragement, Godly advice, but he was tongue-tied. Why couldn't his wife be as compassionate? As loving? Winston weighed his words, knowing the conversation had to stay decent. He took Aruba's hands into his.

"Aruba, don't stop doing what you're doing. James is so fortunate to have you in his life. I…" Winston paused. "I will keep the two of you in my thoughts and prayers. Trust me, things will work out for you."

"Thanks, Winston. It's good to know you and Victoria have my back."

Winston sighed.

Aruba, sensing his tension, his passion, enjoyed the effect her enticement was having on him. "Did I say something wrong?"

"It's just…never mind."

"Oh no, you don't start a comment and not finish it," Aruba joked.

"I've been offered a position at Cedars-Sinai Research Center and I'd love to accept it. My journey in cardiology has never been about money. I love what I do and I love impacting lives. However—"

"Victoria would hit the roof if you mentioned it, right?" Aruba asked.

"Whoa, how much has she said about my workaholic ways?"

"I'll never tell."

"I know she's displeased with the moving, the different cities. I'm sure it's stressful, but I work hard to make sure Victoria and Nicolette are safe and secure. Which would you rather have, Aruba? A man who worked regular hours and was home for the family, or a man who worked a lot but whose mission was to leave a legacy?"

"You doctors have such a way of putting things. Hmmm, let me think. I'll take the legacy man for five hundred dollars."

They both chuckled at her comment. Winston's phone rang. He looked down, cursing his luck as Victoria's ringtone, "Who's That Lady," trilled in the office. He gave Aruba a *shhhh* gesture and put Victoria on speakerphone.

"Victoria, how are you?"

"I'm calling to see what you're doing for lunch today."

"Just working on some documents and fielding calls for new clients. Where are you?"

"I was headed to your office, but got a call from Charlotte. I actually called Aruba earlier to meet her, but I couldn't reach her."

"What's with the call from Charlotte?"

"Oh, she had to go out of town suddenly. Jack is up for some film award at a festival and he wanted her to join him. I'm filling in for her at Dorcas House."

"What? You're volunteering?"

"You said I should think about others. Besides, if this is the way to get some more shoes and stock my winter wardrobe, count me in."

"Babe, I've got another call coming in. Let me call you back in thirty minutes or so."

"Don't bother, I'll stop by later when I'm done at Dorcas."

Winston ended the call, embarrassed that his wife's desire for things took precedence over her concern for people.

"On that note, I'm slicing you some cake, Dr. Faulk."

Aruba carved a fat slice of banana rum cake for Winston. She cooked extra rum sauce at home, noting people who ate her cake always requested more sauce. She poured sauce on the cake, then passed it to him.

"Since you asked me about James, what advice do you have for me about Victoria?"

"Well, Victoria is luckier than James. She has a good man who works hard, is intelligent, and desires to leave a legacy. Keep being you, Winston. Someday she'll see you for the regal king you are."

I hope she sees it soon.

"I'm leaving after our dessert. I've got to get back to the office. I can't leave without giving you a little something, though."

Aruba handed Winston the gift bag. Flustered, he removed the colored tissue paper. To his surprise, she'd purchased a book he'd been eyeing at Borders. *Take the Risk: Learning to Identify, Choose, and Live with Acceptable Risk* by Dr. Ben Carson was at the top of his To Be Read list.

"Just what I needed for what I'm going through. So this starts the race again."

"Race?"

"I'm really at a crossroads right now, and I know this is one thing that will help me make the decisions I need to make about my future. I'll find a way to pay you back for this one."

"No need, Winston. You already have."

Aruba had set her bait and her work was done. She packed the picnic lunch, left the cake on Winston's desk, and kissed his cheek.

Winston watched her sway out of the office. *Aruba's a risk I'd be willing to take, come what may.*

[12]
For the Love of Money

James rubbed his sore jaw and popped the cap off a bottle of Ibuprofen. The root-scaling procedure done at the dentist's office was excruciating. He'd hobbled in from Dr. Morton's office, plopped down on the sofa, and tried to get a nap, but his phone vibrated so much he couldn't rest. He snatched the phone from the coffee table, then grunted. Seventy-eight text messages. Thirty-five missed calls. "Damn, can't you take a hint," James muttered as he scrolled through the calls and messages from Tawatha. Tawatha was the first woman James met whose traffic signals were all screwed up. Red was a definite green for State Fair. He purposely slowed communication with her after the night of the accident. Too risky. He thought he could keep her at bay with an occasional email or text about Aruba's cancer, but when she offered to help take care of Aruba, he ceased communication with her. He hoped she'd buy the grieving husband bit, find a new man. She wasn't going away quietly and he had to do something.

He grabbed the remote, turned to CNN. Aruba would never believe that he enjoyed watching *Headline News* or anything financial, but lately, time on the sectional had turned into an introspective party. For the first time since the early years of their marriage, he actively sought employment. He'd sent out at least fifty résumés, drummed up a few contacts from his previous jobs, and registered with two upcoming job fairs. He wondered if his dreadlocks were getting in the way of finding a job, but he decided to hold tight to his locks for now. Bills continued to roll in each day as he recuperated from the accident. Gas. Lights. Car notes. Insurance. ER expenses. The list went on and on, but his baby was still doing the damn thing. Taking care of them and not complaining about it. The least he could do was find a part-time gig to help alleviate Aruba's fears. He'd keep the job prowling to himself for now, surprise her when a good prospect came his way. He didn't want to think of how disappointed she must have been in him and his inability to keep a job. He wasn't sure why he couldn't keep a job himself. Time in front of the television, watching *Divorce Court* and *Judge Joe Brown*, made him wonder when it became acceptable to let his lady foot the bill, finance the major purchases, steer their destiny.

Growing up, he had witnessed equal give-and-take between his parents. His dad turned the bill-paying reins over to his mom, and said, "You can make more sense outta these numbers than I can. Take care of everything and give me a little something for my pocket." James sat with his mother at the dining room table the first Friday of each month. She spread the bills out, smallest to largest, and wrote checks for each item. James was accountable for double-checking the numbers and making sure they balanced in the checkbook. She told him no woman wanted a man who couldn't manage money. He laughed at his mother then, told her she was trying to spook him. He wished he'd paid more attention to her. Maybe his marriage would be different now.

"The fuck?" James bolted from the sofa, panic-stricken.

Silence, then darkness, jarred James's memory.

"Shit! I can't believe…"

James ran to the front door, called to the utility worker.

"Brotha man? What's up? You gotta do this shit today?"

The Indianapolis Power and Light representative walked back to the door to greet James. He hated confrontation. He wanted to resolve the matter quickly and attend to other homes in the subdivision.

"Sir, a disconnect notice was sent," he looked down at his clipboard, "a month ago." He added, "You'll have to go to our office on Illinois Street to settle the matter. Of course, you'll have to pay the delinquent charges as well as a reconnect fee." He pointed to the yellow sticker on the door. "Have a good day, Mr. Dixon."

James yanked the notice off the door, then went back inside. In an attempt to smooth things over, Aruba gave him one task after the accident: make sure the utility bill is paid each month. How did he forget to pay the bill? What the hell did he do with the money? James rushed upstairs to Aruba's secret stash. She always kept money nestled between DVDs in their bedroom. He dug through several movies and came up empty.

"Damn!"

He rambled through several coats in their walk-in closet, hoping he'd left some money in his pockets, or that she'd paid some bills and forgot to empty hers. He searched the glass pickle jar in back of the closet, usually filled with silver coins. Empty. He refused to let her come home to no lights. The last thing he wanted to hear *again* was how irresponsible he was, how he couldn't handle the simplest tasks. James paced the bedroom floor, thinking of a way to pay the bill.

"The account," James murmured.

He connected the old standby touch-tone phone and called Chase Bank to check the balance on their joint account. He waited for an account representative, paced back and forth.

"Thank you for calling Chase Bank. This is Whitney Jamison. How may I assist you today?"

"I was calling to check the balance on my account."

"Your name, sir."

"James Dixon."

"May I have the last four digits of your social security number or your bank account number?"

"Six one eight, four two zero, one one one."

"And what was the date and amount of the last deposit made to this account?"

James eyed a wall calendar, remembering Aruba's direct deposit payments on the fifteenth and thirtieth of each month.

"The fifteenth. The amount was one thousand, forty-five dollars and forty-three cents."

James concocted lies to tell Aruba as he marched the bedroom floor. He would make an automatic payment from the account to IPL and replace the money from one of the job prospects. No way would he allow her to step through the door with no lights. He'd tell her he used the money to buy Jeremiah a few outfits.

"Mr. Dixon, I'm so sorry to inform you that account has been closed."

"Pardon me."

"Yes. It appears your wife closed that joint account about a month ago. She opened a new account several months ago, though. However, I am not able to give you any information about that account as she is the sole account holder. Again, I'm so sorry. Have a good day, Mr. Dixon."

James slammed the phone down. No wonder she'd been walking around, pretending everything was okay. She was holding out on the money. He was tired of her holding the purse strings, dictating everything financial between them. James knew what he had to do.

[13]
Long Time No See

Tawatha nuked a Lean Cuisine meal as she read *Black Enterprise*. At first she hated that Hinton and Conyers didn't have a wider variety of magazines. Everything splayed on the tables had something to do with finances, current news, or pets. Out of sheer boredom, she picked up a *Black Enterprise* a few weeks ago and was hooked. She particularly enjoyed the "Wealth for Life" section and the financial fitness contest winners. She loved reading about people her age working to get their financial houses in order. Sometimes she felt as if life had passed her by because lots of the couples and singles featured made four to five times more money than she made. Once the dust settled and she married James, she planned to sit down and complete the financial snapshot numbers just to see how her assets and liabilities looked on paper. She knew she didn't have much, but they made her want more. Her phone vibrated. She broke into giddy laughter when she saw James's number on her caller ID. Maybe his wife had died. Maybe he was calling to tell her about the arrangements. Maybe he and Jeremiah could move in with her and the kids. Who would want to live in a house where their spouse passed? The one thing she admired about James was that he never told her his wife's name. Truth was she didn't want to know. She was going to be the new woman in his life and her name was the only one that mattered.

"I think someone has the wrong number. I don't know a James Dixon. You sure you're calling the right person?"

"Come outside and see."

Tawatha dropped her magazine, dashed to the parking lot. She rushed into James's arms, planting kisses on his cheeks. She wanted to give him a deep, passionate kiss, but she knew her nosy coworkers were probably gazing at her from their offices.

"Turn around, let me look at you," said James.

Tawatha twirled for her man, pleased that her makeover would make him think twice about proposing to her. James watched Tawatha strike a pose, noting she seemed different. Gone were the tight, form-fitting clothes she wore when they first met. She'd traded in the silky, tight skirts showcasing her ample bottom and tops barely holding in the headlights for a sleek, two-piece gray skirt suit. A string of pearls adorned her neck. James knew Tawatha had long hair, but he was blown away by the sleek, layered cut she sported. No more streaks or highlights. Just the natural beauty he saw while working at Hinton and Conyers.

"Tawatha, you look beautiful. I came to take you to lunch, but I'm not sure you want to be seen with me looking like this."

"Don't be silly, you look fine. Gorgeous. Sexy. Yummy. Need I say more?"

Tawatha swatted James on his bottom, went back to the office to get her purse, and told her boss she'd be back in an hour. Her lunch break had just begun and she decided to utilize accrued time from a project that went overtime a few weeks ago. She joined James in a different vehicle than the one he'd driven during the night of the accident.

"What happened to the Sequoia?"

"Insurance company totaled the vehicle. This is my wife's vehicle. She's driving the company car."

Satisfied with his response, Tawatha sat back in the passenger's seat and smiled at the man she loved. Minutes later they were at Tea's Me Café. They ordered a BBQ Chicken and Swiss Panini, Corned Beef and Swiss with sauerkraut, and hot oolong tea.

"James, I've missed you so much. I know why you haven't called. This must be hard for you. Please don't leave me in the dark."

"Thanks for understanding. I can't tell you what this is doing to me. I've been out of work, taking care of things—"

"I told you I'd help. I know it would be awkward, but I can help feed and bathe your wife." *If that woman on* Widow on the Hill *could do it, I can, too.*

"That would be too creepy for me. I mean, we did, well, you know…in the house."

Roberta's words came rushing back to her. *"What goes around comes around, Tawatha. You can't disrespect another woman and not expect to pay the cost."* Tawatha shooed the thought away. Things had been going great for her. She'd accompanied Lasheera to Dress for Success and walked away with lovely suits of her own. She never guessed a wardrobe change would make a difference at the office. Mr. Conyers began to take her seriously, asking her opinion in staff meetings and giving her challenging assignments. A new place, new job title, and a small raise boosted her confidence, gave her a greater sense of hope. Now if she could only get her man. He would fit into the puzzle she imagined for herself and the children. She knew she had to take it slow. She'd stop sending so many text messages. She wouldn't call as often. She almost felt sorry for his wife, the lovely woman in the photos on the mantel. She had long hair in the photos. Tawatha envisioned her with a short, curly Afro after chemotherapy.

"So what's it like?"

"What, T?"

"Going with your wife to the visits?"

James sighed. His firsthand experience with cancer occurred when his Aunt Eunice had succumbed to it four years ago. He felt horrible using her experience to meet his needs, but he had business to handle. He'd face the music later.

"Well, she goes through a machine that looks like a chamber. I guess the radiation is hard to bear because the last time, she asked them to stop."

"What are the doctors saying?"

"It's not looking too good right now. I hope I'm not being disrespectful, but can we change the subject? It's difficult for me to talk about this."

"I'm sorry. I've just been concerned about you and wanted to see if there was anything I could do."

"You've done enough. I can't tell you how much I appreciate you coming out. Especially since I haven't been able to communicate with you that much."

"Not a problem. I figured you were knee-deep in appointments and visits with her cancer. I'm a very patient person. I can wait." Tawatha sipped her tea. "Ohh, I've got some good news for you."

"What's new with you?"

"I got a different place! My mother's boyfriend, Mr. J.B., let me rent one of the properties he owns. You wouldn't believe how gorgeous it is. The kids love it. You've got to stop by and see me sometimes." Tawatha scribbled her address and new number on a slip of paper and tucked it inside James's wallet sitting on the table.

"I'll do that. I can't promise you it will be soon, but I'll make it my business to visit you."

"You mean *us*, right? You haven't met my kids yet. I haven't told them about you, but I know they're gonna love you."

James chewed more of his panini. He stared at his watch.

"I'm not keeping you from work, am I?"

"Course not. I got a little extra time from a project we did a few weeks ago. I told Mr. Hinton and Mr. Conyers I'd be back a little late. You really think I'd miss a chance to spend some time with you?"

Tawatha took off her left shoe and rubbed James's leg. She had vowed not to sleep with him anymore without a commitment, some form of a closer relationship. However, that didn't stop her flirting. She grew moist thinking about their intimate times and looked forward to the night they could resume their action between the sheets. Her toes traveled closer to his penis. At that moment a beautiful woman wearing a pink T-shirt emblazoned with *Save the Tatas* passed by and said hello to them. She froze when there was no response.

"This thing really has you down, doesn't it?"

"Maybe I shouldn't have come hounding you like this. I think I'll head back to the hospital. Let me take care of this for us."

"I got it. You don't need the hassle of paying for lunch."

Tawatha fished thirty dollars from her purse, paid the bill, left a tip on the table, and locked arms with James. They headed to his vehicle.

"You mind riding with me to pay a few bills?"

"Wherever you go, I'm there."

James headed to IPL. He cued up music in his CD player, then made small talk with Tawatha. He found a space in front of the building and parked.

"T, look in the glove compartment and give me my checkbook."

Tawatha flipped through insurance papers, bills, and deposit slips. "Baby, it's not here."

"It's gotta be. That's where I keep it."

She searched the glovebox again. "Seriously, James, it's not here."

"Damn, I musta left it home after paying some other bills. I'll just pay the bill later."

"James, it doesn't make any sense to go back home and come back. Let me give you the money."

"You know I can't take anything from you."

"Boy, please. I just got a raise and I'm doing okay. How much you owe?"

James paused. "Really, I can't."

Tawatha whipped out her wallet. "I won't take no for an answer. You've been good to me. You helped feed my kids with the money you gave me. Please, let me pay you back. We're gonna walk in here, pay this bill, and drop the subject. Got it?"

"How can I say no to that kind of assertiveness?"

Tawatha and James entered the utility company to pay his bill. When they settled the matter and retrieved a receipt from the cashier, Tawatha walked out feeling a sense of accomplishment. She was cementing her place in his life, showing him she could be trusted. She'd never experienced an equal partnership with a man and refused to let this opportunity pass her by. He dropped her off at Hinton and Conyers, kissed her left cheek and promised he'd call in a few days. As she sashayed into the office, she made a mental note to call Roberta later for money to pay for Aunjanue's and Sims's uniforms. IPL had just received the money she had set aside for the children's clothes.

[14]
The Gift that Keeps on Giving

Victoria slid her Mercedes into a parking space at Dorcas House. The only reason she agreed to volunteer at the domestic violence shelter was out of respect for her neighbor and friend, Charlotte Nicholas. Charlotte and Victoria enjoyed shopping, lunch, and occasional trips out of town. To Victoria's dismay, Charlotte had grown tired of sitting around watching television or spending countless hours at the mall. She'd found a greater purpose through volunteerism and declined a lot of Victoria's invites over the past few months. Victoria moped at first, but decided she'd give volunteering a shot. She wasn't convinced helping others was good for the soul, but peering at the massive, stone façade of Dorcas House, now was as good a time as any to see what the volunteering hype was about. She freshened up her makeup in the mirror, tightened her clip-on ponytail, and exited her car. She walked toward the entrance of the building, clutching her new Louis Vuitton bag. She'd enjoyed a full-body massage and cleansing at the Flowing Nile salon two days ago. She also shopped for new clothes and a few household items. She knew the items she bought a few days ago were too glitzy to wear to a shelter, so she dug in her closet to find the cheapest garments she'd purchased in months. She'd dug out a pair of Dereon jeans, a pullover sweater, and matching ballerina flats. She wanted to be comfortable for the day. She pulled on the front door, stunned to find it locked. Someone peered from a window inside and pointed to the buzzer. Victoria rang the buzzer near the door, leaned into the intercom.

"Hi, I'm Victoria Faulk. I'm filling in for Charlotte Nicholas today."

Moments later, the lock clicked and Victoria was welcomed into the facility by Miriam Jacob, the shelter's Outreach and Community Initiatives Coordinator.

"Mrs. Faulk, welcome to Dorcas House. I'm Miriam Jacob. Charlotte told me you'd be with us today."

"It's so good to meet you. Please call me 'Victoria.'"

Victoria suspected Miriam devoted her life to the shelter by the way she ushered her inside, as if she were about to take her on a tour of Egyptian artifacts. *I wonder what she does in her spare time.* Victoria observed Miriam's weathered countenance. Although she wore a snazzy burgundy pantsuit, a matronly chignon bun, and a colorful pair of Donna Karan glasses, Miriam's face signaled so much beyond her warm smile. Victoria followed Miriam to the front desk where she was instructed to sign in. Two women were seated in the lobby, watching HGTV and neatening magazines. The woman wrapped in a blanket gave Victoria a vicious once-over and turned her head. The other never looked up from the magazines.

"When Charlotte told me she had a replacement, I was a little leery. I'm very protective of the women and children. We can't let everyone roam the building. But when she told me who you were, I felt at ease."

"I understand the sensitive nature of what goes on here."

"I'm so grateful for everything. Please tell your husband we couldn't have completed the last phase of our renovation without him."

"Excuse me?"

"I bet you're so knee-deep in philanthropy, your accountant keeps track of what you donate." Miriam pointed upstairs. "I'll show you the Dr. Winston Faulk computer lab on the second leg of the tour. The children are grateful to have such a wonderful area to study."

Victoria blushed. *I can't believe he spent our money without saying anything about it.* "We try to meet the needs of the community as best we can," she managed through a tight smile.

"Most areas of the building are locked and require a passcode for entry."

"Oh, I see."

"Tell me what you know about domestic violence, Victoria."

"Unfortunately, not very much, Mrs. Jacob."

"Call me, 'Miriam.' I hope today won't be the last time you're with us. I've got pamphlets for you to take home, but the quick and dirty is that domestic violence affects women, men, and children."

"Men live here?"

"No, our facility houses women and children only. If a man comes here, we refer him to another shelter in our network. As far as women are concerned, we've housed women from trailer parks, mansions, black, white, Latino, rich, poor; you name it, we've seen it. Most people assume abuse is only physical, but it takes many forms."

"How so?"

"Well, a woman can be fiscally abused. A man can hold the purse strings and dole out money how and when he feels like it. We've had clients come with just the clothes on their backs and lacking essentials like sanitary napkins and toiletries."

Miriam's words stung Victoria. She struggled to manage her three-thousand-dollar-a-month allowance, but that was what it was, her mad money. Winston was always generous in supplying their needs and many of their wants. *How could a woman be so weak as to not stash away any money while she was married? Of course, it could be those maverick working women who had to contribute to the household funds like Aruba.* She thought how lucky she was to have landed a life of comfort and luxury. If only Winston didn't pull stunts like the computer lab, they'd have even more.

Victoria tuned Miriam out as she fixed her eyes on striking wall murals. The vulnerability and innocence of the art captivated her. She was positive children had painted the designs. She recalled childhood paintings created with her aunt as they drank sparkling grape juice and nestled beneath the orange trees in their California backyard.

"Over here is our kitchen," said Miriam. "A lot of women share specific duties outlined on the schedule posted on the wall. We serve three meals a day. Will you be joining us for lunch?"

"I've eaten already, thank you."

Victoria pictured burgers, fries, and all manner of fattening calories in the kitchen. She refused to fall off the wagon and gain weight.

Miriam continued the tour, pointing out the computer lab, the play area, staff offices, and the TV area. As they exited the TV room, Victoria glimpsed a heavyset woman limping toward a leather chair. She scratched a Barack Obama bandana on her head; the rhinestoned words *YES WE CAN* moved with the motion of her fingertips. A little girl, whom Victoria imagined to be eight or nine, followed the woman, touching the hem of her tattered housecoat. The woman eased in the chair, holding her stomach and wincing while she sought a comfortable spot. The girl pulled a footstool close to the woman.

"Alice, just prop my leg up a little."

"Yes, ma'am."

Alice placed her mother's left leg on the footstool. She pulled a small jar of shea butter from the pocket of her faded-out, denim jumpsuit. She removed a slipper from the woman's wrinkled, worn foot and massaged it carefully, taking care to rub around the visible burns.

"Ouch, not so hard, baby."

"I'm doing it soft, Momma."

The mother removed dark shades, revealing a swollen shiner and a jagged, fresh scar that ran between her eyes and nose. Exasperated, she allowed Alice to soothe the pain that seemed second nature to her. As Alice rubbed her mother's foot, she stared longingly at Victoria in the doorway.

"Ma'am, you smell good and you're so pretty," Alice's raspy voice called to Victoria.

"Not half as pretty as you are," said Victoria.

Alice's face reddened. She returned to massaging her mother's feet and wondered what it would be like to live with Victoria.

Miriam redirected Victoria's attention to the tour. Victoria kept stride with Miriam as they entered a small room marked *Donation Center*.

"What happened to Alice's mother?" Victoria whispered.

"They came about a week ago. Sylvia, that's Alice's mother's name, drove here from Cincinnati, Ohio. After ten years of marriage, being burned with hot water, curling irons, and enduring countless beatings, she walked out. Sylvia said Alice's classmates taunted her about the beatings, the black eyes. Bullies pushed Alice in her back and said her mother was dressing up for Halloween before the season started with all that black makeup on her face. She said that was enough for her to flee."

Victoria took in Miriam's words, unable to give a response.

"Sylvia is a tough cookie. She'll make it."

"I hope so."

"Hey, you have a job to do," said Miriam, trying to soften the atmosphere. "This is Charlotte's pet project. She said you're fabulous at organization. As you can see, we get countless donations from the community. So many in fact, they're strewn about and need to be straightened out. Think you can handle it?"

"I most certainly can."

"I'll leave you here to get started. Charlotte usually devotes two hours, three days each week. Do what you can and don't feel compelled to do it all at once. It will take time to get all these items together."

"I'll at least knock out the toiletries and some of the small electronics."

Victoria placed her purse in a cubbyhole in the room. Grateful for the stepladders in the room, she surveyed the stacks of lotions, soaps, shampoos, and plastic bags spread throughout the room. Always equipped with an electronic labeler, Victoria removed it from her purse. She made sure she'd label the items, so they'd be easy to identify. She'd even take the time to separate them by brands. The room was like a corner in her closet, she so was certain she'd do a great job. Twenty minutes into organizing, a familiar voice called from behind her.

"Excuse me, Miss, what type of shampoo do you have? I asked last week about—"

Victoria spun around, certain her ears were playing tricks. Both women stared at each other, one in surprise, the other in horror.

"Joy, did Charlotte recruit you as well? She's working us overtime, isn't she?"

Joy backed against the wall. Victoria Faulk was the last person she expected or wanted to see at Dorcas. In fact, no one from the neighborhood knew she'd checked out of desperate housewife land.

Here stood her former acquaintance, flawless as ever and probably enjoying the highlife without a clue of what she'd endured with Walter.

"Victoria, I didn't know you volunteered here."

"So, does Miriam have you doing kitchen duty? It's my first day here, but I really like her a lot."

"Victoria, I live here."

"Joy, you're so silly. Really, when did Charlotte call you? She caught me just as I was going to Winston's office this morning. I tell you, I really planned to shop at Restoration Hardware—"

"Victoria, this is my temporary home. Walter and I are getting a divorce and I had no place else to go."

Today was too much for Victoria. She'd only planned to spend a little time at the facility, go visit Winston, and go back home. Now Joy sprang this surprise on her. The more she thought about matters, it had been a while since she'd seen Joy at outings, at play dates, or in restaurants in the neighborhood. The inner circle assumed Walter's plastic surgery practice kept her busy, since she did a lot of work from home. Victoria blurted the first thing that came to mind.

"But you guys were perfect. I can't imagine what might have happened."

Joy held her breath, stared at Victoria. She hated the word perfect and abhorred it more when people used it to describe blemished, normal people. How could anyone have ever thought her marriage was perfect when he was always away? If having a husband who made her account for every dime was perfection, she fit the bill. Joy thought of the other elements that made her *perfect* marriage: No children because Walter felt a child would ruin their time alone—although he was never around. Add to that his mother's feeling she wasn't good enough to carry on the bloodline. Having sex with condoms he purchased because he was paranoid she'd poke holes in them. Making her stand on a Weight Watchers scale every two days to ensure she didn't gain weight, then charging her fifty dollars for every pound she gained. Joy thought of those *perfect* vacations where Walter brought his laptop and made her go to the beach, dinner, and shopping alone because his patients were more important. Let's not forget that *perfect* waterfront home that she had to clean from top to bottom with no help. *How sad when others on the outside looking in are totally clueless about the way you really live.*

"Let's sit down over here a minute," said Joy.

Victoria trailed Joy to chairs scattered about in the room. They straightened them up, took a seat.

"No disrespect to you, Victoria, but I can't imagine how you ever thought life with Walter was perfect. Sure, we all enjoyed a good life in our set, but did you ever take the time to delve deeper into what was going on with me?"

"I guess I didn't. I just thought—"

"Doesn't everyone? Everyone always thinks they know the particulars about everyone else's relationships." Joy paused. "Do you remember when the six of us traveled to Cancun and dined at La Habichuela after the snorkeling junket?"

"Yes. I remember you left early because the food didn't agree with you."

"No, the way Walter kicked me in my stomach didn't agree with me. When we got back to the beach, he accused me of looking at some other man while we were in the water. It was all I could do to down that glass of wine at the restaurant. I was down for the count and returned to the house we rented."

"Come to think of it, I didn't see you much after dinner. I blamed it on the food and weather conditions. Why didn't you ever say anything? I would have listened to you."

"I made the mistake of confiding in Linda once. Actually, she just happened to stop by after Walter and I had a terrible fight. By the time she read me the riot act about how lucky I was and how a woman has to put up with a little discomfort to enjoy the high life, I didn't share anything with anyone else after that time. And Victoria, your world is Alva, Winston, and Nicolette. I doubt you would have believed me. I like your friend, Aruba. I wanted to tell her because of the things you shared with me about her husband, but I never got a chance to tell her."

"Aruba? You would have shared that with Aruba before talking to me?"

Joy pursed her lips and raised her eyebrows. "Victoria, you're not exactly warm and fuzzy when it comes to other women. Other ladies seem like a pastime instead of a passion for you. I figured you didn't have a lot of girlfriends growing up."

Victoria recalled conversations shared with Joy. She constantly nitpicked about Winston never being around, his practice, his hesitance to buy her bigger, better toys. She understood why Joy didn't want to open up and share anything. Those complaints must have paled in comparison to having an abusive husband. She felt awful for not being there, for not doing more for Joy.

"No, I didn't have a lot of girlfriends because…well, that's water under the bridge now. What can I do to help you? What do you plan to do?"

"Well, Walter made me sign a postnuptial agreement, so I can't get any money. I managed to squirrel away about fifteen thousand dollars over the five years we've been married. I'm moving back to St. Louis with my grandmother until I can figure things out. I plan to fight him tooth and nail, but I doubt I'll get anything. Funny, huh. I've been married to a plastic surgeon all this time and he never bothered to fix up his wife."

Joy pulled up her shirt sleeve, exposing various scratches and cuts. "I guess Charlotte must have missed last week also because I didn't see her. I would have been mortified. I know the rest of the circle would have known about my being here."

"Your secret is safe with me. I won't tell anyone, Joy."

"Well, I've got lunch duty. We have the best salads and fruits. A lot of the farmers from surrounding areas give us wonderful foods. If you keep volunteering, I'll fix you a great meal before I spring out of this joint," said Joy.

Victoria examined Joy exiting the room. Even battered, she wasn't broken. She exuded confidence that Victoria hadn't seen in the five years their husbands mingled at parties and on trips. *Why don't I pay more attention to people?*

Victoria returned to organizing. She took her time making sure everything was in its place, but the conversation with Joy left her spent. When she placed the hair dryers, nail-decorating kits, and foot spas on the top shelf near makeup compacts, she was amazed at what she felt. Tears streamed down her face. She hadn't seen any in a long time.

[15]
Old Before My Time

"Onnie, what did you tell me about square roots?"

"You already know what I'm going to say, right?" Aunjanue snapped at Sims.

"I know. Try to figure it out first, then ask you if I can't get it," said Sims. He returned to his math problems, Aunjanue to her conversation.

"Where was I, Tarsh? Oh, Mr. Carvin said he loved the drawings. I'm saving my money for watercolors and an easel. My Grandma Bert and Grandpa J.B. told me if I saved half the money they'd help me get the supplies I need."

"Onnie, you're supposed to comb my hair. I want two ponytails," whined S'n'c'r'ty.

"Don't you see I'm on the phone?" Aunjanue spied the clock. "Tarsh, I gotta go. My momma's coming home soon and I have to cook dinner." She hung up the phone and called her brothers and sister into the kitchen.

"You know Momma will be here in about an hour and we don't want her fussing tonight, right?"

"Yes, Onnie," they sang in unison.

"Are your chores done?"

"Yes, Onnie."

"Grant, you come in the kitchen and wash the lettuce for the salad.

Sims, you take out the trash. S'n'c'r'ty, you get the pasta sauce and spaghetti out of the pantry."

They complied, happy to take orders from their oldest sister. Aunjanue was their rock, and next to their grandmother, their only example of stability. As happy as they were to take orders, Aunjanue was happier to give them. She vowed motherhood wasn't in her future. At twelve, she felt twenty-five. She loved her brothers and sister, but she'd grown tired of paying for Tawatha's choices. While other girls her age played basketball, soccer, or shopped, she was home helping with homework, hairdos, and cleanup. Aunjanue knelt, pulling a silver stockpot from the bottom cabinet. She filled it with water and eyed her siblings with a mix of love and resentment. She placed the pot on a burner and turned up the temperature. She found the cast iron skillet Roberta had bought them recently. She slit open a three-pound packet of ground beef, dumped it in the pan, and turned the heat to medium, so the meat would brown perfectly.

"S'n'c'r'ty, when the water boils, what are you supposed to do?"

"Break the spaghetti and put it in the pan."

"Grant, get the salad bowl down. Chop up the grape tomatoes like I showed you last week. Do we have any more bacon bits?"

"I think so. I'll check the fridge."

Aunjanue looked around for Sims. Since moving into the new house, she often spotted Sims staring at or talking to Rochelle Hudson two doors down. Aunjanue told him that girls didn't like guys who seemed too anxious or willing to please. But every day, she saw him with his hands in his pockets, leaning on the oak tree in the Hudsons' front yard, and laughing at Rochelle's tired jokes. She didn't care what he was doing tonight. She had to make sure dinner was done and on the table before Tawatha made it home.

She'd been a tornado the last month or so and Aunjanue wanted to protect the clan from their mother.

Aunjanue gave her work the once-over, making sure everything was in its place. Grandma Bert had come over when they first moved in with cleaning rags, twelve bottles of Terminator deodorizer, and *The Cleaning Bible* by Kim and Aggie, a book by the zany Brits they watched on BBC. As the four of them watched *How Clean is Your House?* with Grandma Bert and Grandpa J.B., Aunjanue shook her head in disgust because she knew they were candidates for the show. After they moved into the new place, Grandma Bert sat the four of them down, told them how important it was not to go back to the way they lived at the old apartment. Aunjanue asked her grandmother to help her with a schedule, so everyone could have a chore. This neighborhood was different. Everything was open; people stopped by unannounced from time to time just to say hello or drop off something nice.

The most popular girl in Aunjanue's class, Tarsha Mosley, lived across the street. Aunjanue would be embarrassed if Tarsh knew how she used to live. She quickly adopted rituals in the new house Grandma Bert firmly required them to follow while visiting her home: Don't put it down, put it away; wipe up stains the moment you spill something; the floor is no place for your clothes, hang them in the closet. The list seemed endless but necessary since Tawatha never taught them much of anything. Then again, the lessons she taught them were ones Aunjanue vowed to forget. She vowed to never have children because children were expensive little souls that required time, attention, money, and a stable male presence. She felt the sting of playground taunts at the old apartment complex when someone would say, "Y'all must have different daddies 'cause your brothers and sister don't look nothing like you."

Or, "We don't see no men around you all 'til the nighttime." She vowed to get a degree, a house, a car, and a dog named Superman. There was no need to complicate matters with the broken promises that wafted between the walls at night when Tawatha moaned or screamed as the knocking headboard kept them awake or prompted S'n'c'r'ty's bedwetting because she thought the men were hurting Tawatha. She vowed to make her own money and not ask men for help. Johnathon Boyce, the last man they got to know, made Tawatha beg for money for the kids' lunches, shoes, and clothes. No way would she ever ask a man for anything. Grandma Bert showed her how to budget, balance a checkbook, and anticipate problems as they arose. She hadn't mastered all the particulars her grandmother spoke of, but she knew with time, trial and error, she'd get better at it.

She also knew if she ever had children, it would be with one man. The name Gipson was on their birth certificates, but Aunjanue deduced who their fathers were by physical traits. Each man left a little of himself with the children. Her father, Bobby Whitlow, left her with his dark-brown complexion and fiery attitude. He was the only man who stood his ground and put Tawatha in her place during arguments. Aaron Briggs, Grant's father, left behind freckles, an overbite, and the start of towering height. At ten years old, Grant was already five-eight. Melvin Spanger, Sims's father, left behind a lazy eye and a love for reading. Aunjanue kissed Sims's lazy eye when he was small and told him how special he was and that she envied his unique eye. At nine, he felt gluing his eyes to books would keep others' attention from his left eye. Nathan Porter, S'n'c'r'ty's father, left behind spunk, laughter, and his short stature. He seemed to be so busy laughing, writing poems, and planning on being the next Walter Mosley that he didn't have time to come around in the daylight. He convinced Tawatha to take the vowels from Sincerity's name because it would make her popular, unique. Aunjanue decided there would only be one man for her *if* she ever had kids.

"Onnie, we have bacon bits," said Grant, interrupting her train of thought.

"Thanks. We can pull those out just before dinner."

Aunjanue set the table for five. She loved the pub-style dinette set Grandpa J.B. picked out. In addition to eight chairs, he purchased a bench for the table. S'n'c'r'ty loved dining at the bench. Tarsha's mother, an interior designer, gave them a gorgeous set of teal and brown accent pieces which Aunjanue placed on the table in the design similar to the layout in Tarsha's house. She'd learned so much from Tarsha's mother about how a house should look just by observing her work. Aunjanue set S'n'c'r'ty's place at the bench, adding her *Dora the Explorer* dishes.

"Onnie, the spaghetti strings are ready. I'm too little to pour that hot water out and drain them."

"Too little or too lazy?"

S'n'c'r'ty giggled at Aunjanue's question. "You know I can't pour out the water."

Aunjanue grabbed a dishrag and swatted S'n'c'r'ty's behind. "Lil bit, get the square pan out and program the oven like I showed you. We bake the spaghetti for thirty minutes, okay?"

"Okay."

Aunjanue finished her homework at school, so she could help her brothers and sister at home. She'd grown afraid of Tawatha's bizarre behavior and wanted to make sure she shielded the kids from her moods. Her latest obsession was a man named James. She'd never seen the man, but she heard Tawatha calling him throughout the evenings. When Aunjanue and her siblings went to bed, she listened as Tawatha dialed his number several times.

Sometimes she'd leave messages. Other times, she'd hang up repeatedly. The men her mother dated normally came around, got to know them a little better. This man was elusive. Aunjanue wondered how a wedding would take place if the potential stepfather never came around. Tawatha had purchased several *Brides* magazines. She cut glossy ads of dresses from the magazines and started a wedding project file that sat next to her bed on the nightstand. A representative from David's Bridal had left a message for Tawatha on Tuesday confirming an upcoming appointment to view new arrivals in the shop.

"The oven beeped, Onnie. We can put the spaghetti in now," said S'n'c'r'ty.

Aunjanue mixed the strings, sauce, and beef in the baking dish and slid the pan in the oven. Thirty minutes was more than enough time to check everyone's homework, make sure they washed up for dinner, and iron their outfits for the following day. She would insert days-of-the-week tags she had made and laminated at school, so they wouldn't get confused when they selected clothes each morning. It was Aunjanue's assignment to wash and iron their clothes for the upcoming week. She closed the oven and headed toward the laundry room. Tawatha startled her when she came through the front door.

"Hi, Momma. You're home early."

"Did James call today?"

"No, Momma, he didn't call."

Dejected, Tawatha tossed her purse on the sofa and headed to her bedroom without speaking to the other children. She slammed the door, knocking down an African print hanging on the wall at the entrance of her bedroom. Grant and S'n'c'r'ty huddled near Aunjanue.

"What's wrong with Momma?" asked S'n'c'r'ty.

"Probably had a hard day at work," offered Aunjanue. The less the others knew about this new man, the better. She was in no mood to explain another man. Leave that to Tawatha this time around. "Grant, tell Sims to come in, so we can finish our homework. S'n'c'r'ty, go get the workbook I brought you from school. We're going over the Spanish vocabulary again."

"But, Onnie, I don't want to."

"How are you going to communicate with Blanca if you don't speak Spanish?" Aunjanue reasoned.

S'n'c'r'ty poked her bottom lip out, went to her room, and brought the workbook to the desk in the living room. They completed their homework in silence as the scent of spaghetti flowed through the house.

"Onnie, I'm hungry. Can we eat now?" S'n'c'r'ty asked.

"Go wash up, so we can eat, everybody."

As they washed up, Aunjanue snatched a serving tray from the side of the refrigerator. She pulled Tawatha's favorite platter from the cabinet. She piled Tawatha's plate with spaghetti, taking care to sprinkle the food with parmesan cheese. She fixed a salad, dousing it with Italian dressing and bacon bits. She scooped two garlic bread sticks from the cookie sheet and put them on the plate as well. Tawatha had sworn off desserts, so she left the caramel cake in the fridge. She stepped lightly toward Tawatha's room, then rapped gently on the door.

"Momma, it's time to eat."

Nothing.

"Momma, I fixed your plate. May I come in?"

Still nothing.

Aunjanue tiptoed in Tawatha's room and placed the tray near the bed. Tawatha stared out the window just as she had the last four nights. Aunjanue didn't know how to reach her, find out what was going on in her head. She simply wanted Tawatha to say something. She definitely didn't want to wake up again in the morning and throw away uneaten food. Nor did she want Tawatha to spend all night dialing the phone, hanging up, and repeating the name "James."

[16]
Somebody's Got a Secret

"So, you talking or do I have to wrestle it out of you?" asked Bria.

"Wrestle what out of me?" Aruba grew nervous with Bria's inquisition.

Bria blocked the entry to Aruba's office, twiddled her fingers on Aruba's nameplate.

"You never schedule mornings off unless you're taking Jeremiah to the doctor or working from home. The glow of your skin is saying so much more than a pediatric visit."

"Would you move, Bria? I've got a ton of work to do."

"Not until you spill the beans. Where were you? How can I make Sidney do this for me?"

"If you must know, I had personal business to take care of, then I went to the post office to handle some things for my territory. Check out these certified mailing receipts if you must. By the way, what does your husband, Sidney, have to do with my morning off?"

Bria opened the door to Aruba's office, watching her smirk melt to speechlessness. Aruba scanned six dozen roses of various hues spread throughout the office.

"James must have spent a fortune on these flowers. I told you to have a little faith and he'd get back on his feet. If I weren't a busybody in recovery, I would have swiped those note cards."

"Thank God for deliverance," said Aruba.

"He sent you a gift as well. I've heard of afternoon delights, but early morning?"

"Yeah, yeah, get out of my business. Don't think I forgot about Sidney sending a limo to the office four months ago and whisking you away to South Beach, then to Taiwan just because."

"It was our wedding anniversary."

"Let's not mention your 'just because' bling-bling that shows up on your wrists, or ears, or—"

"Okay, I get you."

"You think you're the only woman who deserves goodies, a little affection?"

"I never said that. I'm happy that James is handling his business, that's all."

"Don't stand in my doorway, get back to work. Stop taunting me."

"Open one card and I promise I'll leave."

"If you leave, I'll share them all with you later."

"You're lucky I've got a lot to do. Don't leave those cards unattended."

Aruba laughed as Bria returned to her office. Fate always lurked in the shadows of life; reconnecting with Bria was no exception. Aruba shopped at Castleton Square Mall that snowy day six years ago when Bria approached her. Neither knew they'd relocated to the Midwest, since they'd lost touch after graduating from college. At step shows, parties, and various social functions around Atlanta, they ran into each other, waxed poetic about their childhoods. Although Bria attended Emory University, they shared common birthplaces. Bria's family moved from Harlem to Atlanta when she was three. Bria spent her summers in Harlem, though. Each year, neighbors anticipated the reunion of chocolate and vanilla, pet names everyone gave them because of their closeness and hues. The girls played together, since Bria's grandmother's house was across the street from Aruba's parents. They ran to the ice cream truck, spied on Mrs. Ransom with her male friends, and carved their initials in at least five trees in Harlem.

They became reacquainted at the mall; their old friendship was cemented when Bria called Aruba crying at the sight of bleeding patients and the smell of antiseptic cleaner in the hospital. Aruba ribbed Bria, the registered nurse, about her career choice. She called a few friends in HR and got Bria on at State Farm. She enjoyed outings with Bria; her husband, Sidney; their friend Renae; and her husband, Darnell. As much as she loved Bria, she couldn't share Winston with her. She'd know about him when the time was right. She was fine with Bria thinking things were good with James.

Aruba sniffed the deep burgundy, yellow, pink, coral, lavender, and white roses. She opened the cards attached to each dozen, radiating at the single word each card contained. *Magnificent. Brilliant. Captivating. Bewitching. Sweet. Caring.*

She gushed as she ripped open the gift bag. The bag contained a fragrant envelope emitting the scent Winston wore earlier. She read the invitation.

Mr. Winston Faulk requests the honor of your presence in Chicago for drinks, dinner, and a night of entertainment at the House of Blues. To RSVP or for more details, please email me at unchainmyheart@yahoo.com.

Aruba turned to her computer to respond to Winston when Bria stuck her head in the door. "Did you forget the interviews?"

"Interviews? Today?"

"Oh, you don't need an assistant anymore? I'm just glad they're letting us choose our own people this time. I didn't care for the last guy they stuck me with. All he did was surf the net, eat, and tell me what *wasn't* in his job description. You're lucky. I did the last three interviews. You can have the last one."

Bria placed the résumé-filled manila folder on Aruba's desk. "I had some pretty impressive candidates. All of the candidates are overqualified if you ask me. I think your person, though, was handpicked. You be the judge of the qualifications."

Aruba was in no mood to interview anyone. Her mind raced with thoughts of what she'd wear to Chicago, what lie she'd tell James. How good her poker face would be with Victoria. She leafed through the folder, glanced at the résumé, then walked to the lobby to get the candidate. She mentally shopped her closet for outfits for the special occasion, hoping just the right thing would make Winston consider spending a lifetime with a woman who appreciated him. As she reached the young woman watching *Dr. Phil*, she looked over the résumé once more.

"Ms. Lasheera Atkins, follow me."

[17]
Your Office Hours are 9 to 5

Lasheera fidgeted with the charm bracelet Tawatha and Jamilah had purchased for her interview. She jumped when the elegant woman beckoned her.

"Hi, I'm Aruba Dixon and I'll be interviewing you for the Administrative Two position."

"I'm Lasheera...oh, you know my name. Nice to meet you," Lasheera said as she stood to shake Aruba's hand.

"My office is this way."

Lasheera walked behind Aruba, past a long corridor of offices. She wondered if John Coffey felt this way, walking the *Green Mile*. The double cheeseburger she had wolfed down at McDonald's churned in her stomach. She felt nauseated and wondered where the hints and tips provided by her job coach disappeared. The one thing Lasheera remembered Brenda, her job coach, saying was to be candid but not too honest. Brenda said a good interviewer's job was to make a candidate comfortable enough to reveal unsavory work habits. The questions she'd rehearsed came and went. She wondered why she'd let her attorney, Mike Requeno, talk her into working in an office setting. The other options were culinary arts or corrections. She feared salmonella outbreaks and was too vulnerable to be around prisoners. She could see herself giving some handsome D-blocked brother the key to escape if he said the right words to her.

She felt inadequate walking behind Aruba. *I wonder if someone ridiculed her about her name*. Everything about her was refined and chic. Lasheera looked down at the oatmeal-colored suit her girls had selected and wondered if she looked professional. They even sprang for a new hairdo. She felt good about the haircut and had asked the beautician for The Rihanna. She had visited the MAC counter for a consultation and walked away with a new face and a complete palette for the new Lasheera. Her stomach churned again at the thought of having to address the lapses of employment on her résumé. She hadn't held many jobs because of her addiction, and now she wondered if she could learn a new skill set. The only job she'd held was a six-month stint at Panera Bread which ended when she was a no-call, no-show three days in a row. Up until her disappearance with Lean On Me those three days, she'd done well with the company. She had begged the manager for her job back, but he said if he gave her a second chance, the other employees would be livid.

"Have a seat, Ms. Atkins."

Lasheera sat in a chair across from Aruba's desk. As Aruba scanned Lasheera's résumé, Lasheera looked at the photos lining the credenza. She eyed the tall, dreadlocked man on whose lap Aruba sat, smiling. Next to that was a family photo of the beauty king, Aruba, and a handsome little boy whose cheeks Lasheera could kiss for days. *Damn, her dude is so fine. How'd she get that lucky?*

Aruba eyed her watch. Twenty minutes for the interview was a waste of her precious time because Lasheera already had the job. When Mike Requeno spoke, the company president listened and complied. Dan Cholly golfed with Mike in the evenings and everyone in the office joked about their bromance. She perused the yellow sticky notes Bria had placed on the résumé per Mike's conversation. She knew Lasheera was trying to get her life back together and had little job experience. She would be delicate in the questioning process. Looking at the skinny young woman before her, she sought what the makeup, haircut, and suit couldn't cover. She seemed frail, unsure of herself. She decided to put her at ease, make it an informational interview, since she was going to hire her anyway. She had to get back to Winston and the Chicago trip. Aruba passed a laminated sheet of paper toward Lasheera.

"Ms. Atkins, these are the essential job functions for the position offered. Please take a look at them and let me know if there is anything on the list you're unable to perform."

"Mrs. Dixon, you can call me 'Lasheera,'" she said, taking the list.

Lasheera read the list, then passed it back to Aruba.

"I'm confident I can perform all the tasks listed."

"Good. So, Lasheera, of all jobs on the planet, why are you at State Farm?"

"I want to learn something different. I'm looking for a new career, not just a job. I would like to have a decent income, health insurance for my son, and the possibility of a promotion in the future." Lasheera recited the prompts from coaching sessions.

"How much money do you expect to make from this job?"

"The advertised position is twelve dollars an hour. I think that is a good salary."

"How long do you plan to stay with the company?"

"At least four years. I read about the tuition reimbursement and I want to utilize it for school. I'd like to pursue a degree in marketing or business."

"Why should I hire you?"

Lasheera took in a deep breath. She knew the answer to this question could be interpreted so many ways. She didn't want to sound too arrogant, but she didn't want to sound as if she lacked the confidence or ability to perform the job.

"I'm hardworking, willing to learn new things, and I've always respected State Farm as a company."

Aruba continued her questions, impressed that Lasheera answered everything. She seemed genuinely enthused about being her assistant. The job was filled with filing, data processing, and a few other duties she'd teach Lasheera in the coming months. She had a good feeling about her and looked forward to getting to know her better. After Lasheera produced a list of questions from her purse about State Farm and the job itself, Aruba knew the interview was a good one. She'd have to call Mike and thank him for sending such a wonderful candidate.

"Welcome to State Farm, Lasheera. How soon are you available to start?"

"I can start today if you'd like."

Lasheera walked around Aruba's desk, then hugged her.

"No, we've got to get your paperwork together and there are a few things I need to do before you start," said Aruba. She wasn't a touchy-feely person, but felt compelled to embrace Lasheera. "Let me take you around the office, show you where everything is and introduce you to some folks."

Lasheera fought hard to contain her grin as she followed Aruba, shaking hands with several people in offices and cubicles. Try as she might, she couldn't. She'd been unemployed so long that she'd almost given up. She had the thank-you note Brenda had helped her write in her pocket, but she would write a new one for Aruba. She appreciated the opportunity to begin anew and felt a sense of loyalty to the woman who made it possible. The minute she left State Farm, she'd tell Tawatha and Jamilah about the woman responsible for helping her get Zion back.

[18]
Leads, Leads, Leads

"Mommy, I want pizza!"

"You do? Jerry, how about something from the house?"

"Awww, Mommy!"

Aruba tickled Jeremiah's stomach in the Angels in Halos parking lot. After interviewing Lasheera, conducting a meeting, and helping Bria crunch numbers, there was no time to respond to Winston. Maybe he'd think she was pondering the notion.

Aruba lifted a flyer from her windshield and placed Jeremiah in his booster seat.

"Where's Daddy?"

"He's home, Jerry." *At least that's where he'd better be.*

Aruba's heart sank when she unfolded the flyer. She knew she should be happy for the success of others, but announcements like the one in her hands kept her stuck in the past, constantly wondering what if. Mitch Coleman, the father of one of Jeremiah's classmates, was on tap to open a third salon in the city. The others were adult hair salons; the current opening was a kiddie salon, specializing in hair care for girls only. Divas in Training promised to be the one-stop shop for girls ages five to seventeen for hair care services, nail and spa treatments, and free promotional items. She remembered James mentioning the idea of a kiddie salon years ago, but never following through on the seed. She forwarded him business plan information, funding sources, and found a few contacts through Bria's husband, Sidney, but nothing ever came of the effort. She looked at Jeremiah in the rearview mirror and hoped her son would grow up to be a more responsible man than his father. Aruba called James at least seven times after leaving Winston and returning to the office. Her calls went unanswered, her text messages ignored. She wanted him to pick up Jeremiah so that she could run a few errands before returning home. He finally called at five-thirty to say he'd been out paying bills. His curt tone managed, "I made baked chicken and seasoned green beans" before hanging up. A twinge of guilt rose in Aruba. Had she been supportive enough? Had she done all she could to back him up, to bring his goals and dreams to fruition?

When she looked back over the years they'd shared, the emotional war inside resumed. James had experienced so many false starts and setbacks, many of which were self-imposed. Their early conversations over Chinese take-out brimmed with the possibility of owning a business or two, buying a home, purchasing rental properties, and traveling. People who saw them together always told her how lucky she was, that she had snagged a fine husband. Where were they when she was left to pay the bills when he was unemployed, or field calls from other women who said they could love him better? Or when, in a surprise show of generosity, Victoria had allowed them to use her Brown County cabin as a wedding anniversary gift and James spent most of the night on the phone with a woman whose name she didn't know. It was definitely time to pitch a new tent elsewhere. Winston was the perfect camping partner.

Aruba pulled into the garage, lifted Jeremiah, and went inside. The smell of James's famous chicken permeated the house. She would eat salad and drink a raspberry Crystal Light green tea for dinner. She was full from lunch and had shared the leftover food she'd cooked for Winston with her coworkers.

"Hi, James, how are you?" Aruba's attempt at small talk was met with silence.

"Daddy, did you miss me?"

"You know I did, little man," said James. He smiled at Jeremiah, then rolled his eyes at Aruba.

"What's the problem, James?"

"That's what I'm trying to figure out. It's time to eat. You and Jerry should get ready for dinner."

Aruba headed upstairs with Jeremiah, changed into comfortable lounging gear, and carried Jeremiah on her back to the dinner table. She was in no mood for James's games, his silence, or his pity party. He was probably in a sour mood about being unemployed. She didn't know what he'd been doing all day, but he must have been honest about paying the bills. The lights were on and she knew this was disconnect day. She was tempted to call IPL to see how he paid the bill, but she decided to back off, let him exhibit responsibility, since he swore she didn't trust anything he did. The house was spotless as usual, so maybe he'd spent the day cleaning. Either way, he had no right to give her attitude. Lately, he seemed more miserable than she remembered. Maybe it was time they both admitted their marriage wasn't working, admit they should call it quits.

Jeremiah jumped in his favorite seat next to James, and said grace. The table was set, a candle lit, and the food splayed about as if they were in a restaurant. She eyed James as he cut a breast in small pieces and stacked roasted potatoes atop his green beans. Stacking food was always a bad sign. She'd grown accustomed to his habits over the years and knew sinister thoughts were lurking.

"Would you at least talk to me?"

"Not right now," James said.

Clinking silverware was the night's conversation. After dinner, James cleared the table as Aruba retired upstairs. She hated the silent treatment, but refused to be the peacemaker tonight. She bathed Jeremiah, then went to bed. Throughout the night, she felt James's presence in the bedroom. He walked in, stared at her, and walked downstairs again. Her heart raced. She gawked at the alarm clock. Two-fifteen in the morning. She had to get up at seven. She slipped into a robe, then headed downstairs. The smell of coffee hit her nose. When she reached the dining room, the sight of the contents of her purse strewn about enraged her. She approached James with quick steps, her fists balled in a tight knot. James sat at the head of the table, rifling through her wallet, sipping a cup of coffee.

"James, what are you doing with my purse?" Aruba snatched her bag from James.

"I don't know. Trying to figure out why my wife feels the need to open a separate bank account without my knowledge."

"What are you talking about?"

James stood in her face, waving a business card. "Who is Mitch Coleman? Is he the reason you need to hide money from me?"

Aruba snatched the business card. "*He* is the father of one of the boys who attends Jeremiah's daycare. He opened a new salon and I thought he might be someone you could hook up with for work. *Work!* You know, that thing you do so very little of these days?" Aruba gathered the items from the table and stuffed them in her purse.

"Answer me, Aruba, why are you hiding money?"

"Answer me, James. Who is Ms. T. and why is my son mentioning her?"

"I don't know a Ms. T.! Don't try to put this back on me."

"James, you are such a liar. I guess the thong I found under the sofa just walked in here and decided to take a nap, huh? My ass isn't *that* big, so I know it doesn't belong to me."

"I don't know what you're talking about!"

"Of course you don't. I found it the night of the accident when I came home. The thong is the reason I opened a new account. Bounced checks, no savings, and no unity are the reasons I opened a new account. As soon as I get enough money, Jerry and I are out of here!"

James advanced a few steps and stood in Aruba's face. "You're not leaving me!"

"Why? It's not like you want to be married, James. You have more than enough women to step in and take my place. I'm sick of putting up with your bullshit, James. I should have left years ago!"

Aruba walked away from James, surprised by his swift footfalls. He jerked her left arm. "Don't fucking walk away from me! You're not leaving me and you're not taking my son away from me!"

"Don't touch me, James!"

Aruba headed upstairs with James on her heels. She walked into their bedroom, stepped into the closet, pulled down an armful of clothing. She dragged a set of luggage from the closet. The most she managed to do was unzip the first bag when the first punch met her face, knocking her to the floor.

"I said you're not going anywhere, so let me see you try it!"

Aruba held her face, kicked James in the groin, and ran to Jeremiah's bedroom. She gathered him, a few of his things, her purse, then zipped to the garage while James was still down. She backed out the driveway, her hands trembling, Jeremiah crying. She didn't know where she would go, what she would do, but she was thankful she had enough money to hide out for a while. She exited the subdivision, then pulled into a gas station parking lot. She took a deep breath, knowing now was the time to make her move. There was no way she could go back home again. It was time for Jeremiah to get used to the new life he was entitled to. From her Black-Berry she texted:

Chicago will have to wait. James and I had a fight. Jeremiah and I are going to the Conrad. Please get in touch with me as soon as possible. Please don't tell Victoria.

[19]
Protector, Provider

"Tori, the hospital just paged me. I need to go in."

Victoria peered from her eye mask and waved her arm as she always did. She never questioned his whereabouts, pages, or practices. For that, Winston was grateful. Aruba's text infuriated him. Had he not been so consumed with her safety, he would have driven to her home and settled matters with James, man to man. How could he mistreat her? Aruba was the kind of woman men dreamed of having. To watch James handle her the way he did… forget James. Aruba was his main concern.

Winston headed downtown to the Conrad. He made a note to pay for her stay at the hotel for two weeks. That would give him enough time to help her find a safe haven. How ironic that Victoria prattled on and on about volunteering at a domestic violence shelter but never tried to shield her friend from abuse. In eight years of marriage, he'd never been unfaithful. He prided himself on avoiding compromising situations that would make him appear a hypocrite. So many of his friends and colleagues were either separated or divorced. When they turned to him for advice or a listening ear, he held fast to the same answer: "I'm committed to my wife and my daughter and nothing can come between us."

Never say never.

Winston thought of Aruba and Victoria. The difference between the two was that one needed protection; the other, showcasing.

His intention was to have a life partner, not a trophy wife. He couldn't remember the last time Victoria needed him, embraced him, or initiated lovemaking. Aruba, a woman he'd met through his wife, made him feel more wanted in the five months they'd gotten to know each other better than Victoria did in the ten years they'd been together. How could he handle his feelings? He smiled as he eyed the CD Aruba placed in the gift bag with *Take the Risk*. He flipped open Kenny Lattimore's *Timeless*, read the note in Aruba's handwriting above Kenny's silhouette: *Whenever I hear track three, I wish you had this place in my life. You are so important to me.* He placed the CD in and skipped to track three. Aruba was too much. Norman Connors's "You Are My Starship" was the only song his parents danced to when he was younger. Now, Kenny put a passionate spin on the song, causing Winston to reminisce about stolen moments his dad shared with his mom. His dad took his mother in his arms as they swayed together on the patio of their summer home, laughter rising and falling as his dad whispered seductive thoughts in his mother's ear. Winston had waited to call Aruba because he wasn't sure what to say. He reached for his cell, then dialed her number. She answered on the first ring.

"What do you need, Aruba? Tell me and I'll do it."

"Where are you?"

"I'm about twenty minutes from the hotel. What happened?"

"I'd rather talk about it here. My eye is swollen from the punch James gave me."

"Punched you? Do you want me to take you to the ER? Is Jeremiah safe? Do I need to bring anything to the room?"

"No, I'm too tired to go to the hospital. I ordered room service. Jeremiah is asleep. He slept through the entire incident."

"That's good to hear. Aruba, everything will be all right. I give you my word."

"Thank you, Winston. I'm in room eight seventy-one."

Aruba hung up her phone and strolled to the bathroom. She placed a bag of ice on her eye, returned to the bed, plopped down. James had hit her in the past, but there was something different about his rage tonight. He'd never gone through her things, never been that silent. She'd tried so hard in the past to reach out to him emotionally, to accommodate his needs. She was certain of two things: she didn't deserve to be beaten and she could no longer make excuses for his issues. Her desire to help him work through those issues had disappeared years ago. She still loved James, but she was no longer *in love* with him. Her head was spinning at the prospect of getting a divorce. There was the cost of filing, mediation, counseling if a judge felt it necessary; the list went on and on. One good thing about the time they'd been together was the fact they'd accomplished little. There would be no division of assets, no lengthy back and forth about furniture and other items couples who worked together enjoyed. They would simply share custody of Jeremiah. *Damn, I won't even get child support.* A knock on the door reminded her that James's money or presence didn't matter anyway. Aruba opened the door for Winston, then fell into his arms. Her light sobs were met with the tightest hug she'd felt in a long time.

"Hey, hey, come on over here," said Winston, leading Aruba to the bed.

He motioned for her to sit. He joined her, careful not to wake Jeremiah. Tonight would be the night the slightest sound would awaken him.

"Let me look at your eye, Aruba."

Winston kept an array of medical supplies in his vehicle for times like this. He'd brought ice packs and meds to help her through the night.

"Did you call in to work?"

"I plan on calling Bria around seven or so to let her know I'm under the weather and won't be in for a few days. I have a new employee to train, but she doesn't report to work until Monday."

"Do I need to take Jeremiah to daycare in the morning? I plan to nurse you back to health today. I don't think you need to go out. James gave you a huge black eye."

"Actually, you can. You and Victoria are listed as relatives or friends who can pick Jeremiah up or drop him off."

"Do you plan to press charges against James?"

"I'm still thinking. Winston, I don't know what to do."

"Your room is paid for, for two weeks."

"Winston, you didn't have to—"

"Shhh…I'm not finished."

"Victoria told me the house is in your name only. I can pay off the mortgage and quit-claim deed it to James. You don't have to answer now. Just think about it."

"Winston, I don't know what to say."

"You never answered my previous question. What do you need? Tell me and I'll do it."

Aruba looked at Winston and could only think of one thing. "Hold me. Lie next to me in bed and hold me 'til day breaks. It's been a long time since I've been held."

[20]
The Well's Running Dry

James threw the covers from the bed, unable to sleep for the third night in a row. He stared at the alarm clock. Nine a.m. He wondered where Aruba was and why she wouldn't answer his calls. In the past, he'd cruise by Bria's, Renee's or Victoria's houses and find her there. They'd go back and forth; she'd pack her things, Jeremiah, and come home. He camped out at all three houses the past few nights, but saw no sign of Aruba. He rode past her job with no luck. He didn't know what to do because every move she'd made lately deviated from her old ways. Perhaps she meant it this time when she said she couldn't take it anymore, that she wanted to start a new life without him. For the first time in their ten-year marriage, he thought of what life would be like without her. The thought sickened him.

Three days had passed since the scuffle and being without her had caused an unfamiliar mix of emotions to well inside of him. There were so many things she did he took for granted. As much as he loved to cook, he was startled to open the deep freezer and find she'd prepared and frozen his and Jeremiah's favorite things. Among the labeled Tupperware bowls were black-eyed pea casserole, champagne salad, braised beef short ribs with rice, and his all-time favorite dessert, sweet potato cheesecake.

The last time he'd ventured out to find her, he'd slipped on some jeans and a hoodie. He had fished through his pocket and pulled out a note from Aruba that read: *No matter what happens, I'll always believe in you.* Through all their ups and downs, she never stopped encouraging him.

"What have I been doing? What have I been thinking?" James asked to no one in particular.

The phone rang, bringing James back to reality.

James snatched the cordless phone from the wall. "Aruba, baby, where are you?"

"Mr. Dixon? Is this Mr. James Dixon?"

James composed himself. "This is James Dixon. Who's speaking?"

"This is Sloan Marks. I'm calling from Franzen Industrial Staffing. You put in an application sometime ago and I was calling because we have some available positions. Are you still interested in employment with us?"

"Absolutely! What do I need to do?"

"I'll be sending some people out two weeks from today on assignment to various sites. Give me a call back next Friday and I'll have a specific location for you."

"Thank you, Miss Marks."

"You're quite welcome, Mr. Dixon."

James hung up the phone, elation and sadness covering him in equal measure. He'd been out of work for months and the moment he found something promising, Aruba wasn't around to rejoice in the good news. He decided to try her once more to let her know what was going on. He dialed her phone, disappointed that it went straight to voicemail again.

"*Aruba, I miss you and Jeremiah. I just wanted you to know I found a job. Not sure where I'm going yet, but I promise I'll work and make good on it this time. I'm about to lose my mind without you and Jeremiah. I love you, baby. Please come home to me. I know we can work this out.*"

"*I love you, baby. Please come home to me. I know we can work this out.*" After reluctantly checking her voicemails, Aruba placed her BlackBerry in its case, repulsed by the sound of James's voice. His desperation was enough reason to get on with the business of divorcing him. Hearing his voice didn't garner the emotions she'd felt in years past. This, her first day back at work, would be the start of something new. She was enthused about training Lasheera, seeing Winston later that night at the Conrad, and browsing the web for a new apartment. Aruba didn't allow people in her personal business, so she couldn't risk Jeremiah seeing Winston and blabbing to James. Not yet anyway. She'd shared with Bria the night of the assault, pleading with her to watch Jeremiah until she felt the coast was clear. Bria never imagined James being so cruel, although she'd had her suspicions over the years about him as a husband and a father. Bria's husband respected and loved her, so she felt the least she could do for a friend in need was provide childcare, secrecy, and a shoulder to cry on. She cloaked for Aruba the three days she was absent, picked up Jeremiah from Angels in Halos, and assured her that things would be okay.

Aruba had Lasheera sit in conference room A to study the first set of training materials Bria prepared. Bria had been a godsend. Aruba made a mental note to do something special for her once the drama died down and her new life with Winston began.

"Aruba, line one," said Doris.

"Thanks, Doris."

Aruba picked up the phone with a smile on her face. Winston had called her every hour on the hour to inquire about her well-being. He'd sent more roses to the hotel room, visited each night, ran her bath, massaged and oiled her body, made her feel like a queen. His upfront admission that he couldn't make love to her raised the stakes and strengthened her resolve to get closer. He'd reasoned he was wrong and didn't want to further complicate the situation with intimacy. The emotional affair they were having was new territory for him. He'd fallen under her sway with her grace and charm as weapons; he feared what making love to her would do.

"Hi, beautiful. Were you ready to go back to work today or was that your attempt to stay away from me?"

"Both. I need to get back to business as usual. I told you I have a new employee to train."

"I've been thinking about you all day, Aruba."

"It's just nine in the morning."

"You're on my mind twenty-four/seven. What do I need to do to convince you of that?"

"Speaking of convincing, what did you tell Victoria about your absence the last four days?"

"Sadly, if it isn't about shopping or something that concerns her, she doesn't care. After my page, I told her I had to fly out to Phoenix to examine a patient who may need open heart surgery. She didn't bat an eyelash."

Time spent with Winston had been everything Aruba desired. He was thoughtful, loving, and attended to her needs in a way she couldn't have imagined. As she and Winston spooned at the Conrad, listening to Victoria on speakerphone that second night, Aruba thought it odd that Victoria asked for a fur coat, a pair of

Jimmy Choos, and reservations for the Arizona Biltmore Resort and Spa. She never told Winston she loved him, nor did she ask about his well-being. Aruba held him tighter then because she realized Victoria was handing him over on a silver platter.

"That speakerphone conversation blew my mind. Please let me say something as a friend. You're a wonderful man and a great father. Someone I'd treat like a king if I had the opportunity."

Winston ignored the ego stroke because it felt too good to hear from someone other than his wife. "I'm on my way to the hospital. Do you need me to do anything for you today?"

"Just dinner later tonight. We can eat in the room."

"I miss you, Aruba."

"Same here."

Aruba hung up the phone, then headed to the conference room for Lasheera.

"Psst," said Bria, sticking her head out of her office.

"What now, girl?"

"Going to get your groupie?"

Aruba stepped into Bria's office and closed the door. "What are you talking about? Why are you so caustic?"

"I don't know. I guess I'm a little jealous, since no one worships me."

"Maybe I shouldn't get sick anymore, since your imagination runs wild while I'm away."

"Make fun of me all you like, but you made quite an impression on Lasheera. She called several times while you were away. She asked whether she really had the job, about the dress code, if she'd be working directly with you. Sounds like she wants to make a good impression on you."

"Don't make fun of her. I think I'd be nervous reentering the workforce after a long time."

"What happened?"

"You know I can't divulge her personal business."

"You take confidentiality to extreme measures! Come on, Aruba, why has she been out of work so long?"

"How would you feel if I let it slip to folks around the office you're a nurse afraid of blood?"

"Ouch! Point well taken. I have to give it to you, you can keep a secret. What will you take to your grave?"

"Wouldn't you like to know? I'll see your nosy butt for lunch."

"If you don't eat with Lasheera."

"Jealousy doesn't suit you, Bria."

Aruba exited Bria's office. She headed to the conference room and attempted to stop the smile creeping across her face. She liked the fact Winston wanted to honor his vows, but she also wanted to make love to him. How much longer would the lie about him being out of town hold up, anyway? She had ignored Victoria's calls the past few days. After Victoria's last message about being concerned where she was since she wasn't home, she'd sent a quick text message and told her she was working late since auditors were in town. Aruba knew Victoria would back off, since she was allergic to work. She would do lunch with Victoria to impede any suspicion. Victoria and Nicolette would miss their good thing soon enough. Now wasn't the time for any slipups. Aruba stepped into the conference room as Lasheera perused training materials.

"I hope you're not overwhelmed by all the information. If it's any consolation, it took me several months to catch on."

"I'm up for the challenge, Mrs. Dixon."

"Lasheera, we're gonna be working closely together. Please call me 'Aruba.'"

"May I call you Mrs. D. until I get more comfortable?"

"Sure, if that's better for you."

Lasheera shifted in her seat, flipped through more pages in the binder. Earlier, Bria had given her a Post-it pad for notes, and she made sure to insert the neon squares where she needed most help or felt confused. The materials overwhelmed her; how on earth would she ever learn all she needed to be successful at the job?

"Are you nervous?" asked Aruba.

"A little. It's been a while since I worked."

"You'll get the hang of everything in no time. You'll be working with me today. The materials are for you to take home and study. Today's training will be showing you how to do my scheduling."

"What will I be scheduling?"

"My travel dates. I handle the Indianapolis territory, Columbus, and Bloomington."

"Bloomington? My girlfriend Jamilah attends IU. I'm proud of her."

"I bet you two are thick as thieves."

"No. It's more like the Three Musketeers. I have another girl-friend, Tawatha. We've known each other since grade school."

"I'd love to meet the two of them sometime."

"I've known the two of them since we were young. I can't imagine my life without their love and support. You know what it's like to have good friends, Ms. D.?"

"I do. There's nothing like someone having your back."

Lasheera smiled and wondered if Aruba's friends were as so-phisticated and kind as she. Lasheera answered the phones, learned the scheduling ropes, got to meet a few other people in the office, and wondered how soon it would be before Jamilah and Tawatha met her cool new boss.

[22]
Sista Spa Night

Bria and Renae made a pact to get Aruba out of her funk with a good old-fashioned Sista Spa Night at Bria's house. Aruba's funks were frustrating because she denied anything was going on in her life. When a crisis occurred in her life, Aruba got busy working in the office or bringing in juicy dishes from home. She'd pretend she found a great recipe to share with everyone, but Bria knew something had gone wrong at the Dixon household. She also knew Aruba wouldn't spill the goods because her mother, Darnella, admonished both of them when they were children about sharing marital business. Ms. Darnella's perceived paranoia about sharing personal business gained credibility after it was discovered her good friend, Sheila Mills, secretly spilled a few revelations to Mr. Lance when Ms. Darnella went on a church flea market trip. Aruba's father didn't speak to Ms. Darnella for two days and would have continued his silence if Ms. Sheila hadn't gone in for the kill. After Sheila said she would make the better wife, Mr. Lance realized Sheila was up to her old high school tricks. Ms. Darnella called Aruba and Bria in from playing one day, forbade them from visiting Ms. Sheila, and pointed her fingers in both their faces with these stern words: "I don't care how bad things get in your marriages when you grow up. If your life isn't in danger, and if you and your husband can make it to someone prayerful and tactful, only go to that individual. People begrudge you the smallest things. Before you know it, a little secret shared can be hurled back in your face and cause your relationship a world of hurt." The girls clutched their jump ropes, not sure they'd ever get married and upset they'd been interrupted for grown folks' business. Bria brushed the words off; Aruba allowed them to sink in. Bria watched as Aruba hid dates, relationships, and juicy tidbits about her whereabouts over the years.

After Aruba married and relocated to the Midwest, Bria hoped she could be trusted, that Aruba would confide in her. Darnella's words proved stronger than Bria's trust. Bria caught the slight scratches that appeared on Aruba's forehead. Scratches Aruba swore Jeremiah placed there. She watched the frantic check-balancing routine Aruba mastered during lunch breaks and the anger she displayed when whipping out a red pen to denote the balance status. Aruba couldn't hide the heated conversations with James that flowed out when Bria walked past the office door from time to time. The saddest memory Bria had witnessed was the double-date night at Peterson's. Sidney wanted to pay for everyone's meal, but James insisted he'd pay. It was a pricey dinner, and Sidney didn't mind since James was unemployed. Bria almost burrowed a hole in Sidney's knee when she saw Aruba slide her credit card to James under the table. Bria was done when James placed the card in the meal-ticket holder, signed her name, and put the receipt in his wallet. How could she convince her friend that she was worth so much more without sounding intrusive? Or worse, a hater. Spa night would be the start of tearing down Darnella's words. She loved Aruba like a sister and wanted her to know she was there for her for more than just babysitting Jeremiah.

"Baby, how long you want me out of the house?"

"Sid, I thought you were going to hang out with Joshua and Marcus."

"We're going to Jillian's, Nicky Blaine's, then I'm going to check on my mom."

"Have fun and drink a sour apple martini for me."

"Baby, it's good to know you still care about me and my where-abouts."

"I love you, Sidney Allen Hines, and don't you forget it."

Bria planted a kiss above Sidney's left eye, their signal that all was well in their world. She loved the language they'd created over the years that was exclusive to their marriage. She'd seen wonderful marriages and relationships in her life and she wanted to continue the goodness. She was hesitant to share their love language for fear someone would say she was boasting. She didn't like it when couples who were doing well looked down on those who were struggling. That's why she wanted Aruba to know she was more concerned than she'd ever been about the state of her marriage.

"So, you ready for the big talk with Aruba?"

"I don't know, Sidney. She won't admit anything about the situation with James. I can't bring myself to tell her I saw the fax come across our machine in the office from Attorney April Morris. She's one of the most visible divorce attorneys in Indy and is a fighter for women getting the most they can get in a settlement."

"How many years they been married?"

"Ten. Eleven in March."

"That's a lot of time to throw away. You sure spa night is appropriate for this kind of talk?"

"I thought of a different approach."

"Why are you looking at me? Why do I feel like a lamb being led to the slaughter?"

"Baby, our pact is we never discuss personal things in our marriage without each other's permission, right?"

"I don't like where this is going." Sidney gave Bria a devilish grin and encouraged her to proceed with a light nod of his head.

"If I pounce on Aruba, she'll shut down and I'll never get anything out of her. I'll play the hypothetical game like we did when we were younger."

"You mean I have a friend who…" said Sidney.

"Exactly. The biggest struggle we've had thus far in our marriage was the rehab incident. It was mild compared to what I hear other couples go through, but it was touch and go with the drinking."

"Job stress got the best of me. I'm glad we went through counseling to help us through that time. I'm sorry for what I put you through."

"I'm not fishing for apologies. I need your permission to share the story tonight. It would pain me if you shared something intimate about me without my knowledge, so I just wanted to double-check."

"I don't mind. I'm glad you asked me first. I'm blessed to have you as a wife and I try to show you what you mean to me as much as I can."

"You do. I appreciate you more than you know. I just hope we continue growing together. I can't imagine my life without you."

"So did your man get enough food?"

"Yes. You hooked us up! The station volunteers will be here soon. I hope the girls will enjoy the treatments I planned. Cutcha Right was gracious enough to let us have five of their students tonight. Their services will go toward their credits. Lisa Cosby of Heavenly Make-up by Lisa will offer makeovers and facials, and Sharron B. of Fingerprintz II will be here just in case someone wants twists done."

"Who's coming to spa night?"

"Aruba, Renae, Joycelyn, and Lasheera."

"Lasheera?"

"She's the office newbie. I thought it would be good to have her mingle with us. She thinks the world of Aruba and I didn't want to leave her out."

"I can't believe you guys pulled Renae out the house on a Friday night."

"It's for Aruba, so Greer gave her a pass for the night."

"Wait, is Lasheera pretty?" asked Sidney.

"Yes."

"Is she skinny?"

"Yep. I'm sure Joycelyn will be on the war path. If you weren't good friends with Dre, she wouldn't be invited to any functions at this house." Bria shook her head at Joycelyn's insecurity.

They embraced and kissed. Bria waved to Sidney and watched him leave the house. She would think of an extra special gesture to thank him for supporting the night's efforts.

Two hours later, the girls laughed, sipped champagne, and enjoyed the beginning stages of their pedicures. The pampering overwhelmed Lasheera who felt out of place among Bria, Aruba and their married friends. She tried not to stare at Bria's belongings, but she couldn't help wondering how it felt to have a husband. Lasheera knew Bria and her husband didn't have children. *Why does a childless couple need such a large home?* Lasheera wondered if she'd ever meet anyone special. As Renae and Joycelyn compared vacations, talked about their spouses, and made plans for the coming weeks to do something as couples, Lasheera sank lower in her seat as her feet were massaged with a pumice stone. The only thing she could contribute to the night was revisionist single mother stories. No way would this sista circle know about how much she'd been through. She sipped champagne, bit into a Godiva chocolate-covered strawberry, and blinked back tears forming from feelings of deep-seated inadequacy.

"Honey, Dre is the last man on earth who enjoys heavy cooking.

He still hasn't gotten the nerve to tell his mother to stop sending those cooking tips. She said I'm starving him and he needs some meat on his bones," said Joycelyn, as she grabbed a strawberry from the fruit tray.

Lasheera's forehead creased. *I know that baby voice didn't come from that big woman.*

Bria forgot to warn Lasheera about Joycelyn's high-pitched voice and regretted the faux pas when Lasheera placed her hands over her ears. She gave Lasheera a sympathetic nod and held back the laughter inside.

"Greer's mother gave up on me a long time ago," said Renae. "I can do take-out like nobody's business and that's all there is to it. Now, Ms. Aruba Crocker over there needs to take some tips from us and stop slaving in the kitchen like she owns a restaurant."

"I like cooking for my family. What's wrong with that?" asked Aruba, shifting her toes in the sea salt and eucalyptus foot soak.

"Nothing at all if you want to forgo having fun and games, if you know what I mean," said Joycelyn.

"Ladies, we have a new, *single* woman with us tonight. Let's not run her off with our crazy tales," said Bria.

"Oh, you're not married?" asked Joycelyn. She looked at Lasheera as if she had three heads with Buddha tattoos.

Not this again. It's not a lie if it's finessed. "No. Things didn't work out with my son's father, so I'm single and loving it."

"There is nothing wrong with being single, Lasheera," said Renae. She cut her eyes at Joycelyn as if to say *don't start tonight.*

"I guess. I like having the comfort and security of a mate. Having someone to talk to, to share my day with, someone to help carry the load," said Joycelyn.

"Marriage isn't for everyone, Joycelyn. How many times do we have to remind you of that fact?" asked Aruba.

"What woman in her right mind wouldn't want to have a man around to help take care of things and her? I don't know of one!" said Joycelyn.

"Actually, I didn't grow up planning a wedding or thinking of getting married. I don't want to be pressured into a union with someone just to say I've got a man. If the right person comes along, fine. If not, that doesn't make me less of a woman or mean something is wrong with me," said Lasheera. She pointed to the Jamaican rum nail color as the volunteer doing her feet anticipated the conversation heating up.

"You work with Aruba and Bria, right?"

"Yes."

"Do you mean to tell me you wouldn't want to be in a position to keep your paycheck, let your husband handle everything, and do what you please with your money?"

"I'm telling you if I had a husband, I'd want us to work together and share the load. There shouldn't be a mine-and-yours mentality in a marriage," said Lasheera, becoming more irritated by Joycelyn's attack.

"People, people, we don't have these discussions at Sista Spa Night," said Bria, diffusing the argument.

Bria knew Joycelyn's issue. Joycelyn derived pleasure when meeting a skinny sista who wasn't hitched. Lasheera's model-thin frame, snazzy hair cut, and warm personality wasn't lost on anyone in the house. Joycelyn's three-hundred-pound-plus frame, squat stature, and boisterous personality could be disarming for some. Joycelyn took pride in her appearance. She kept her hair done, nails tight, and feet together. Somehow, that was never enough to satisfy her or the notion that Andre, or Fabulous Dre as Joycelyn renamed him, wanted someone smaller. No matter how much he complimented her, she always shrank in front of smaller, single women. Bria, Renae, and Aruba joked they'd be in trouble if they didn't have husbands. During a Circle Centre Mall visit, a precocious boy pointed at Joycelyn and Dre, and said, "Look, Mommy, they look like the number ten standing next to each other," as they strolled by. Dre's six-three, lithe body next to Joycelyn's round-figure frame could have been mistaken for the number. Dre spent the rest of the night calming Joycelyn down and telling her how beautiful she was to him. Renae and Aruba witnessed the metamorphosis in Joycelyn when smaller women were around. If the women were married, she'd back down. If they were single, she'd harangue the hell out of them until they left her presence.

"I have a question for you all. I have a circumstance that needs to be addressed," said Bria.

"Out with it," said Aruba.

"I have a friend—"

"The hypothetical game, Bree?" asked Aruba.

"I have a friend whose husband is this really nice guy. He's crazy about his wife, but I don't think they can have children. For a time, the husband thought he was the problem and was reluctant to seek advice or help from the doctor. My friend said because the husband was so disappointed about his wife not being able to conceive he started drinking. And drinking. Soon, the wife found herself in rehab with the husband, so he could pull it together."

Aruba performed a process of elimination. Dre was too busy to have children. Greer was strapped with child support from his previous marriage and wasn't thinking about having any children. James didn't drink. Sidney was too righteous to drink. The woman Bria was talking about must have been someone new.

"Well, did he make it out of rehab?" asked Joycelyn.

"He did. I think the incident made them stronger," said Bria.

"So what's the problem?" asked Renae.

"During the ordeal, the wife didn't have anyone to talk to. She felt alone and wished she had confided in someone about the incident."

"She doesn't have friends?" asked Aruba.

"Yes. She just wasn't sure how they'd take the news. If they'd support her. Visitors and fish smell in three days. She didn't want to be a burden."

"That's absurd. You all get on my last nerve, but you know if something jumps off between Greer and me, I'm calling the posse. I don't know what I'd do without my crew," said Renae, high-fiving Aruba, Joycelyn, and Bria.

"That's how I feel about Jamilah and Tawatha. We've been friends since grade school and I rely on their love and support. Especially…" Lasheera paused, forgetting these women were new. "Especially after the break-up with my son's father."

"I hope you all know we can share anything with each other. That's why we're here," said Bria, cutting her eyes at Aruba.

"What if a woman keeps her business to herself because she doesn't want to be judged or criticized?" asked Aruba.

"What do you mean?" asked Renae.

"Don't act so innocent. How many times have we sat around saying how stupid a woman is for staying with a spouse who isn't ideal, or how dense a woman is for trying to leave a man who either provides a good life or makes a lot of money?"

The ladies sank in their seats, guilty as charged.

"I'm just saying women can be so hard on each other. In a moment of weakness, one woman might share something in confidence with a sista, then she, *out of love and concern*, tells your business to someone else in the group. Then it goes on and on. And my goodness, woe to the woman who has the nerve to say she's having an affair or thinking of having an affair. We rake her over the coals like nobody's business."

"Ahuh, I sure do," said Joycelyn. "As good as I am to Dre, I would kill him and his mistress if I found out he was cheating on me."

"Aruba, cheating is different. You know the rule of thumb is stay away from another woman's man," said Renae.

"A marriage is complicated enough without a third wheel. These single wenches think they can march in and pick up the slack while you're doing the best you can to hold it together. Cooking, cleaning, working, trying to create a decent home, and then someone else thinks she can wave a magic wand and fill your shoes," said Joycelyn. She tried to steady her feet for her pedicure, but the conversation enraged her.

"Please be still while I apply your color, ma'am," said the student.

"Single wenches. What's that supposed to mean?" asked Lasheera. She hated the way married women wore halos, as if they did everything so well, so perfect, that a man shouldn't get his needs met elsewhere. "What if a wife isn't on her J-O-B? I don't know what happens to you all after you get a ring and a roof over your heads, but you stop having sex and being attentive to your husbands. It's no wonder they cheat!"

"Sounds like someone is speaking from experience. A single wench no less. Guess I pegged you right," said Joycelyn.

"Calm down, Joycelyn and Lasheera," said Bria. This was the craziest spa night she'd ever hosted. She wouldn't have invited Lasheera if she'd known things would get this heated. "Your opinions are valuable and necessary. Let's find a better way to express ourselves, okay."

Joycelyn exhaled deeply and placed her feet back on the stool to be painted. Lasheera, upset she'd allowed Joycelyn to get the best of her, picked up a magazine from a table next to her and flipped through the pages.

"I'm sorry for calling you a wench, Lasheera. I see so many

marriages breaking up due to adultery and I get angry. Please accept my apology."

"I'm sorry for what I said as well. I'm not a wench, but my son, Zion's father, is married. We made a horrible mistake when I was younger and lacked better judgment. If I could erase that time from my experiences yet have Zion, I would."

"You heifers are gonna make me call a group hug," said Renae, air-blowing her nails.

Aruba added, "The bottom line is no one wants to open up and be betrayed. For example, I know a young woman at a rival company who adores her friend's husband. According to Sabrina, the wife doesn't sleep with the husband, she shops 'til she drops, isn't very encouraging to the husband, and feels she's got the marriage so locked up that he'd never cheat. What advice would you give her?"

"The wife or Sabrina?" asked Bria.

"Sabrina."

"I'd tell her she's getting herself into something she's not ready to handle. The grass is greener on the other side, but the water bill is higher," said Renae.

"I'd tell her she's just hearing one side of the story. I bet if she talked to the wife, she'd hear some things about Mr. Olympia that he's not telling," said Bria.

"She seems to know a lot about the wife," said Joycelyn. "Please don't tell me she's friends with the woman."

"I think she is," said Aruba.

"That's a different kind of trashy. Let her go ahead and have him. She'll get more than she bargained for and will regret it for the rest of her life. No good will come of that situation," said Joycelyn.

Lasheera chimed in for good measure. "She'll have his attention for a while. Then they'll both realize the promises and fantasies they've whispered to each other are just that, promises and fantasies.

The time they stole away from their families and friends would have been better spent working through their issues at home. Once trust is broken, it's hard and nearly impossible to get back."

Lasheera held her head back, thought of Zion, and wondered why she ever believed Marvin would marry her.

Bria sliced through the moment with a deep breath. "For the record, ladies, we're still childless, but I'm proud of my Sidney for not drinking anymore."

The ladies reflected on her words, wondered how they could be better to the men in their lives from this point forward.

[23]
My Name Is

"**M**iss, the total is two thousand, four hundred, eighty dollars." The sales clerk contained her excitement as Victoria slid her black American Express card across the counter. This sale exceeded her monthly quota. It would also net great store incentives.

"Thank you," she looked down at the name on the card, "Mrs. Winston Faulk."

"Thank you," said Victoria. "You've been most helpful. I'll have to drop your manager a line as kudos for your great service."

"Wait a minute. Is your husband, Dr. Winston Faulk? The doctor who separated the conjoined twins? Oh, my God! You're Dr. Faulk's wife?"

Here we go again.

"My brother received the Dr. Winston Faulk scholarship at Butler University. He's a pre-med student. I know he'd love to meet your husband." The sales clerk trembled as she handed Victoria the card.

"Well, I wish him the best of luck. I'm sure he'll go on and do great things. Have a good day," Victoria read her nametag, "Marie."

"You, too, Mrs. Faulk."

Victoria exited Saks and headed downtown. She refused to let Marie spoil her day. Of course she couldn't blame Marie for the name on her credit card. She'd chosen the name printed on it. Just as she'd chosen the license plate on her Mercedes that read, *DOCTOR'S GIRL*. She'd been so wrapped up in being Mrs. Faulk that she didn't know who she was anymore. She enjoyed the perks of being married to a successful man, but lately, she felt empty. Aruba was working all the time and couldn't get together for drinks or fun; Charlotte and her husband continued to travel; Winston was back and forth in Arizona with new patients.

Maxie's words continued to haunt her. *"I see you helping others."* Victoria perused the items she'd purchased. Since the last shelter visit, Sylvia had become a permanent fixture in her mind. Inter-action at Dorcas made her realize how blessed she was to have the life she lived, to have a man like Winston. The thought of fleeing in the middle of the night for shelter tied her stomach in knots. *What kind of man neglected his family the way Sylvia's husband had?* With grit crowding out reservation, she phoned Miriam at Dorcas to see if it was okay to form a closer relationship with Sylvia. Victoria hoped Sylvia didn't see her attempt at friendship as a charity bid. She really wanted to do something good, to get to know someone outside her circle of friends. When she learned Sylvia was only a few years older, she wondered what life must have been like for her. Bit by bit, she learned Sylvia gave up college for marriage, had several miscarriages, was forbidden to work, and truly believed she'd grow old with her estranged husband, Gerald. That was Sylvia's yesterday. She recently had enrolled in Butler University and was pursuing a degree in education..

Victoria performed a mental checklist of the day's activities for Sylvia and Alice. Alva prepared Sylvia's favorite meal for lunch: smothered chicken with gravy and garlic butter mashed potatoes. Victoria wasn't sure what other items went with the meal, but the food smelled wonderful when she left. Nicolette stayed behind to help Alva. Alva and Nicolette would also remove the gifts from the trunk and put them under the Christmas tree. Christmas was two months past, but Alva brought the tree down from the attic, decorated it, and made nametags for Christmas in February. Sylvia and Alice were their special guests, and she wanted to make sure they felt welcome.

Victoria parked in front of Dorcas. Sylvia and Alice were expecting her, so she didn't have to go inside today. Alice peered through the front window. She pulled Sylvia's shirt when she recognized Victoria. They both walked toward Victoria's car, with Sylvia placing her hand over her mouth to stifle the shock of how stylish their ride to lunch would be.

"Miss Victoria, it's good to see you again," Alice said, hugging Victoria.

"I'm glad to see both of you." Victoria opened the passenger and backseat doors for Sylvia and Alice.

"Victoria, is this your car? I've never been in a Mercedes before. Gerald and I did all we could to keep that jalopy of ours going. I feel like I've died and gone to heaven." Sylvia slid in the front seat, beaming.

"I wanted to do something nice for both of you today, so I'm taking you to lunch."

"McDonald's?" Alice asked.

"No, I'm taking you to my house."

"No offense, but you don't look like the cooking type, Victoria. Am I gonna have to whip us up something?" Sylvia asked.

"I can't lie, Sylvia, I'm not the cooking type. My housekeeper, Alva, already cooked your favorite foods."

"Hush your mouth, a housekeeper? Miriam said your husband was a doctor. I don't know that I've ever met another black woman like you. I mean one that would want to be friends with someone like me."

"What do you mean, someone like you?"

"When I lived in Cincinnati, I'd run across your type shopping, lunching, spending your money like it was running water. Gerald and I had a hotdog cart and I'd gaze at those women, wondering what it would be like to live the life they lived. I never bought the notion that the grass wasn't greener on the other side because money can provide opportunities, no doubt about it."

"I do feel blessed to do a lot of the things I do."

"It's good you got your head on straight about it."

"Ms. Victoria, do you have any children?" Alice asked.

"Yes, I have a four-year-old daughter, Nicolette. You'll get to meet her today. She stayed behind to help frost your brownies."

"How did you know I like brownies?" Alice's eyes lit up with the question.

"Oh, a little bird told me." Victoria winked at Sylvia.

Laughter and chitchat made the ride to the house a swift one. As they neared the driveway, Sylvia cupped her mouth with her hands, unsure of what to think of the majestic home before her.

"How many of y'all live here?" Sylvia asked.

Victoria pressed her garage door opener. "Four. My husband, Alva, Nicolette, and me."

"And Alva cleans all this up herself?"

"The house practically cleans itself. Although we have help, we're sticklers for picking up after ourselves and making sure things are easy on Alva. She's a godsend and I wouldn't want to drive her away."

"Like I said before, you sure are a little different than your kind I've met in the past."

Alva and Nicolette met them at the garage door. Alva had taken the time to bake an assortment of muffins, cookies, and breads for the guests. The smell of the goodies floated throughout the garage, welcoming them in. Alva wanted to make sure they'd have a snack for now and something to take to the shelter later. Nicolette sidled next to Alice, grabbed her hand.

"You gonna be my big sister?" Nicolette grinned.

"If you want me to be." Alice studied her surroundings, embarrassed that she didn't know how to act in such a place.

"Let's go up to my room. We can have a tea party."

"We'll be eating in about fifteen minutes, Nicolette, so don't keep Alice too long."

"Okay, Mommy."

Sylvia trudged behind them as she breathed short breaths caused by the beauty of the welcoming house. To the right of Sylvia's vision, she marveled at what looked like storage for days. The cherry hall tree held coats that hung as if they, too, enjoyed living there. Some creative soul had taken the time to not only place the shoes in cubbyholes, but to arrange them by color. *Ain't that something.*

"Make yourself at home, Sylvia. I'm going to put my things down, slip into something comfortable, and check messages. I'll be back shortly."

Alva motioned Sylvia to join her at the breakfast nook.

"May I offer you something to drink?"

"I know I'm going back to my Mississippi roots, but how 'bout some sweet tea?"

"Coming right up."

Sylvia sat with caution. Everything about the day was a dream to her. Why had this pretty woman invited her to such a grand home? Why was the housekeeper, who could be her big sister, being so nice? And who taught her how to make smothered chicken and potatoes so well? Sylvia hadn't smelled chicken like that since the family's 2003 reunion in Vicksburg. When Miriam first told her Victoria wanted to know what size clothes she wore, she assumed this suburban housewife had a few friends who wanted to empty their closets, do something good for the less fortunate. Then Victoria began calling, checking on her once or twice a week. She offered a gym membership when Sylvia expressed a desire to lose weight, to be high school skinny again. She treated Alice to a pampered princess spa day at Divas in Training, the children's salon. She suggested housing referrals in the city and told Sylvia when she was ready, she would put her in touch with someone at the Indianapolis Neighborhood Housing Partnership if she felt homeownership was something she wanted to pursue. "Why me?"

"Did you say something, Sylvia?" Alva asked.

"I guess I did. Why me is what I asked. I've never had someone be so generous to me."

Alva joined Sylvia, sweet tea in hand.

"Victoria and Winston are wonderful. She's like a daughter to me. When I came to Indianapolis, I'd worked for two families that made me feel like an outsider. Being new here and missing Antigua—"

"I knew you had an accent," Sylvia interrupted.

"...I was referred to the Faulks by my last employer. I was a little surprised at first because they were so young and wealthy, but they took me in and made me feel so at home. Winston's a noted cardiologist who has done amazing things in the medical community. They even insisted I call them by their first names. I could just freeze Nicolette in time because she's such an angel. She's bright, inquisitive, and a joy to take care of."

Sylvia took a swig of her sweet tea, then leaned into Alva. "Okay, girl, you can spill the beans. Is her husband white?"

"Heavens no." Alva blushed. She stood, removing a photo album from a drawer beneath the island.

Sylvia flipped through the photos. Joy and satisfaction rose as she turned each page.

"Good Lord, he's handsome!"

"Yes, Winston is a good-looking man. And he's nice. That's a rare combination in this day and age."

"You go with them on all the vacations?"

"Yes. Last year alone we went to Brazil, Paris, and Australia. I really enjoyed Brazil."

"I bet you did. Those are lovely." Sylvia slid the album back to Alva.

"We have digital photo albums, but I guess I'm old-fashioned in that I like to have these near."

"I'd have to get used to all this technology around here. My soon-to-be ex-husband, Gerald, wasn't open to exploring anything new. We moved from Mississippi to Cincinnati, Ohio, and that was it. No growth, no progress. Did Victoria tell you what happened?"

"I just know you live at Dorcas. She didn't fill me in on any details."

"You ever been married, Alva?"

"I was. I lost my husband in a car accident when he was thirty-six. I never wanted to remarry."

"I lost Gerald to the Grand Victoria Casino and Jack Daniel's. I hoped he'd stop drinking, but it never happened. I'm ready to move on, now. It's time I make a better life for Alice and me. After all she's seen, it's the least I could do."

Victoria, Nicolette, and Alice disturbed the light banter and fun between Sylvia and Alva.

"Look at me flapping my gums. Let me get this food on the table," Alva mused.

Alva fixed the table, then joined them. An hour passed as the four laughed, swapped stories, and enjoyed each other's company. Sylvia chuckled so hard tears streamed down her face. She wasn't allowed to laugh, to be, to live when she was with Gerald. The tiny slice of freedom she was experiencing strengthened her resolve to get her life in order.

After lunch, Alva packaged the sweets and gave Sylvia her number. "Call me when you need to talk."

"Don't hang up when I call you on a regular basis."

"I wouldn't dream of it."

Victoria coughed, nodded her head toward the theater room.

"Yes, where are our manners?" Alva asked. "You all have something waiting for you downstairs."

As if the day hadn't been enough to dispel any myth a cynic had about mankind, Sylvia and Alice held hands as they descended the stairs.

"Momma, it's a movie theater!"

Alice ran toward a leather seat, plopped down, and reclined.

"Alice, come out of that seat!" Sylvia hissed through clenched teeth.

Nicolette grabbed Alice's hand, pulled her near the Christmas tree. "It's Christmas in February. You have to open your presents."

"You did all this for us?" Sylvia asked.

"We sure did," Victoria answered. "And you can't go back to Dorcas until you open every single one."

They sat Indian-style on the floor, opening gifts and *oohing* and aahing as each present created a tad more distance from past Christmases. Christmases when Gerald promised gifts, but reappeared December 27th. Lunch was wonderful; Christmas in February was divine.

Sylvia froze when she opened the largest box before her. "No. You. Didn't." Sylvia dragged out the words as if they'd make the box disappear. "I...I..."

"Well, you said Foxy was your pride and joy and that you missed her, so there you go," said Victoria. "I hope she's a good substitute."

Sylvia pulled the fur coat from the Elan Furs box. She ran her fingers over the beautiful, floor-length coat, then stood to try it on. "I've never had something this nice in all my life."

Victoria remembered Sylvia saying Gerald had pawned the frayed, faux fox jacket he'd given her. She wanted to make sure Sylvia kept warm the rest of the winter.

"This is too much. We can't take all this from you," said Sylvia.

"You're not taking anything. It's our gift to you for being so wonderful."

Sylvia sat now, crying, trying to regain her composure. She watched as Alva placed the gifts in bags.

"I'll put these in the trunk of your car, Victoria."

"Victoria, I can't thank you enough. You have to let me do something in return for you."

"You came for lunch. That's all I needed you to do."

Alva watched them load into the car and drive away to Dorcas. She was thrilled to meet Sylvia and Alice. It had been a while since she'd had enjoyable guests, people she deemed as equals. Whatever had gotten into Victoria, she hoped it would flourish and spill over onto Winston.

[24]
Make It Wiggle, Make It Jiggle

Winston heard low thumping coming from the media room and wondered what was going on. He'd been gone so much the last five months he wasn't sure what to make of the noise tonight. Most nights he'd slip in bed with Victoria, lightly kiss her forehead, and fall asleep. Darkness helped ease his guilty conscience. The situation with Aruba was getting out of hand and he knew he had to do something before they were exposed. He was proud that he still hadn't been intimate with her, but a man could only take so much before he gave in to his desires.

Winston pulled a bottle of wine from the refrigerator, sat at the kitchen table, and pondered his circumstances. Since Aruba fled her home, he'd been on a roller-coaster ride. He got her a room at the Conrad just to help out. The thought of her going back to James incensed him, so he rented her a condo. He knew Aruba's house was in her name and didn't want her to shoulder the expense of two households, so he thought it best to pay her mortgage up for a year as well as find a safe place for her and Jeremiah. She'd worried enough about money the last ten years and he felt contemplating a divorce and juggling finances was too much for her. If only he could get her out of his head. Two months ago, she took the afternoon off to go furniture shopping and he accompanied her. The furniture was where she drew the line. She insisted on paying for her own furniture because the fresh start would be a reflection of her tastes, her style. She selected gorgeous pieces from Ashley Furniture, Kittle's, and ordered a living room set online from Holley House Furniture. He loved the freedom she displayed.

Winston sipped wine, thought of Aruba, and noticed a turquoise and tan envelope taped to the microwave with his name written in gold calligraphy. He figured it was another request from Victoria for something. It seemed she always wanted something.

"Let me get this over with." He opened the envelope and read the note.

I know you've been craving affection and I've got just what you need. Join me in the theater for a sexy surprise.

Winston descended the stairs, cautiously, not sure what to expect. Hadn't he given her the bag she requested, the trip to Arizona, a $2,000 gift certificate to Nordstrom, a fur coat? Although she'd never offered a sexy surprise, he was sure it came with a string attached. Winston found a pole, not a string, at the bottom of the stairs in the center of the room. The low thumping he'd heard earlier was music, unfamiliar music that belonged in a strip club, not a suburban home. He had to admit that he liked it. He spied Urban Mystic's CD cover sitting on the table next to the entertainment center. A quick scan of the songs let him know the tune "Back It Up" was streaming from the speakers. When Victoria spotted him, she approached him, took his hand, and sat him down in a plush theater chair. He looked at Victoria, speechless. She'd slicked her hair back in a ponytail and wore makeup. She donned a black T-shirt with the words, *I'M NOT A STRIPPER, I JUST DANCE LIKE ONE*, in silver rhinestones and hip-hugging black shorts. Before he could ask what was going on or protest, Victoria turned the music up and began to dance for him. He

eyed her going back and forth in what was obviously a choreo-
graphed routine. He loved Victoria, but knew she didn't have an
ounce of rhythm.

Stop. Make it wiggle, make it jiggle.

Somehow, she managed to fool him and stay on beat with the
tune, glorifying the reasons a woman should back it up. *She's
counting the beat of the music.* He smiled as she took four steps
backward, faced the pole, then leapt onto it. She twirled around
it, stopping in the middle as she turned upside down. He figured
this was every husband's dream, but all he could think about was
Aruba performing the routine for him. He saw Aruba in the T-
shirt, the shorts, bending down and backing it up with her vicious
body. By the time he snapped himself back to reality, Victoria had
crawled toward him on all fours, touching him, and beckoning
him to make love.

Winston stood, unenthused, and walked toward the stereo. He
turned the music off and sat down again.

Flushed with embarrassment, Victoria sat next to him.

"What did I do wrong? I hoped you'd enjoy something...differ-
ent. You've been complaining about things we don't do intimately,
and I just thought—"

"When was the last time I complained to you about anything?
When was the last time I attempted to touch you?"

Victoria thought about the question a moment and couldn't
answer. She'd neglected his needs so long she couldn't recall the
last time he brushed her shoulders, and whispered, "You're the
most beautiful woman in the world, Tori."

Nor could she remember when she returned from a shopping
spree to find Alva and Nicolette gone, soft jazz playing, and scented
candles blazing a trail to the bedroom.

"Are you saying you don't desire me anymore?"

Winston dreaded this moment. He knew he couldn't tell her the truth, but he knew distance had to be created between them to sort things out. "I guess I'm going through something right now. I wonder if you've been dismissive because of the sacrifices you've had to make for my career. Don't you know I only wanted to make a good life for you and Nicolette?"

"I know that, Winston. I mean, I know that now. I've complained in the past and been so selfish. The past few months have been eye-opening for me. I've taken so much for granted. Will you give me and us a chance to start again? I want to make things up to you."

If only she had said those words nine months ago. This moment was difficult enough. Victoria's complaints and ramblings made it easier to contemplate leaving her. But looking at her made him reconsider the reasons he wanted to abandon the relationship.

"Winston, you're scaring me. Are you telling me things have gotten so bad between us you're not willing to work at it?"

"I'm not saying that, Victoria. I need space to think things through. This home has become a safe haven for you and Nicolette. I wouldn't uproot my family or disrupt your safety or hers."

"Are you moving out?" Silence enveloped their shared space. "Well, are you?"

Winston rose from the sofa without responding. He knew one more look at her might deflate his courage. He climbed the stairs to pack an overnight bag. Victoria followed him, hands trembling, wondering if she could find a way to convince him they were worth salvaging. She'd never seen him so determined to stand his ground where their relationship stood. She always found a way to manipulate the circumstances in her favor. What on earth had gotten into him?

"What am I supposed to tell Nicolette?"

Winston eyed Victoria, incredulous she'd chosen to leverage Nicolette. "Well, for starters, tell Nicolette her absent father is thinking things over and trying to determine if he's wanted around here for more than his paycheck."

"What's that supposed to mean?"

Winston pointed to the settee in the sitting area. Reluctantly, Victoria joined him, chewing her nails. "Do you know how embarrassed I felt a few weeks ago when Stan Marshall said his wife joined you for brunch at Palomino?"

"Kathy?"

"So you remember? Do you also remember what Nicolette told their daughter, Grayson?"

Victoria tried to remember what had transpired. One minute the girls were playing, sipping orange juice. The next, Grayson was crying about something Nicolette had whispered to her. Neither she nor Kathy ever got to the bottom of the matter.

"Well, it seems Nicolette told Grayson her father needed to work more since our house is bigger, our cars are better, and we have more money. Funny thing is, I knew she was repeating things she'd heard you say before."

"Winston—"

"I'm not done yet. I've tried to compensate for my absence over the years with getaways and romantic overtures, hoping that you would understand to live the way we live requires sacrifice. You don't have to work, Alva makes sure you don't have to worry about cooking or cleaning, and it still seems that's not good enough. Whatever it is you want, I've accepted that I can't give it to you."

"I want us. I want us to have a good relationship, to talk, to…"

Winston didn't wait for her to complete the sentence. He walked away as she spoke, headed to the garage, tossed his bag in the backseat, and drove away. Maybe a ride would cool him off, clear his mind. The one place he couldn't go to was Aruba's. He wanted to make love to her and feel that sweet release in her arms tonight. It was much too soon to do that.

[25]
The Hardest-Working Man in Indy

James watched training videos at Franzen Industrial staffing with eight other applicants and diverted the gaze of a sexy, young woman staring at him. This was his third successful temporary assignment. No way would he screw up this opportunity with another woman or negligent behavior. He was on a roll with Franzen. He'd even been requested to work for the latest company. Aruba would see once and for all that he had every intention of making things right between them. His misdeeds had cost him a legal separation from Aruba and estrangement from Jeremiah. To make matters worse, he'd succumbed to Tawatha's advances in a moment of weakness and spent the night at her place. James was floored by the lovely home she now occupied. James couldn't shake the feeling of discomfort after sneaking in during the middle of the night, having sex with her, then slinking out as one of her sons rubbed his eyes and gave him a who-the-hell-are-you leer. Seeing Tawatha's son made him miss Jeremiah even more. He still smelled the scent of the freshly waxed floors and Tawatha's perfume. He'd spent the previous night nursing a half-eaten box of strawberry Newtons and avoiding her texts. He knew it was wrong to play games with her, but he was sure by now she would have gotten the hint that he wasn't leaving his wife.

James recalled a saying his mother often made while deadheading flowers in her garden: "It takes two people to make a marriage go bad." It may take two, but he knew he was largely responsible for the disintegration of his union. James anticipated the temporary assignment would become permanent. He would work hard at reestablishing his life with Aruba. Randy Jacob, Franzen staffing coordinator, drew his attention back to the training.

"I want to remind you that although we're sending you to various work sites, you are a Franzen representative. We expect each of you to report to your assignments in a timely manner and to call in at the number in your orientation packet if you're unable to work."

"How long will this assignment last?" This came from a stocky man donning a scowl, faded jeans, and a black overcoat two rows over from James.

"The current assignment will last eight months to a year. The pay is sixteen dollars an hour, no benefits. You'll be working throughout the city, cleaning out foreclosed properties.

Shelby Arvinson, owner of Arvinson Renovation, has the need for more workers due to the number of properties being abandoned. If you work hard and establish a good rapport with the owner, this assignment could become permanent."

Young Sexy gazed and smiled at James as she raised her hand. "Are we all working the same sites or will we be separated?"

James acknowledged her stare with a smile as he read a pamphlet he'd taken from his welcome packet.

"Arvinson has provided a van for its workers, so transportation shouldn't be an issue or a reason for call-ins. Is that understood?" Everyone nodded and clipped on ID badges Randy passed out.

"The van leaves from the front parking lot in ten minutes. Please make any calls, take a restroom break, or grab a snack before you leave."

Randy's dismissal of the group was Young Sexy's cue. She sidled next to James, her expressive, dark-brown eyes fixed on his. James took in her oversized Columbia University sweatshirt, fitted jeans, and steel-toed pink and tan boots. Her shoulder-length bob accented her delicate face and rich, mocha skin.

"Hi, how are you?" she asked.

James stirred hot chocolate and met her gaze. Her boldness excited him, but he kept his mind on Aruba.

"I'm good. And you?"

"I've been thinking about you, wondering where you've been."

"Do I know you, Miss…"

She extended her hand. James noticed her wedding band.

"I'm Katrina Benford. Don't tell me you don't remember me, James?"

James had flirted with so many women over the years, taking their numbers, promising to call, that he spaced out at moments like this. He knew it would be better to let her reveal where they'd met.

"James, it's me? Trina. You really don't remember me?"

"Of course I'd remember someone as lovely as you, but a brotha's getting older. Help me out."

Katrina playfully jabbed James's arm. "You were at a barbershop off Fifth and College four years ago. Shear Bliss." Katrina placed her hands on her hips. "That was the only shop I found specializing in great short cuts. This bob is okay, but you cut my hair in the style Halle Berry wore hers in *Die Another Day*. Man, my husband was livid that guys were approaching me left and right. Everybody loved it when I rocked that cut!"

Katrina pulled a silver photo album from her purse and handed it to James. He flipped through the photos, admiring Katrina in various poses as he slowly remembered his short stint at Bliss. He'd almost forgotten about the time spent there. He was popular with the ladies, a little too popular for Aruba's taste, but she never complained. He made more than enough money to pay his monthly booth rental during those days, but he wanted to party and hang with the fellas. Several missed payments and he was outta there. Aruba encouraged him to explore working at other shops, but he belittled her for suggesting he wasn't man enough to keep a job doing what he loved. *Did she say that, or was it me?* As always, she tried to spur on his efforts.

"So when can I sit in your chair again? I'll go short again if you do my hair."

"Well, I'm not actually doing hair right now."

"Not doing hair? That's like Beyoncé saying she's not creating new music or booty-shaking. You're kidding, right?"

Emboldened by her enthusiasm, James answered, "I've been looking into it. I'd rather own a shop instead of working for other people."

Katrina was about to comment when Randy announced, "The van is out front, everyone. Please gather any items you're taking and board as quickly as possible."

Katrina and James put on their coats and piled into the van with the other workers. Katrina nestled close to James, continuing their conversation.

"Like I was about to say inside, I feel you. I'm not doing this job because I need to work. I'm here scoping out the competition."

"Really?"

Katrina removed a business card from an elegant card holder in her purse. James read the card and was impressed by what he saw. Benford and Associates boasted they'd rehab any home. Large or small, they guaranteed they'd modernize any residential property in Indianapolis and the surrounding areas.

"We're taking Arvinson down," Katrina said, leaning into James conspiratorially and winking.

"So tell me how you'll manage that."

"Simple mathematics. The recession and current housing market have been bad for some, good for others. People who are still working and holding on to their property know that selling it might take some time, so they're rehabbing. The pie-in-the-sky purchasers who got in over their heads with too much mortgage are walking away from properties. That's where we come in. My husband, Isaak, was doing great as a real estate developer in the private sector, but he knew he had the know-how to start his own business. He's been acquiring properties left and right, making a name for himself, and racking up development and design awards along the way."

Isaak Benford. James knew the name sounded familiar. He recalled seeing the clean-cut brother wearing the hell out of a Brooks Brothers suit and a Rolex on the cover of the *Indianapolis Business Journal* last year. Beneath the caption, *Benford Does Green Best*, Isaak stood in front of a massive home that had been rehabbed with repurposed materials and boasted an eco-friendly design. The home sold for $800,000 and received the 2007 Design Award for Innovative Renewal, $200,000-$300,000 Category. James watched Katrina's eyes light up as she revealed their scheme to put Arvinson out of business.

"I'm all about applauding the competition. Arvinson is smart because he's bringing the workers to him, endearing them by providing a van, making sure he establishes trust. I want to go on site to see how the actual…James, I'm sorry. There I go again."

"What, Katrina?"

"I get so excited that I take over a conversation talking about the things that Isaak and I do, what he wants to accomplish. I didn't mean to bore you. Enough about Isaak's obsessions. What's going on with you?"

"You weren't boring me. I actually enjoyed hearing about some-one taking charge and handling his business by using his God-given talents."

"Oh, don't let me sugarcoat things. We've had our ups and downs trying to get Benford and Associates off the ground. I actually had to cut back on a lot of shopping, hairdos, and nights out with the girls, so I could have pristine credit. No way was I going to embarrass him going to the bank. Don't get me wrong, I didn't have bad credit. I just wanted to be his partner in every way."

"Gotcha."

"I remembered you said you and that pretty wife of yours might open a salon. What happened with that?"

James thought it odd he'd be having this conversation with a former client/semi-stranger. He was about to ask her how she knew what Aruba looked like, but he remembered the photos he had of her in the shop. Everyone complimented his gorgeous wife from the photos and the few times she'd brought him take-out or stopped in to say hello. He tried to project an image of confidence, but then as now, James was tired of lying and pre-tending to be something he wasn't. How could he say to Katrina what he really felt without sounding like a loser?

"I've been dragging my feet a little. I'm not sure what's holding me back, but talking to you has lit a spark I haven't had in a long time."

"Do you, boo."

"I'm being selfish again. I've been yakking all this time about Isaak that I forgot to mention my cousin, Mitch Coleman. He opened up a salon for little girls last year. I don't know how he does it, but he's making money hand over fist with Divas in Training. He says he's bringing up the next generation of women who don't mind doing what they need to do to stay beautiful. I'll put you in touch with him. The least you could do is talk to him and see what he's doing to keep multiple facilities afloat. You know you won't be working for Arvinson too long, since Benford will steal you away." Katrina winked and playfully poked James's side.

Divas in Training. James remembered Aruba mentioning the owner of the shop before she'd left home. He flushed with embarrassment after receiving the same tip twice. Aruba always had his back when it came to uplifting him. There was something about Katrina that reminded him of Aruba. James loved the way Katrina's eyes lit up when she talked about Isaak. Maybe Aruba would give him one last chance so that she could speak of him in the same way to a stranger.

[26]
Do Me This Solid

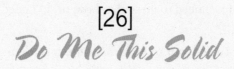

"Can you believe Mr. J.B. had the nerve to take Momma to the Bahamas?"

"And the problem with that would be? I think it's sweet." Lasheera shook her head and softly chuckled at Tawatha's selfishness.

"He could have waited another week. They're making things difficult for me."

"What's going on?"

Tawatha paced back and forth in her office, cell phone in hand. Mr. Hinton had requested she be present at a late dinner with Craddack Development. In addition to staving off the rumor mill buzzing with speculation and innuendo as to why she was asked to go to dinner and not senior project managers, she had to find a fill-in for Aunjanue's art show. Tonight was too important to decline Mr. Hinton's invite.

"I can't make it to Aunjanue's art show. Remember I told you about Craddack Development? We've been wooing their CEO for a contract for months now."

"Yeah."

"Well, Mr. Hinton wants me to sit in on the meeting tonight."

"How'd you score that?"

"You sound like the clowns in the office. He thinks I could learn a lot about the business."

"I'm sure he does."

"Sheer, stop. This is serious. You think you could go to the art show for me? I'll do anything if you could do this favor for me."

"You know my transportation's kinda shaky. I could find a ride, though. Do I just need to go to the show, or do I need to take them home as well?"

"Actually, I need you to pick them up, take them to the show, and bring them back home. The show is at Onnie's school. I'm sure she's cooked dinner, so you don't have to worry about feeding them."

"Oooo, you're gonna owe me big-time!" Lasheera joked.

"You know I got you. I don't want to miss any opportunity for advancement."

"You know I love seeing my babies and I don't mind getting them. I'll call you and tell you about my arrangements."

"I owe you big-time. Thanks, Sheer."

"Yeah, yeah, yeah."

Tawatha released a sigh of relief. She was nervous about going to dinner. What would she say? What if Mr. Hinton fielded her with questions? He'd given her Craddack's annual report and a portfolio about the company. She was well versed in all things Craddack, but she worried most about disappointing Mr. Hinton. No one in the office would ever understand how much she wanted to please him. Royce Hinton was old enough to be her father. The first time he called her into the office to reprimand her about the short skirts she wore, she figured he wanted to score. She waited for him to make his move. He sat behind his desk, his crisp, starched dress shirt hugging his muscular frame. She looked into his dark-brown, sad eyes, wondering if his wife satisfied him at all. He was a handsome man, the kind of man she'd fantasized about when she was younger. His honey-colored skin was weathered, and even when he smiled, the creases in his forehead foretold hidden regrets, unexplored thoughts. He was fiercely private, so no one knew a lot about personal matters on the home front. He took a deep breath, and quicker than Tawatha could devise a plan to get Royce comfortable and satisfied, he began to cry. Through his tears, Royce expressed Tawatha's eerie resemblance to his daughter, Ramona. She'd died in a car accident at twenty-three. Since the accident, he and his wife had been estranged, mere strangers navigating a mortgage, social calendar, and contemplating divorce. He wanted Tawatha to slow down, to be the young lady God called her to be, to stop selling herself short. She appreciated him from that day forward and wanted to make sure she took advantage of every opportunity to flourish at Hinton and Conyers. She knew the children would be disappointed that she couldn't attend the show, but at least they were seeing the fruits of her labor. When James joined the picture, they'd all understand the importance of her sacrifices.

"Mrs. D., may I talk to you for a moment?"

Aruba stared at Lasheera and waited for her to say the appropriate name.

"Aruba, may I ask you for a favor?"

"That's more like it. What's up?"

"Well, my girlfriend, Tawatha, has to attend a meeting tonight for work. Her oldest daughter has an art show at her school." Lasheera paused, suddenly embarrassed that she was always without transportation or thumbing a ride. "Tawatha needs me to pick the kids up, take them to the show, and drop them off."

"Do you need to leave early?"

"Actually, I don't have a way to get there."

"Do you need to borrow my vehicle?"

Lasheera closed the door. "I can't borrow your vehicle or anyone's because my license is suspended. I know you're married and busy, but I wondered if you could help me tonight. I need you to take me to pick them up, go to the art show, and take them home."

Aruba kept her composure. She and Winston were meeting for dinner at Ruth's Chris Steak House at eight and she didn't want to be late. Sidney and Bria were keeping Jeremiah for the weekend, so this snafu would seriously dig into her time with Winston. He still hadn't made a move to make love, but this weekend would be different. She'd see to it.

"Aruba, it's not like I'm putting my girl's business out there, but she needs me. She's a single mom, raising four kids alone. She's made strides at her job, she's gotten a new place, and she has a new man she's been hiding from us for a while. She's turning her life around and I want to be there for her."

Aruba pondered Lasheera's words. She could say the same thing about Bria right now. Bria never asked questions about her separation from James, never pushed for details about their problems. She pledged to be there for her, help in any way needed. Lasheera spoke highly of Tawatha and Jamilah. Maybe it was time she met one of the musketeers.

"I'll make a call to cancel an appointment I had. I'll do it for you. If it's an art sale, I might purchase something."

"Onnie's a talented artist. I mean, Aunjanue. That's Tawatha's oldest daughter. She's really good. You're gonna like her drawings and sketches."

[27]
Out of the Mouths of Babes

"Auntie Sheer, Auntie Sheer," yelled S'n'c'r'ty as she dashed out the front door. Sims and Grant followed closely behind.

"How are my babies doing?" Lasheera hoisted S'n'c'r'ty in her arms, spun her around, and placed light kisses on her cheek.

"We'll be doing better when Momma gets here. Aunjanue is worried."

"Who's the pretty lady?" Grant asked. He smiled at Aruba.

"You know we're not supposed to talk to strangers, Grant," S'n'c'r'ty chided.

Lasheera, embarrassed by S'n'c'r'ty's blunt nature, made the children form a semicircle around her. "This is my boss, Aruba. Your mom can't make it to the art show, so Miss Aruba's taking us to Onnie's school tonight."

Aruba greeted the children, admired the love and affection they showered on Lasheera.

"Can't make it?" Grant's bottom lip poked out at the news.

"I thought we were going as a family, then eating out afterward," Sims offered.

"Hold your horses, I can feed you. Your mom has important work tonight. She's been working hard, trying to make more money, so she can do special things for you," said Lasheera.

The children nodded in agreement. If Tawatha's working meant being able to do more things they all enjoyed, the kids saw no need to argue.

"Let's go inside to see if Onnie needs some help."

Aruba followed them inside the house, surprise and amazement debunking the myths she secretly held about Tawatha. When Lasheera shared her friend's plight, Aruba expected to drive her to a roach-infested crack den with drunks milling around outside, asking for cigarettes or bus fare. Maxie was right; stereotypes belonged in Hollywood, not in black people's minds. Just because a woman had lots of children didn't mean the worst should be thought of her situation. Aruba, reddened with embarrassment, admired the tasteful home she entered. *Wow, four children live here?*

"Lasheera, your friend has a lovely place," said Aruba. She sat on the sofa and watched S'n'c'r'ty scroll through a list of DVR-listed shows, settling on an episode of *Family Matters*.

"She's doing so well. I don't know that I would have taken you to her last place. Honey, that apartment was guttermost! Food and clothes everywhere. She's really been working hard at getting herself together. I wasn't kidding when I told you I was proud of her."

"As you should be. That's what good friends are for."

Aunjanue entered the living room, fidgeting with the suspenders on her corduroy dress. S'n'c'r'ty ran to Aunjanue.

"You look pretty, Onnie," said S'n'c'r'ty.

"Thanks, girl." Aunjanue scanned the room. "Auntie Sheer, can you help me with my ponytail? Where's Momma?"

"Sit down at the dining room table. I'll fix it. And don't be so nervous. We've got lots of time to get you there."

Aunjanue plopped down in a dinette chair, removed the top from the styling gel, and handed Lasheera the clip-on ponytail.

"Please make sure my edges are slicked down. I want to look good tonight just in case the art show is featured in the paper."

"You'll look fine. By the way, wave to my boss, Aruba, in the living room, Onnie."

Aunjanue waved to Aruba, then shot Lasheera a what's-she-doing-here look. Lasheera braced herself, plowed forward.

"Miss Aruba is taking us to the show tonight. Your mom has an important meeting tonight and she can't make it."

"I hope it's not with that James man." Aruba tensed. *Another James is causing confusion.* If she ditched my show for—"

"She's working, Onnie. Her boss needed her to sit in with a big developer. You know she's working hard to make things better."

Aunjanue smacked her lips. Disappointment clouded her face as she thought of Tawatha. *She's missing the one thing I worked so hard to do.* Aunjanue steadied the jar of gel for Lasheera.

"Aunjanue, tell me about some of your pieces that will be displayed tonight." Aruba tried softening the atmosphere.

"My drawings are colorful and filled with flowers. Sometimes I do people," said Aunjanue, her countenance radiating. "They're only for display right now, but next month, we'll be able to sell our best works for a spring art fundraiser. The seventh-grade art class is going to Washington, D.C."

"I heard you're good. I'll be your first patron. Will you autograph my drawing?" asked Aruba.

"Of course."

"Take a look at the mirror and tell me if this is good for you." Lasheera passed the mirror to Aunjanue.

"I love it! Let's get to the school. I want to be the first one there standing next to my work. S'n'c'r'ty, did you put your socks up and fold your underwear?"

"Yes, Onnie."

"Grant, did you take out the trash?"

"Yes, Onnie."

"Sims, how 'bout the lemons? Did you rub down the counter?"

"Yes, Onnie."

"Good. Go grab your coats, so we can go."

When they gathered their coats, the children filed out their home in a single line, just as Aunjanue taught them. Aruba shuttled the children into her vehicle, allowing S'n'c'r'ty to use Jeremiah's booster seat. She recalled Lasheera saying Aunjanue was twelve, but the young woman sitting behind her exhibited maturity that belied her years. Aruba admired the way the children respected and obeyed Aunjanue. Out of her rearview mirror, Aruba caught sight of Aunjanue giving S'n'c'r'ty the black mother stare, making her tamp down and stop tugging Sims's ear. Aruba wondered how busy Tawatha was that she crowned her oldest daughter surrogate mother. *Maybe I can reach out to her when my life calms down.*

On the ride to Lincoln Middle School, Aunjanue quizzed Grant with history questions on three-by-five cards. He answered them correctly, almost fearful of Aunjanue's wrath. Her face beamed with each correct response.

Aruba and Lasheera were impressed with the artwork. Who knew children were taking on such adult paintings and sculptures? Other parents commented about Aunjanue's work. In the cafeteria, parents and students congregated, chatted over gourmet cookies and sparkling punch flowing from an ornate fountain.

"I remember cheap butter cookies and tropical punch at functions like this. When did it change?" asked Lasheera.

"It's the moms and dads with free time," whispered Aruba.

Aunjanue didn't want to disturb their conversation, but she couldn't contain her excitement. "Did you like my work?" Lasheera's approval meant the world to Aunjanue. She chewed her nails, waited for Lasheera's response.

Lasheera swallowed the last of a pecan toffee cookie. "I'm biased, but you had the best prints out there."

"Yes, she did," said a deep, rolling voice not too far behind them.

"Mr. Carvin! I didn't know you were here." Aunjanue smiled, grabbing him by the arm. "Auntie Sheer, everybody, this is Mr. Carvin, my art teacher. Mr. Carvin, this is my Aunt Lasheera; her boss, Miss Aruba; and my brothers and sister."

"It's a pleasure to meet you all." He spoke to the group, but his eyes stayed focused on Lasheera.

"You must be proud of your students, Mr. Carvin." Aruba extended her hand to shake Mr. Carvin's.

"I can't express the joy. Especially when some students think they can't master simple lines, then create a complete masterpiece."

Lasheera knew the food had changed, but so had the teachers. She averted her eyes from Mr. Carvin's gaze. She'd been embarrassed in times past, thinking a man was paying attention to her when he was in fact looking at the most beautiful woman in the room. Lasheera figured Aruba was commanding his attention. Still, she caught another glimpse of him from the corner of her eye. She looked him up and down. His face said I'm running off to recess, since it was so youthful, so cherubic. His body, however, said former NFL player on the injured reserve list. The elegant cardigan sweater he wore outlined a six-pack she knew came from somebody's Bowflex. His fitted jeans made Lasheera blush. He was the same gentleman she'd noticed earlier whose swagger hinted a nice package beneath his boxers. She and Tawatha always did a teeth check when meeting guys. It didn't matter how handsome or sexy, if his teeth were jagged, chipped, or resembled any color of a Crayola box besides white, he was ousted. Mr. Carvin passed inspection with Chiclets whites. He towered over Lasheera and made her wonder what he'd be like for walks in the park or to hold in the middle of the night. She admonished herself, though, because he looked fresh out of college, probably an early high school graduate. An art prodigy whose parents had too much time and money on their hands and made sure their only son fulfilled his promise.

"So how'd you manage to escort the kids out tonight?" asked Mr. Carvin.

Lasheera's mind, still at Northwestway Park and walking with Mr. Carvin, was lulled back into the conversation by Aunjanue. "Earth to Sheer, Earth to Sheer," said Aunjanue.

"Onnie, did you say something?" asked Lasheera.

"I didn't, but Mr. Carvin did. He wants to know how you came to be our escort for tonight."

"Kids, let's look at some other drawings in the exhibit room," said Aruba, wanting to give the two privacy. Lasheera's eyes protested. She didn't want to be left alone with the handsome stranger for fear words might escape her. She watched Aruba and the kids exit the cafeteria to rejoin the other students and parents. She'd give Aruba a piece of her mind once they got back in the car.

"Well, Mr. Carvin—"

"Lake. Call me 'Lake.' My name is Lake Joseph Carvin."

"Okay, Lake. Aunjanue's mother had to work, so I was asked to bring them out. Tawatha and I help each other out as best we can."

"When she said aunt, I got excited. A lot of kids are here solo tonight. Parents are working. Don't have time to be involved. Believe me, I love consistent parental involvement. So…do you have children as well?"

Lasheera shrank under his comment and question as Zion immediately came to mind. "Would you like a blood sample and my credit report, too?"

"Did I say something wrong?" Lake remembered the golden rules the women in his family taught him. Never ask a woman her age, how many children she has, or if her hair is real. He didn't mean to step across any of those lines.

"No. I'm sorry. I feel what you're saying about parental involvement, is all."

"I wanted to talk to her mother, but since you're here, I can run my idea past you. You can be the middle woman for me."

I should have known he wasn't interested in me.

"Are you familiar with the Penrod Arts Fair?"

"Can't say that I am."

"It's a local arts fair that takes place the second weekend of September. I'd like to sponsor Aunjanue for this year's fair. She can gain exposure and I can get rid of art supplies my ex-wife left packed in the garage."

So he's single.

"Ex-wife? I thought you were nineteen or twenty." Lasheera surprised herself with the outburst.

"Thanks for the compliment. I'm thirty going on sixty. I'm the oldest young man I know."

"So why art? And why teaching?"

"Would you like a blood sample and my credit report, too?"

"Touché."

They both laughed at their protectiveness. "Art is how I kept my single mom entertained back in the day. She called me the J.J. Evans of the block. Later, she corrected that and called me Ernie Barnes. She's always been about giving credit where credit is due. I know it's a hackneyed phrase, but I wanted to give something back to my community. Being a black male with teaching aspirations got me a free ride through college, great fellowships, and a chance to revive shriveling art programs in our school systems. Good enough for you?"

"I'm speechless. I think I've missed that window of opportunity. College, I mean."

"Never say never. My mom is working on a Master's degree at fifty-two. You can do anything you put your mind to, Lasheera."

They were so into their conversation that they didn't see Aruba and the children return. Aunjanue looped her arm with Lasheera's.

"Auntie Sheer, Miss Aruba said she's taking us to the Cheesecake Factory. I've never been there before. She said it's for my brilliant artwork. You ready?"

"Um, I was just talking to Lake…Mr. Carvin about selling some of your art. I'll wrap this up in a few minutes. You guys wait in the car for me."

On cue, Aruba guided the children to her vehicle. She was elated that Lasheera was getting much-needed attention from someone who seemed genuinely nice. Lasheera's horror stories over lattes and caramel cappuccinos made her shudder at the thought of Lasheera's and her own missteps. Lasheera deserved a slice of happiness. She wasn't pushing her down the aisle or toward a baby carriage, but she hoped Lake Carvin would take her on a date, compliment her, convince her that life always offered a second chance to willing participants.

Aruba's BlackBerry vibrated. She opened the text message, tried to conceal her smile.

HURRY HOME, SWEETS. I'VE GOT A BIG SURPRISE FOR YOU. WF

[28]
All in My Lover's Eyes

When Aruba turned the lock, stepped into her home and smelled the oils, saw the candles, eyed the strawberries dipped in chocolate next to the bottle of champagne, she apologized to the ancestors. Dead and alive. She apologized to Aunt Diane, her mother's sister who drove to Augusta, Georgia, to get the good liquor off Wrightsboro Road for the basement parties. She bowed in deference to Alita Ruth, her mother's second cousin who wore the strapless, camel tan jumpsuit and the Farrah Fawcett wig to the basement parties and always asked the uncles to invite one of their friends from Lockheed to meet her 'cause she needed a man with some benefits. She said sorry to Darshelle, Kinsey, and Mayella, her father's sisters. Aunts dubbed the BBC—the Bitter Bitches Club—by her dad. As DK&M sat on her paternal grandma's wraparound porch, shelling peas, peeling peaches, or shucking corn, freshening up highballs of scotch and chomping on peanut brittle, yelling out to the cows, chickens, and pigs on Grandpa Willie's twenty-five acre farm that men weren't shit and weren't worth the spit it took to cuss 'em. Aruba remembered her dad blowing smoke rings from a Prince Albert cigar and roaring, "Yeah, the BBC would say something stupid like that!"

As Winston met her with a plush robe, took her purse off her shoulder, and led her to the bathroom, she realized all the fussing, Al Green crooning while confronting other women in the wee hours of the morning, and vowing to drown their hurts in bingo, scriptures, and a good flea market trip had more to do with wanting to be loved than hating men. If only Diane, Alita Ruth, Darshelle, Kinsey, and Mayella could see her now. Diane and Alita Ruth would ride her about being with someone else's husband. Ah, but Darshelle, Kinsey, and Mayella, the Stanton voices of reason, would assure her that she was getting what she deserved since his wife wasn't taking care of her business. The Stanton women were strong believers in the adage: "one woman's trash was another woman's treasure." And what a treasure Winston was.

"Winston, what—"

"Don't talk." He silenced her with a soft finger to her lips. He removed her clothing, then led her to the Jacuzzi filled with bubbles.

On the ledge of the tub sat a decorative basket of body scrubs, scented oils, and lotions. Winston presented them to her, a gift for the hard day she'd had.

"I started your bubble bath, but I want you to choose which scrub you'd like me to bathe you with, which scented oil you'd like to freshen the bath, and which lotion you want me to rub you down with when I'm all done."

"Aren't you going to join me?"

"No. It's all about you tonight."

"Afterward, will it be all about you?"

"Afterward, we'll lounge in bed and chat. I've thought about you all day. I just want to hold you in my arms."

With that, Winston led Aruba into the tub. She dipped her toe in the water, amazed that the temperature was just right. She eased in, allowed Winston to douse a washcloth in the sudsy rinse. *Why didn't James do something like this for me?* she thought as Winston squirted blackberry currant body scrub on the cloth. He washed her body with gentle care. She wanted to fall asleep right there, thought about it until he told her to stand.

"Winston, do I have to?"

"What? You embarrassed all of a sudden?"

"It's just that I haven't…It's been a while since. You know, maintenance."

"Stop worrying. I like a woman with a little fur coat on down there."

After he dried her, Winston carried her to the bedroom, placed her on the bed, and returned to the living room to get the strawberries dipped in chocolate and champagne. How many nights had he dreamt of doing this for Victoria? All he ever wanted was to get her attention, let her know that he was the same romantic man she'd met as a med student. How did money change matters so much? Why was he showering this attention on another man's wife and not his own? He wrestled with his emotions daily. He also felt it was too late to turn back. He hadn't felt so loved, so wanted, so important in years. He didn't know where their journey would end, but he was thoroughly enjoying the ride.

"So what do I owe the pleasure of this grand treatment?" asked Aruba, her eyes brightening at the sight of the platter of delicacies. She bit into a strawberry, then sipped champagne.

"It's my thanks to you for helping me see the light."

"The light?"

"The light of being a fool all these years." He motioned Aruba to turn around. He rubbed shea butter on her back.

"You haven't been a fool. You've been a good husband, a good provider, and a wonderful role model to lots of people. What more could a woman ask in a man?"

"You tell me. The one person I've wanted to see those qualities all these years has ignored me. I don't think I've been too much of anything. I'm an absentee husband and father. Oh yeah, I'm a paycheck, too. How's that for creating a loving family?"

Aruba faced Winston, took his hands in hers. She looked into his eyes and asked a few questions of her own.

"How would you have accomplished all the surgeries, break-throughs, or gained acclaim without sacrificing? If you were sitting in the house watching Victoria paint her toenails or nursing Nico-lette, how would your dreams have come to pass? I…" Aruba paused.

"What? What were you about to say?"

"I wish I'd met you first. I think we would have made a great team."

Winston wanted to concur, wanted to tell her she was the type of woman he needed, wanted by his side. Instead, he asked, "What are we going to do about our situation? I think about you all the time. When we're apart, I worry about your well-being and your safety. I think about Jeremiah and pray he hasn't been scarred for life by what he's seen. Could you live with yourself knowing we betrayed Victoria?"

Hell yes. "Could you live with yourself knowing we betrayed James?"

"I struggle with that. A part of me wants to write a check to send you both to marital counseling. Then there's the other part of me. The side that wants to take you and Jeremiah with me to start over. I know Victoria would fight for custody of Nicolette tooth and nail. She'd also want a fat chunk of child support and alimony. That would be a lot for you to take on. I'm not sure I could put you through that."

"Guess that's a lot to think about, huh?" Aruba suddenly felt defeated. In all she desired, she'd forgotten about Jeremiah. The thrill was gone for her where James was concerned, but he was

Jeremiah's world. She hated bigger issues, the hard questions. How would Jeremiah react with Nicolette as his sister? How would a physical separation from James affect him? If Jeremiah ever got married, would he be paranoid about his wife's friends and associates?

"I guess the good thing is we've done everything except make love. You know what they say about soul ties, right?" asked Winston.

"I bet this saying's a good one."

"Seriously. Have you ever dated someone and your head was clear until you made love? Then everything went out of the window. I can't lie. I've been waiting to make love to you since the Conrad. But I don't want to create that soul tie right now. When I said for better or worse, I meant it. I didn't know worse would be like this, but I don't want to jump ship too soon."

"Touché."

The Isley Brothers lulled them to sleep, both in each other's arms, both thinking of truth and consequences.

[29]
That's What Friends Are For

Victoria rang the doorbell a third time. It didn't matter that she stood outside in the cold, restless, afraid. She needed to talk to her friend. She heard footsteps nearing the door from inside. She would apologize to Aruba for waking her so soon. The door swung open, and James looked her up and down before speaking.

"Vic...toria, what are you doing here at seven-thirty in the morning? Is everything okay?" James held the door as if he were a bodyguard. He didn't invite her inside.

"I came to see Aruba. May I speak to her?"

James glanced over his shoulder nervously, maintained his bodyguard stance. He made sure the space between them was narrow. "She's not here right now. I'll tell her you stopped by, Victoria." James tried closing the door, but Victoria was insistent.

"May I please come in for just a minute?" Sensing his reluctance, she added, "I won't stay long."

James barely cracked the door open, allowing little space for Victoria to squeeze in. To her surprise, James was fully dressed. She thought she would awaken them both. The smell of sausage and eggs lingered in the foyer. She was too uncomfortable to remove her coat, so she quickly pleaded her case.

"James, I imagine Aruba's really busy with work, but if you could let her know I'd like to meet with her ASAP, I'd appreciate it. It's life or death."

"Victoria, Aruba and I are separated. Have been for several months now." James rifled through some papers in a wicker basket on a table in the entryway.

"I had no idea. I'd been calling her with no response. I'd like to be there for her. Where is she?"

"I'm searching for the address now. I know where she lives, but I'm giving her some space." He rambled a few seconds more. "Found it." James pulled out the letter that had come a month ago. The postal letter confirmed her forwarding address; however, they had obviously sent it to their home by mistake. He thought of driving by the new place to plead with her to come home, but he couldn't blame her for wanting to be apart. He had a lot of making up to do and he'd show her how serious he was when the time was right. James scribbled the address on a yellow sticky and slid it to Victoria.

"James Dixon, are you coming back down here or do I need to come getcha? You know you've got a lot of taming—"

The voice rising from the basement startled Victoria. She dropped her purse.

"Sorry. I didn't know you had company."

Victoria eyed the leggy woman wearing skintight corduroys and a fitted pullover sweater. She had an interesting look: braids on one side of her head, the other side loose. She didn't want to imagine how it got that way. She would have labeled her attractive were it not for the snarl on her face.

"Paris, I asked you to wait downstairs."

"Is she joining us?" Paris pointed to Victoria. "She looks like she could use some of your magic."

"Go!" James instructed playfully.

"All right. I'm just saying! Thought she might like to get in on the action, too."

Paris went back downstairs, humming a tune under her breath. Victoria was at a loss for words. James said they were separated, so that didn't give her the right to say anything. Then again, it did. Guilt consumed her when she thought of how loyal Aruba had been to her. She was out early in the morning seeking her counsel and shoulder to cry on. The least she could do was say something to James about how he was mistreating his wife.

"James, how could you do this to Aruba? She's been a good wife and mother. The least you could do—"

"This isn't what you think, Victoria."

"A woman flounces up your stairs, asking you to tame her, and it's not what I think?"

"She's—"

"Save it! I'm going to see Aruba now, and I'll think about whether or not to tell her what I've seen. It's amazing how men think they can get away with random bullshit like this!"

"What? The doctor's wife can curse? Imagine that. Look, I don't owe you an explanation for anything. Tell my wife I love her and I'm waiting for her to come home. Good day, Victoria."

Victoria stormed out of the house, jumped in her vehicle, input Aruba's address in her GPS, and headed out to visit the only real friend she had. Her aunt and mother were wrong; women were to be more than tolerated. She shuddered at all the times she looked down on Aruba in judgment when all she wanted was a listening ear. How many times did Aruba set aside time to listen to her desperate housewife woes with empathy? How many times had she watched Nicolette with no questions asked, but she always found an excuse when it came to watching Jeremiah?

Her thoughts journeyed back to the first time she met Aruba eight years ago. Aruba had contemplated purchasing a home in their old neighborhood. It was decent enough. The homes in the neighborhood went for the mid $300,000's. Certainly not a place she'd want to call home forever, but she hung in there with Winston's conservative ways until she convinced him a larger home was befitting a man of his status. Back then it was rare seeing a black face in the neighborhood, and particularly so young. After spying Aruba in the information center, she waltzed in for a look-see and chitchat. Victoria stopped in her tracks as she heard snippets of the conversation between the Realtor and Aruba through a half-cracked door. Victoria gathered the financing had fallen through due to bad decisions on someone's part. The words "credit score," "payday loan," and "repossession" tumbled out in the same sentence. Aruba pulled Kleenex from a decorative box on the desk as she uttered disbelief over her husband's marred credit history. Victoria continued eavesdropping as the Realtor suggested that Aruba purchase the house alone. In that moment, Victoria decided the young woman needed a friend. She waited until the conversation ended. She casually stepped to Aruba—still wiping tears and staring at a smaller floor plan—and asked her to come over to her house for a cup of tea. That day was enlightening and equally scary for Victoria. Reaching out to another person, and especially another female, was murky terrain. How many times had Marguerite staved off friendly advances from other Hollywood actresses? Marguerite's paranoia probably had cost her valuable contacts, leading roles, and hip pajama parties filled with good old-fashioned signifying interlaced with discussions about men and purses.

"Who knew why Marguerite was so guarded?" Victoria asked aloud. She turned into the parking lot of Aruba's new place, knowing she could no longer operate on Marguerite's beliefs. Now more than ever, she and Aruba needed each other. She'd see to it that their friendship would become stronger.

[30]
Clueless

"Summer Ermine."

"How many letters?"

"Five."

"Any cross clues?"

"Aruba, just give me a word, babe."

"Try 'stoat.'"

Winston filled in the crossword puzzle and smiled at Aruba. The *Indy Star* crossword puzzle was their first of the morning. They'd tackle the *New York Times* and the *Los Angeles Times* puzzles next. Music, crossword puzzles and Sudoku were his weaknesses. Having a woman like Aruba working with him to complete the brain teasers pleased him all the more. Victoria often wrinkled her nose at the puzzles, said they were for old fogeys who didn't know the value of a good sale.

Aruba sidled closer to Winston. "Twenty-eight across is 'A-B-E-T.' To assist in a crime. Bet you know some abettors."

"I may have met a few in my time. Ask a patient needing healthcare and they'll likely say HMOs are abetting the system in denying quality."

"Shall we continue using the word in sentences?" Aruba asked, kissing Winston's cheek.

A kitchen timer buzzed, interrupting the intimate moment.

"I'll get your breakfast, Winston. Don't finish the puzzle without me."

"When did you start—"

"You're not the only romantic one around here. I think you'll like everything I've prepared."

Aruba slid out of bed, then headed downstairs to the kitchen. She kept the oven temperature warm, so his turkey bacon would be crisp, just the way Winston liked it. She had given up showing Victoria how to cook bacon when she said the cast iron skillet was too heavy and too much trouble to use. Aruba scrambled eggs and added shredded mozzarella cheese to the skillet. Winston liked his juice freshly squeezed, his coffee with two sugars and hazelnut cream, and his grapefruit sliced in quarters and sweetened with Splenda. She collected his likes and dislikes over the years in a journal she kept locked in the glove compartment. She hoped he'd be pleased that she'd noticed. She skittered up the stairs, breakfast tray in hand, smiling from ear to ear. How long would Winston be able to spurn her advances? This was just the beginning for them. She'd show him just how much he needed her in his life.

"What have we here?" asked Winston.

"Just a little nourishment for your tired soul. I figured—"

The doorbell startled them.

"Are you expecting someone? Do you think it's James?"

"He doesn't know where I am. I ordered a few things online, but I didn't expect the items 'til next week. Amazon's getting faster, eh?" Aruba slipped on a pink fleece housecoat to hide her lingerie. Didn't make sense to let the UPS man see all her wares.

"I'll be right back. Enjoy your breakfast." Aruba kissed Winston's hands and headed downstairs. The doorbell rang twice more. "I'll have to sign for the package. Damn, what *did* I order?" she muttered under her breath.

Aruba swung open the door, gasping at the sight of Victoria.

Victoria was too distraught to receive the same chilly reception from Aruba she'd received from James, so she blew past Aruba quickly, plopping down on the sofa and kicking her feet up on an ottoman.

"Victoria, how did you find me?" Aruba's eyes darted up the stairs. "What are you doing here so soon?" *Breathe, Aruba, breathe.*

"I don't mean to disturb you, but I have no one else to talk to. Please just hear me out."

Aruba stood a few seconds, then sat across from Victoria. She looked at Victoria, wondering what had happened to her friend. Her standing appointment hadn't been honored in at least three weeks. Her short hair, normally curled and teased, was standing over her hand and appeared brittle, unconditioned. She ran chipped nails through her unkempt hair, searched Aruba's eyes for sympathy.

"I stopped by your house and James told me where to find you."

"Did he?"

"He said he wouldn't bother you and that he'd give you your space. Why didn't you tell me the two of you were separated? I could have helped in some way."

"I guess it's been hard to find the words to express what I feel about the situation." *One Mississippi, Two Mississippi. She's going to say something stupid.*

"We're in the same boat right now. Winston…Winston left me. He's not returning my calls, he's not at his office, I can't find him; I'm so lost right now."

Aruba leaned forward, feigned shock. "No, when did that happen? I thought you two had the ideal relationship. I know you had issue with him being gone so much, but I never thought he'd leave you. I'm sure it's just a misunderstanding."

This was the confusing part. Victoria didn't know how to proceed. How much of your business were you supposed to share with someone else? She shrugged her shoulders.

"Let me get you some tea, Victoria. Orange-pomegranate or blackberry?"

"Blackberry, please."

Aruba sauntered nervously to the kitchen. Luckily, she'd left her cell phone in the kitchen charging. She'd text Winston and beg him to stay put. She felt so awkward, so dirty. Maybe this wasn't such a good idea after all. She could barely look Victoria in the eyes. The word *homewrecker* rolled around in her mind as well as the hard questions Winston had proposed the night before. She stole glances at Victoria while preparing the tea. She snatched her phone from the counter when it vibrated. She sighed with relief as she read Winston's text: *Got your message. I'm staying upstairs.*

Aruba rejoined Victoria on the sofa with piping hot tea, yogurt, and fruit.

"Thank you, Aruba. I don't think I can hold the fruit and yogurt down, but I appreciate the tea." Victoria took a sip, leaned back on the couch.

"Before we go any further, I want to apologize to you."

"Apologize?"

"I've been a lousy, horrible friend to you and I'm sorry."

"Where is this coming from? I'm not quite sure what—"

"Please let me finish. From the time I met you, I knew you were someone special. We didn't become acquainted under the greatest circumstances, but I admired so much about you the day you came by for tea. You have strength and drive I wish I possessed. You're beautiful. You're intelligent, and I wish I had half your determination.

"I'm just a housewife who latched on to a good thing, and I've taken him and you for granted. Do you think you could ever forgive me?"

Aruba exhaled. Those were the last words she expected to hear.

"You don't owe me an apology. People get busy, have things to do. Friendships aren't tit for tat, deed for deed. We all get preoccupied from time to time."

Victoria took in Aruba's words. Aruba was doing it again, letting her off the hook for crazy deeds. "I agree that friendship isn't tit for tat, but it should be reciprocal. I haven't been a good friend and I want to make it up to you," said Victoria. She sipped her tea. "Tell me what happened with James."

"I…I don't even know where to start."

"Wherever you want is fine. I barged in here asking for your shoulder with no consideration for what you might be going through."

"Well, let's just say I'm not sure how much longer I'll be married. James and I had a big fight this time and I don't see us patching things up."

"What was the fight about?"

"James thought I was cheating. He rifled through my purse, found some business cards, and assumed I had a thing with one of the male business owners whose son goes to Jeremiah's school."

"If that's not the pot calling the kettle black," Victoria blurted.

"What's that supposed to mean?" asked Aruba. She shifted uncomfortably in her seat.

"Slip of the tongue. I didn't mean it."

"Hey, the cat's toe is dangling out of the bag; you may as well let her out."

Victoria sighed. "When I stopped by your house this morning, James had…there was another woman there. He tried to assure me nothing was going on, but I didn't give him a chance to explain." Victoria inched closer to Aruba, stroked her hand. "I'm sorry, Rube."

Aruba knew she couldn't panic. She remembered her transgressions one story up and willed her knees to stop trembling.

"James is James. We're getting a divorce, so I guess he's testing the waters."

"That's another thing I admire about you. You have character and integrity. You could be with a slew of men, as gorgeous as you are, but you're alone. That's rare in this day and time."

"Enough about my pitiful world. What's going on with Winston?"

Victoria's pensive face resurfaced. "We're separated. I know it's my fault. I pushed him away with my attitude and unrealistic demands. He wanted to share so much with me and all I ever did was gripe about money, gripe about making love to him, gripe about his absence." Tears welled in Victoria's eyes as Aruba's eyebrows arched as if stunned. "Yes, that's right. As good as he is to me I had the nerve to ration sex like food. I just wish I could turn back the hands of time. I don't think he even wants me anymore."

"Don't say that. I'm sure that's not true."

"It is. I took a lap-dancing class to spice things up and I blew it. I don't even think he got aroused."

Aruba's eyes fixed on the cat wall clock in the kitchen in an attempt to stifle the laughter welling inside her. Victoria didn't have an ounce of rhythm, and she'd told her so on those rare occasions they'd ventured out to a nightclub or couples' functions. "So he left you because of a lap dance?"

"No, he packed his things after the dance because he said I made him feel like a paycheck. He said I didn't make him feel loved or wanted, so he left our home for 'space.'"

"Where is he?"

"I don't know. He calls the house to check on Nicolette, but he won't talk to me. He sends messages to me through Alva. I wish I'd done things so differently."

"Such as?"

"Not complain so much. Listened more, talked less. Made love. Cooked dinners."

"You're talking like things are over. Just work on winning him back."

"Winston is very even-tempered. He's never done anything like this."

"Everyone has a breaking point. It's not over 'til it's over, though. Get back in the ring and fix your marriage."

"What would you suggest?"

"Kidnap him. Take him to your cabin in Brown County. Plan a romantic getaway and tell him how you feel."

"I like the sound of that. Why didn't I think of it?" Victoria paused. "And you? Are you telling me there's no hope at all for you and James?"

"Afraid not."

"If you need anything, please let me know. I'm willing to help in any way possible."

Aruba spied her watch. "I'm actually leaving for an appointment. I hate cutting this conversation short, but I have to get dressed."

"May I take you somewhere?"

"No, I'm fine."

"There I go again. I've been sitting here all this time and didn't ask about Jeremiah. Is he upstairs?" Victoria stood as if to head upstairs.

"No...no, he's with Bria for the weekend."

"So when do I get a tour of your new place?"

"When I clean up. The dungeon is not tour-worthy yet. I'm still unpacking. I plan to have a party soon, though. You know you're at the top of the guest list."

"I understand. Again, I apologize for barging in like this."

"Hey, that's what friends are for."

"I appreciate your encouragement. I'll let you know how it goes with Winston."

Victoria took in Aruba's surroundings.

"I love what I see so far. When do I get some decorating tips?"

"Come on, I need tips from you."

"I won't hold you up any longer. I haven't said it in a long time, but I love you, Aruba. I'm grateful you're in my life."

They embraced. Aruba made sure Victoria made it out all right and stood with her back to the door.

"That was a close call," she called to Winston.

"Too close for comfort," he said from the top of the stairs.

They eyed each other in silence, both unwilling to admit that the time to make hard decisions was closer than they'd anticipated.

[31]
Westside Walk It Out

Roberta and Lasheera staged an intervention at Lafayette Square Mall. Aunjanue could no longer hold her worries about Tawatha and felt her grandmother and favorite auntie should do something ASAP. As they made their third lap around the mall, Roberta's patience shortened as she spoke with Tawatha.

"Honey, I'm worried. That's what mothers do. How much weight have you lost? Twenty-five pounds?"

"Thirty-six," Tawatha proudly announced. She waved off the attention of a distinguished, older gentleman wearing a navy blue suit and diving into a cinnamon roll at Cinnabon. The weight loss bolstered her confidence. She didn't mind being thick, but the weight loss made her cartoonish because she couldn't lose her breasts and butt. She knew she was on the right track when a guy yelled out, "Pebblez the Model ain't got nothing on you, ma," a few weeks ago. She stepped up her cardio, squats, and chest fly workouts. She vowed to be the most beautiful bride Indianapolis had ever seen.

"You look healthy. I'm just concerned because the weight loss is so sudden. Why is that?" asked Roberta.

"The kids are worried as well," added Lasheera.

Tawatha took in a few deep breaths. Her unease grew the more they walked. This wasn't the time to let them know about James. How could she explain that her husband was someone else's and wouldn't be fully hers until after the funeral. She could picture Roberta giving her one of those long lectures about waiting on the right man and not lowering her standards. No way was she ready for the criticism Lasheera and Roberta would dish out.

"I'm working, doing well at my job, keeping my place together, staying healthy. What more do you want from me?"

"To be honest about what's going. Does this have anything to do with a man?" asked Roberta.

"Onnie said you have a boyfriend," said Lasheera. "And don't forget you told us to be ready for your wedding."

"Wedding?" cried Roberta.

"Thanks, old refrigerator! Would the two of you stop it! When do I have time for a relationship with my work schedule?"

They pondered her words. Her job was occupying her time and dominating a lot of their conversations in recent months. She was throwing out real estate terminology left and right and talked about owning a slice of Hinton and Conyers someday. She mentioned a seven-year plan.

"You can't blame us for wanting what's best for you. You've come so far and I'm so proud of you, baby," said Roberta.

Roberta and Lasheera continued to walk in silence, praying their concern would register for what is was: concern, not the words of two busybodies. At the third lap, Lasheera grinned from ear to ear at the sight of Lake. He held out a bottled water for Lasheera. This was the usual time he joined her at the mall. She stepped back two paces to allow Roberta and Tawatha private time. Lake said he wanted her to love half of him, so they joined each other every Saturday for walking, chatting, and breakfast afterward. She was taking it nice and slow. She hoped Tawatha was doing the same because she knew her friend. Once a man was involved, she'd stop at nothing to get him. To hell with the consequences.

"So, Tawatha, as beautiful and outgoing as you are, you're trying to convince your old mother there's not a man in your life?"

"What's with the Twenty Questions?"

"If you answer honestly, I'll stop asking." Roberta smiled and wiped away the sweat glistening on her forehead.

"Promise you won't judge me?"

"Do I ever?"

"Every waking minute."

The words stung Roberta. What came out as judgment was meant to be warning signs for Tawatha. She remembered how harshly her mother judged everything about her. She promised she'd never be that way with her children. Here she was, repeating the same behavior without realizing how much she was hurting her daughter.

"I never meant to judge you. If I've done so, I'm sorry. I want the best for you. I want more for you than I've gotten out of life."

"Momma, what do you mean? Mr. J.B. is the nicest man in the world. He loves you, he takes care of you, he likes me and my kids, and he's active in his church. He's one of the few men I've met who walks the walk instead of just talking the talk."

"Yeah, but that came at a heavy price and after a long journey. But this ain't about J.B., we're talking about you. What's going on, Tawatha? You can tell me anything."

"There is someone I love dearly. It's just that we can't be together right now."

"Why not?"

"It's complicated."

"Is he in jail?"

"Would I date a man in jail?"

"No, that's not your speed. You hated being confined in a playpen as a child, so I don't see you visiting a man in a correctional facility."

"Amen! You know me well."

"Is he married?"

Tawatha's silence answered the question. Roberta hoped her child would transcend the foolishness of her youth. Find a good man, get the two-story home with the white picket fence, have a child or two. Although she knew Tawatha was domestically challenged, she was certain the love of a grounded relationship would settle her daughter down. Instead, she tamped down negative comments as Tawatha paraded baby after baby before her with no ring, no commitment, no husband. Although she monitored the things she said, she somehow found a way to slip in a cut or snide remark about Tawatha's lifestyle. Those words came from being disappointed in seeing herself in Tawatha.

"So you'll never marry Mr. J.B.?"

"I didn't say that. Speaking of marriage, what about you?"

"No judging, right?"

"Promise."

"You know my references will be vague, so don't press me for names and details."

"*Okay.*"

"I met a really nice guy at my job. He's a businessman and he has a lot on his plate right now."

"What's on his plate?"

"I'm assuming recession fallout because I don't think things are going well with the business. It's hard for him to work and take care of..." Tawatha paused.

"Does he have elderly parents?"

"No. His wife is terminally ill with breast cancer. I didn't want to bring it up because I was afraid you'd tear into me about being with him."

"You ready to take a break? Let's get some juice. I want to share something with you."

Tawatha stopped short of stomping her feet. She dreaded the conversation about to unfold. They neared Cinnabon and stood in line to place their orders. Before either could speak, Mr. Extravaganza handed the cashier a twenty for their orders and told him to keep the change. He retreated back to his seat, smiling at Tawatha.

"Juice and a cinnamon pecan bun for me," said Tawatha.

"I'll just have juice," said Roberta.

They took their trays to their seats. Knowing Tawatha feared the worst, Roberta took a different approach. She would dispense her words with love and admonition in equal measure.

"Do you know how special you are?" asked Roberta.

"What's the punch line?"

"No punch line. I think you deserve an unattached man who's willing to give you the love you deserve."

Tawatha meditated on her mother's words. She blushed. "You're just saying that. I know you don't mean it."

"I do mean it." Roberta touched Tawatha's hand. "When you described him, I saw the same glow on your face that I had about your father."

"That's good, right? Daddy was a noble man who died in a car accident. I hate I didn't get to know him, but at least you had the love of a husband. I've got a bunch of baby daddies and deep regrets."

"I never married your father, Tawatha. Shirley Gipson was Carol's husband when I met him. I was a young, naïve student who thought I found the man of my dreams. It wasn't until I was pregnant with you and your sister that I found out. His wife came to see me."

"Why didn't you ever say anything? And why are you telling me now?"

"The timing was never right. The only reason I'm bringing it up now is to warn you about the dangers of waiting for something that doesn't belong to you. I never told Shirley about you and Teresa. If your man is sincere, he'll reach out to you when the time is right. Does he have any children?"

"He has a cute son named Jeremiah."

"How do you know he's cute?"

"I've seen pictures of him," Tawatha lied.

"Even if his wife dies, there is so much for you to think about. You'd be blending his child with four others. You're also not sure how much financial devastation her illness has caused. How open is he to your children? What would her family have to say about another woman stepping in so soon after her death? These are just a few things that come to mind. Take your time and don't rush into anything."

If Roberta wasn't crunching numbers, she was spitting logic. Why did her mother always have to be the voice of reason? Tawatha wasn't prepared to answer her mother's questions because she didn't know half the answers.

"Back to Daddy. You're telling me my father is alive and well and living somewhere in this world?"

"Shirley Gipson is alive and well in California. You also have siblings a little older than you."

Tawatha's stomach soured. She set her juice aside. The revelation was hard to digest.

"Did he ever promise he'd leave his wife for you?"

"I didn't know he was married until Carol waltzed into my apartment."

"Momma, our circumstances are different. I know about her and why he can't be with me."

"Tawatha, answer this. If you were gravely ill and married, what would you want your husband to do for you?"

Without hesitation, Tawatha responded, "I would want him to take care of me and my kids. Certainly make my last days bearable."

"Could he do that with another woman on the periphery?"

"I guess not."

"If his wife deserves better, don't you?"

Tawatha remained silent.

"Look at that," said Roberta, nodding her head toward Lake and Lasheera. "Sheer has been to hell and back. She's getting her life on track and I'm so proud of her. Lake is a fine young man and I'm praying their friendship blossoms into a good relationship."

Tawatha looked on with envious eyes. The last two times she'd seen Lake and Lasheera together, she fought back tears. If anyone deserved a little sunshine, it was Sheer. Tawatha's envy came from the way Lake looked at Lasheera. The way he hung on to her every word. The way laughter exploded from their bellies when they shared a joke or funny incident. Then guilt overwhelmed her. It was easier to pity Lasheera than champion her. All the late-night runs to pick her up. All the times when she and Jamilah scrounged spare change to feed her habit in fear she might rob someone. Things were safer then. Now, Lasheera soared. Zion had visited her house several times, and Lake frequently surprised Lasheera with trips and trinkets with an agreement to take things slow. *How did Sheer get such a good catch?* She quickly rebuked the thought. How could she harbor such deep resentment toward Lasheera?

"What kind of friend am I?"

Roberta observed the longing in Tawatha's eyes as she watched Lake and Lasheera.

"If you're patient, you can have the same kind of relationship. Trust me."

Tawatha swigged her juice once more. *Why am I the only one unlucky in love?*

[32]
It's Not What You Think

James waited outside Winston's practice. He wanted to catch him early, before his momentum waned. He'd rehearsed how to approach Winston, but now he wasn't sure if this was the right place or the right time. He thought of driving off or coming back later in the day. He staved off his doubt when he saw Winston coast into his designated spot.

Winston exited his Range Rover, engaged in conversation with Aruba. They'd driven to Ann Arbor, Michigan for the weekend. His morning mission was to allay her fears about Jeremiah seeing them together. They assured Jeremiah the trip was for Nicolette's birthday presents. They did not embrace or show affectionate emotions in his presence. A twinge of guilt rose up in Winston as James advanced him.

"Winston, how are you this morning?" James reached out to shake Winston's hand.

"Babe, let me call you back a little later. Take care." Winston shook James's hand and waited for the nature of his unannounced visit.

"I have an urgent matter I need to discuss with you."

"Now?"

"Yes. I don't think it can wait."

"Step into my office. It's cold out here."

The men stepped in stride toward Winston's building. James quivered at the sight of the bold, black lettering on the door:

Faulk Cardiology. Just one name. Only one man running the show. *Someday…* James allowed the thought to trail off.

"Hold my calls," Winston said to his receptionist.

The appointment schedulers smiled at James as he strolled by. There was a time he would have stopped to chat with the women, but today was about business. He strode into Winston's office, removed his coat, and took a seat. He ran his fingers through his dreadlocks, then set his briefcase on the floor near Winston's desk.

"To what do I owe the pleasure of this visit?" asked Winston. His poker face was in full effect.

"It's about you and Aruba."

"Aruba?"

"Well, both of you."

"Listen, Aruba and I do have—"

"I need to get this out before I lose the nerve. Hear me out."

Winston leaned back in his seat. He wondered the best way to explain the affair. There was no other word to describe the situation. His feelings grew more each day for Aruba. It wasn't fair to either of them to remain in loveless marriages.

"When I saw you and Aruba—"

"I can explain—"

"Let me finish, please." James sighed in exasperation and shifted in his seat. This was proving to be more difficult than he imagined. "When I saw you together at the hospital last year after the accident, I was so angry that I could have fought someone. I know I was at fault, but seeing another man taking care of business where my family is concerned really pissed, I mean, ticked me off."

Winston's shoulders relaxed. "I merely drove her to the hospital. That's what any friend would have done."

"I shouldn't have been there under those circumstances in the first place."

"I never judged you about that night. Go on."

"I've made a lot of mistakes. Most of which I'm sure you know about since Aruba and Victoria are friends. I haven't always done right by my family."

"Who amongst us is perfect, James?"

"Swallowing my pride like this is difficult, but I'm here because…"

Winston sensed his trepidation. "Take your time, James. Thursdays are my slowest days. My first patient isn't due in until eleven this morning."

"You gave me your business card at the hospital and asked me to reach out to you if I needed anything. You said the same thing at the cookout. I'm here to ask for your assistance in a business venture."

"Business venture?"

"For the longest time, I've wanted my own salon, but couldn't get start-up capital. Aruba was always on me about getting my financial house in order, but I wouldn't listen. I can't lie; I want my family back. They say you don't miss your water…you know what I mean. I want Aruba to be proud of me. I want to provide for her."

"How can *I* help make that a reality?"

"I've been turned down by every bank I've approached. Credit issues and no collateral have made it impossible to get a loan. I've been seeking angel investors and thought I'd ask if you'd be interested in assisting me. I'm not asking you to give me anything. I'm willing to sign whatever agreement necessary to assure I'll pay you back. Angels usually give funds, but I don't want to owe you anything."

"What would I be investing in?"

James grabbed his briefcase from the floor. He proudly handed Winston a copy of his business plan. He'd spent the last three months under Katrina's and Isaak's wings, researching his possibilities, investigating demographics, and anticipating the highs and lows of owning a salon. Winston was the third investor he'd approached. With each pitch, he gained more confidence.

"Dixon's Hair Affair will be a full-service beauty salon dedicated to consistently providing impeccable customer satisfaction. In addition to rendering excellent service, quality products, and furnishing an enjoyable atmosphere at an acceptable price/value relationship, we will also maintain a friendly, fair, and creative work environment, which will respect diversity, ideas, and hard work. This will be an upscale salon that caters to our customers' physical appearance and mental well-being. Our motto will be 'Leave Your Worries At the Door.'"

"Where are you looking to house the business?"

"I found a nice location on Illinois Street. The previous owners had begun renovations a year-and-a-half ago, but pulled out due to economic hardship."

"How far did they get on the renovations?"

"About ninety-five percent. The most I'd have to do is buy equipment, hire contractors to complete drywall in the building's exterior, and hire an electrician to assure the wiring is up to code."

"How will you market Dixon's Hair Affair?" Winston asked the question as he flipped from the executive summary to the financial plan.

"Word of mouth is key in the salon business. I don't want to toot my own horn, but I can handle a head of hair."

Winston paused to read through the plan in greater detail. "I'm impressed with your projected cash flow, proforma, and break-even analysis. Take me through the personnel plan."

"I've cultivated friendships over the years with barbers and stylists throughout the city. Quite a few are excited about coming on board to be a part of Dixon's. I plan to have six stylists, two barbers, two nail techs, a facialist, and a massage therapist. Turn to page seven for staff breakdown and salaries."

Winston continued reading. Clearly, James had done his leg-work and was serious about starting a business. He meant what he said when he offered assistance almost a year ago, but things had changed so much. He'd crossed too many lines to turn back, yet James's determination struck a chord with him. He saw in him the same hunger, the same eagerness he himself had when he started his practice.

"Let me keep the plan and get back with you in a week or so. I have to run a few things past my accountant. I also know a few people in the business who might be able to come alongside you and be of help. I don't want to make any promises, but I assure you we'll meet in a week. I'm proud of you and want to see you get your business up and running."

James stood to shake Winston's hand. Isaak's words crept up as he fought to contain his excitement: "Premature excitement is worse than failure because it shows others you have no control over your emotions."

"If you back me, you won't be sorry, Winston. I just ask that you don't share the news with Victoria. I fear that if she knows, Aruba will know."

"Your secret is safe with me. Trust me."

[33]
Let's Get This Party Started

FROM: *Bria Hines*
TO: *Lasheera Atkins*
CC: *Aruba Dixon*
SUBJECT: *Office Assistance*
Lasheera:
I have an enormous mail-out that has to be completed by noon. Please come to my office ASAP to help me complete this task.
Bria

Lasheera's eyes were crossed from the stack of documents she'd edited for Aruba, so a mailing would be a welcomed change. Bria rarely asked for help, so the mailing had to be important. Grateful that Bria had cc'd Aruba on the email, Lasheera felt relieved she didn't have to rush back for anything since Aruba would know her whereabouts.

Bria greeted Lasheera at her office door, ushering her in with a sense of immediacy. Bria locked the door. "Have a seat at the round-table."

"Do I need to make copies of anything? Also, will everything be collated and stapled, or are the documents singles?"

"Do you see any paper around here, Lasheera?"

Lasheera looked around, puzzled by the blank table. "No. I want to know what to get, so we can get started."

"I knew you'd be perfect in helping me. If anyone can keep a tight lid on things, it's you."

"A tight lid?"

"For Aruba's birthday party. I'm planning a surprise party for her at Bella Vita's. Her birthday is in three months and I want to get a jumpstart on the festivities. She is the last person on earth you can fool with a surprise party. She is the hostess with the mostess, and it's hard getting over on her. This year's gonna be different, though. That's why I pulled you in to help with the gag. Trust me, it will be a classy soiree; she just won't know about it."

"What do you need me to do?"

"We'll start with the guest list and theme today."

"Wow…a theme? I can't wait."

"We're having a dream girl party."

"Dream girl? Are you talking Motown, bouffant hairdos, and sequins? I can't hold a tune in a bucket, so I hope we don't have to sing."

"Heavens no. You would probably be surprised to know it's an idea from our childhood."

"You grew up together?"

"Georgia peaches. We were raised in Harlem 'til I moved to Atlanta, but I always visited during the summers. You mean to tell me you never had any Southern relatives you hung out with during the summer months?"

"No. There seemed to be tension between my mom and her siblings in Mississippi. I do have a goal of fellowshipping with them soon."

"When we were twelve, Aruba's aunt, Alita Ruth, came up with the dream girl concept. Our neighbor, Hermilla Jones, got a wild hair up her butt and abandoned her daughter, Maria. Never mind that it was Maria's twelfth birthday, or that Hermilla's mother had suffered a stroke in the wee hours of that morning. Something snapped inside her. Perhaps it was being Leotis's wife, perhaps it was not fulfilling whatever she wanted in life, but Alita was out in her yard planting those azaleas and hollyhocks when Hermilla rambled out of her house with a suitcase in her hand. Alita Ruth yelled out to Hermilla for a progress report on her mom, but Hermilla kept stepping until she was out of Alita's sight.

"That's when Maria came out on the porch, plopped down in a ruby red glider, and turned up the volume on her portable CD player, her birthday gift from Hermilla. She sat there rocking back and forth a while, holding back tears, wondering if anyone saw her. The South is the South, so news of Hermilla's departure spread like wildfire. The girls on the street thought they would shun Maria, but Alita Ruth wasn't having it. In two hours, she planned a party at her house for Maria, threatening all the girls on the street with death if they didn't attend. All the girls had to bring Maria one gift-wrapped item along with a colorful card Alita made. On the card was your dream. Some of the girls wanted to be nurses, doctors, lawyers, entrepreneurs; others had less lofty dreams like planting a beautiful garden, making straight A's the next school term, or marrying and having a good family. Alita Ruth told us whenever we felt doubt, hold on to those cards as a reminder that a dream lived inside us."

"Do you mean Maria Jones, the movie producer?"

"The one and only. I was there when she wrote 'Hollywood movie producer' on that card. Aruba and I flew out to L.A. to see her two years ago, and she still had that card. She laminated it her junior year of high school."

"That's why the industry calls her the 'female Walt Disney.' Most of her movies and HBO specials feature a mother abandoning a child."

"I wouldn't go that far. The community really enveloped her with love and support after Hermilla left."

"What happened to Hermilla?"

"VA Hospital in Augusta, Georgia. Maria visits her whenever time permits."

Lasheera took in the concept. She couldn't remember a time when *lots* of people were part of her life. Tawatha and Jamilah were her aces. She feared having *lots* of folks in her circle until her pastor said one day, "If you're the smartest person in your circle, your circle is too small." Aruba and Bria seemed to know fascinating people as evidenced by the guest list.

"That's a long guest list."

"I know, right?"

"Who are all these folks?"

"Quiet as it's kept, Aruba is very popular. She downplays it, but she has touched the lives of many people and they aren't ashamed to show their appreciation. Before she got married, she was always volunteering. She's also an anonymous donor to people and causes. I can assure you that list ranges from CEOs to welfare recipients."

"I know she's been good to me since I've been working here. I bet every aspect of her life is perfect."

"No one is perfect, Lasheera. You take what you're given and make the best of it. The people who appear perfect are probably those people who are working hard at making the best of what they've got. I won't address the pretenders, just the genuine people."

"Your husband, Sidney, seems like a good man. I see him in and out of here taking you to lunch and bringing you flowers."

"I am blessed. I have a good husband and a good relationship. Again, we work at it. There's no other man on the planet I'd want to share my time, space, and love with other than Sidney."

"I'd love to get there someday. It seems like too much work, though."

"Don't rush it. You'll know when the time is right and when the man is right."

"I am taking it slow with my new boyfriend. This is the first time I've actually *dated* someone. I'm used to jumping in and asking questions later."

"Aren't you glad you've grown?"

"I credit my spiritual growth to the change. I'm not there yet, but one day at a time feels better than flying by the seat of my pants."

Lasheera refocused her attention on the guest list. "What do you need me to do first?"

"I printed out mailing labels at home. Grab those out of my bag and place stamps on the envelopes. I set up a special phone line for the RSVPs. I'll keep you posted as the guests call in. I'm still narrowing down the menu, but Sidney has agreed to buy the first round of drinks for everyone."

"What about these?" Lasheera held up a clear plastic case of blank, multicolored cards.

"Can't send an invite out without those. Those are the cards women will write their dreams on. I'm hoping some of the older guests will join in the fun. Particularly the more successful ones. It's never too late to foster new dreams."

"I know that's right!"

Lasheera busied herself stuffing envelopes, checking names off the list, and anticipating how exciting the evening would be. She was surprised to see her name listed.

"I'm invited, too?"

"Lasheera, you know you're Aruba's right-hand girl. She would crucify me if you didn't come."

Lasheera's cheeks reddened. It had been a long time since she'd felt so special.

"May I ask a favor, Bria?"

"Sure."

"Would it be too much trouble if we could add one more name to the list?"

"I don't see why not. Sidney's budgeted for at least ten more people. It's always good to have someone new in the mix."

"Perfect. My girlfriend Tawatha will enjoy this party so much. It would be just the thing to get her out of the house and away from her job."

[34]
I Am Changing

"Daddy, when are you coming home?"

"Princess, I see you every day."

"I know, but you're not in the house when I get up to pee at night. You disappear after you tuck me in."

"Pee?"

"I mean tinkle," said Nicolette. She muffled her grin with her hands, embarrassed she'd used one of the words from her forbidden list.

Victoria waited for Winston's response to Nicolette's revelation.

"You know I'm busy and have lots of patients to take care of."

"Too busy to be home with us?"

"What did I tell you about sacrifice?"

"You said that in order for people to accomplish goals, they have to work hard and do things they don't always want to do."

"That's part of what I said. I didn't know you listened to me."

"I listen to everything you say, Daddy. And I watch everything you do. I want to be just like you when I grow up."

Winston eyed Nicolette in the rearview mirror. He didn't know whether to be repulsed or excited about the changes he saw. Nicolette's crooked ponytail sat too high with bows that didn't match. Victoria attempted to plait Nicolette's hair, but she was unsuccessful as the top part of the plait was loose, the bottom, tight. Nicolette's outfit matched, but her patent leather Mary Janes were more appropriate for church, not a family outing in Brown

County. Much to his dismay, Victoria had given Alva the month off and a round-trip ticket to visit her children in Antigua. She wore him down with calls and visits to his office about reconciling. A flash of guilt overwhelmed him when he thought of his wife at Aruba's house, pleading for assistance, expressing her love for him. Since that visit, she'd begun to cook, attempt to clean, take care of Nicolette, and beg for a chance to make things right. He couldn't say no to her invitation to Brown County, even though he knew how the trip would turn out. She'd beg for them to stay together; he'd turn her down. He didn't want to jump into a new marriage, but he wanted to explore life with Aruba. He'd muster the courage to tell Victoria on Sunday before driving home.

"Daddy, did you hear me?" Nicolette whirled the ponytail around her fingers.

"What did you say, princess?"

"Mommy said you don't love her anymore. That's what I heard her say on the phone."

"That's not true. I love your mommy very much."

"You're not getting a divorce, are you?"

"Where did you hear that word?"

"Paige Miller. She said her daddy got arrested for 'bezzlement and her mom filed for divorce because she couldn't pay for the things they had."

"Honey, that's embezzlement." Winston turned to Victoria. "Jonathon Miller was arrested for embezzlement?"

"It's been all over the news. You didn't know that? Perhaps you should watch the news where you're spending your time." Victoria bit her tongue, swallowing blood. She'd promised herself she'd monitor her words. What she said and *how* she said it. Winston's absence made her realize how toxic, critical, and fault-finding her words were. Enough to keep any man away. She tried again. "What

I meant to say was it's been sad around the neighborhood with divorces running rampant."

"Are you gonna marry another woman? I don't want a new mommy or a new daddy. I want you to come home and stay with us."

"Nicolette, sweetie, you're talking too much grown-up talk," said Victoria.

Winston nodded in agreement. He couldn't remember the last time they'd seen eye to eye on anything. He looked at Nicolette again. Her face registered concern at the thought of her parents divorcing. For the first time since becoming involved with Aruba, he felt the weight of his deception. He didn't have an ideal marriage, but Victoria's efforts of late seemed genuine. Disengaging himself would alienate her more, and he didn't want to do that this weekend.

"Don't miss the turn, Winston." Victoria folded and unfolded her arms. Her nerves got the best of her when she felt helpless. It took so much convincing to get Winston out of his office and into the scenic cabin they owned. The weekend would be the new start they needed. She wanted Winston to try as well.

"The place looks gorgeous, Victoria. I didn't expect the landscaping to be so pristine."

"Mr. Shoals does a great job at keeping things together." *We pay him enough* stayed glued inside her mouth. She'd worked hard the last month in adhering to her tongue fast.

"I'll grab our bags and bring them in." Winston looked in on Nicolette. "Princess is out like a light. I'll tuck her in after I take everything upstairs."

"Thanks, sweetheart. I truly appreciate it."

Winston stopped in his tracks. Was he imagining things, or did Victoria just thank him for something other than money? "What did you say?"

"I said thank you. I appreciate everything about you. Not just the things you give us, but you."

"You're welcome."

Winston carried the bags inside, partially confused, partially gleeful. Those words meant so much to him. As much as he'd given credence to the thought of divorce, the woman who'd just paid him a compliment resembled the Victoria he'd fallen in love with in California. Her words weren't empty. The glint in her eyes, the broad smile, and her look of admiration deepened his regrets. *What the hell am I doing? I know what I'm doing is wrong and I need to stop.* When he lifted Nicolette from her booster seat, he realized how good it felt to have a daughter who thought he hung the moon. How would she view him if he walked away? He visualized Nicolette in her early twenties, pouring her heart out to some slickster about how devastated she was growing up without a father. He shooed the image away as he put her in bed upstairs, then rejoined Victoria downstairs by the fireplace.

"Shoals started this blazing fire as well. Isn't it cozy?"

"Yes. I love the fact it looks like someone lives here all the time. I'm so glad we didn't sell the property. It was a good investment."

"I realize that, Winston. I also realize there are lots of other good things about us. Are you okay with having this discussion now?"

"Now's the best time since Nicolette's asleep."

Victoria snuggled closer to Winston. "I apologize for allowing Nicolette to hear my conversation with Aruba. I've been a wreck since you moved out. I miss you and I want you to come home."

"I don't know if I'm ready for that now."

"Are you seeing someone else?"

Winston's silence lasted fifteen seconds. "No, I'm not seeing anyone. I don't want to come home to the same thing I left."

"I'm changing. Can't you see I'm putting forth effort to make things better? I'm willing to do what it takes to make this work."

"How do I know this isn't a temporary fix?"

"There's nothing more important to me than restoring our marriage. You have every right to be skeptical. I've messed up over the years. I stopped being your wife, your friend, your lover. I want to be those things again."

"You really are being sincere, aren't you?"

"Do you know how inadequate I feel as your wife?"

"Inadequate?"

"Whenever we're at functions, parties, and socials, there are at *least* twelve women there a hundred times more accomplished than I'll ever be."

"That depends on how you measure accomplishment. Do I meet beautiful, intelligent, driven women? Every day. But I chose you. I wanted to spend my life with you."

"Wanted?"

Winston nodded his consent for Victoria to continue.

"I try to stay abreast of current events, but there's someone at those functions who outtalks me or makes me remember what I don't have."

"What are you lacking?"

"An advanced degree. A job. All I do is volunteer and shop."

"Baby, those are choices you made. I've always encouraged you to go back to school, to broaden your horizons."

"Sit there and tell me you don't think less of me because I'm not Dr. Victoria Faulk."

"Never. If you'd followed our plan we devised from the start of our union, we wouldn't be where we are today."

"I thought you'd change your mind."

"Are you kidding me?"

"I thought you only said you wanted me to stay home to control me."

"Victoria, how many times do I have to tell you—"

"Your parents' union was a competition, not a marriage," said Victoria. She hadn't finished his sentence that way since the good old days.

"Mom felt she had so much to prove to my grandparents that it cost my father's affection for her. They'd picked out the perfect mate for dad, but he loved my mom's desire to transcend the image my grandparents had of her. She was too dark, too thick, and too Southern. Dad wanted a homemaker, not a competitor. That's why I've worked so hard all this time to provide the kind of living that would give you the choice of working or staying home. I don't mind Alva being around, but I'd rather have a home-cooked meal from you. Or a foot massage followed by genuine concern about my day. I want the Victoria I married."

"I'm still here, Winston. I just want time to show you. Would you be willing to seek counseling with me?"

"I'll consider it if you tell me one thing."

"Yes."

"How do I make you feel? You've poured your heart out to tell me how you feel about issues surrounding our marriage, but do you feel you matter to me?"

"Not like I did in the beginning."

"What's different now?"

"You used to include me in your decisions. I used to know where you spent your time and where our money went. Now I'm just an observer."

"I didn't think you cared."

"I do. I stopped expressing my thoughts along the way, but I do.

Imagine how tongue-tied I was at Dorcas House when the director thanked me for *our* contribution."

"I'm passionate about the plight of battered women. I didn't think I needed your permission to give the money. Did you see the Victoria Faulk reading room?"

"I'm sorry for being so selfish. Carol's volunteer request turned out to be a blessing in disguise. I befriended a wonderful mother and daughter there."

The news made his head spin. Victoria was picky about where she shopped and ate. The thought of her mingling with women in a domestic violence shelter beyond a routine appearance startled him.

"While I'm at it, Alice and Sylvia sent me a beautiful postcard from Arizona. They loved the spa visit. I channeled your philanthropic ways and helped them relocate to Texas."

"Alice and Sylvia?"

"Baby, I was so touched by the work being done at Dorcas that I brought Alice and Sylvia to the house. We had a Christmas in February celebration. They loved the spa package and bag you bought."

"Victoria, I thought you wanted those things for yourself."

"Nope. They weren't for me." Victoria eyed Winston. "I think we'd both agree I've had enough spa visits and purses to last a lifetime."

"Amen to that!"

Victoria playfully jabbed Winston's arms. She enjoyed the light moment.

"You in the mood to help out in the kitchen, old man?"

"Old man, eh? I'll show you old."

Winston followed her into the kitchen. When they dated, Winston cooked once a week. His residency kept him on the go, but the weekly meal was his promise to Victoria that no matter how busy he was, he'd always make time for her. How the years had changed that promise.

"Guess what we're having?"

"Steak, right? You asked Shoals if the steaks were marinating."

"That's tomorrow. Tonight we're having Aruba's by the Sea. I got the recipe from her last week."

"Oh?"

"Oh? Is that the best you can do? You've been on me for years to get the recipe, and now you're not excited?"

"How do you know she didn't stiff you on some of the ingredients?" Winston joked. The mention of Aruba's name made his heart ache.

"She's not like that. Truth be told, she's the most genuine friend I've ever had."

"She is very nice. What do you need me to do with this tilapia?" He hoped changing the subject would take his mind off Aruba.

Victoria scanned Aruba's email. "Sprinkle the tilapia with Old Bay and Cajun seasoning in my bag on the counter. I also put Aruba's special seasoning in the bag. She wouldn't divulge *that* secret."

Winston removed the seasonings from the bag and worked on the meat. He wanted to change the subject of Aruba, but was interrupted by Victoria.

"I got an invite from Bria to Aruba's birthday party next month. Sounds like a unique affair."

"I probably won't be able to attend, Victoria."

"You most certainly won't. It's for ladies only."

Winston exhaled.

"I'm excited because it's a dream girl party."

"Like the movie?"

"No, silly. It's women sharing and bonding over their desires. I like that Bria made it about Aruba and all the ladies."

"I'm sure you'll have a good time."

"Will you help me pick out a gift for her?"

"You're the Indy shopping queen. I know you've got it covered."

"We're supposed to be bonding. I thought it would be nice to go out and do something together."

"I'll spring for dinner and a movie once we're home."

Winston went back to seasoning seafood. Victoria came up behind him and delicately sucked his earlobes. That drove him crazy. He thought she'd forgotten how much that turned him on.

"What are you doing?"

"Kissing my husband. For now. If you're good, we can do something freakier after dinner."

Winston took this as the true test. Sure, she could tease him, but she hated kissing. If he turned to her and she recoiled, he'd know this was all a sham and would continue his original plan. He faced her, then kissed her passionately. She reciprocated, locking his tongue with hers and moaning like she did when she wanted him more than anything in the world.

Clapping and girlish giggles interrupted the makeout session. "Daddy, you're kissing Mommy! You're kissing Mommy just like Jeremiah said you kiss Miss Aruba!"

[35]
Toyota Camry Confessions

Tawatha squirmed in her seat as she took in the view. "Whose party are we attending and why the hell are we driving to Geist?"

"Testy, testy! It's my boss's birthday. We're going to Bella Vita's, remember? I'm eating light though because I'm meeting Lake later tonight."

Tawatha's stomach fluttered. Lake and Lasheera had been spending so much time together. She feigned happiness, but she wished James would spend the kind of time with her that Lake was spending with Sheer. He was so attentive, so loving. He even supported her efforts to get full custody of Zion. *That's gonna be me and James when all this is over.*

"So how am I getting home?"

"Lake is coming to pick me up. You're more than welcome to drive my car home."

"Lasheera, I'm so proud of you for getting your license back and buying a car."

"The night my boss took us all to Onnie's art show, I knew I had to step up my game. I'm a grown-ass woman, riding the bus and asking people for rides. It also helped that Lake is good friends with a car dealer at the Plainfield Auction. I got a really good deal with the money I'd saved."

"I almost forgot about her taking the kids. I will let her know tonight how grateful I am for the favor. I'm not too keen about this index card, but it did make me think about my dreams and desires."

"I think it's a good idea. I'll have to share the story behind the story when we have time. Right now I want to know what's going on with you and ole boy. The one you're keeping hidden from us. Is he Secret Service? FBI?"

"Sheer, you're crazy! Funny you should mention him. You and everyone else will get to meet him soon. We're close to a public announcement of our love. He had to get some things tied up, but it's okay now."

"Yeah, like what things?"

Tawatha grunted. "You're not dropping the subject, are you?"

"Not as long as we're friends and not as long as I love you. I've seen you hurt too many times in the past to allow another man to get the best of you. You're a good woman, Tawatha. I've seen you blossom over the last year. You're becoming the woman I always knew you were meant to be. You were meant to do great things. Heck, we're all coming into our own. Jamilah is on the dean's list, I'm drug-free and holding down a steady job, and you're darn near running Hinton and Conyers. I just want the love piece to be intact for you. Feel me?"

"I feel you, big head Sheer. I keep forgetting that I'm not in this alone. I've kept James a secret *because* of the pain I've encountered in the past."

"James. So he *does* have a name."

"Lasheera, he's sooo...I can't describe how I feel about him. I can conquer the world with him by my side. I know we'll have a good life together once..."

"Once what, Watha?"

Tawatha paused. "Promise not to judge?"

"Did we judge you when you took all the vowels out of Sincerity's name?"

"No."

"Did we judge you when you went AWOL five days with Grant's father and worried us half to death?"

Tawatha took a deep breath. "He's married. James is married."

"So is Zion's father. I have no right to judge you."

"I just didn't want to hear all the reasons why I'm a horrible person and a homewrecker. His wife has cancer and she's near death. At least I'm waiting 'til the coast is clear."

Lasheera chose her words carefully. She didn't want to sound self-righteous, but wouldn't wish what she'd experienced on anyone. "Remember, Watha, actions have consequences. You're right; no one has the right to judge another, but I've grown to a place of speaking the truth in love. Do you think you're the rebound woman?"

"No, it's not like that at all. We have a connection. An extremely close bond."

"Do the kids like him?"

"I've been waiting to ease him into their lives."

"Yet you're still anticipating a July wedding?"

Tawatha shifted in her seat. "I was."

Lasheera pursed her lips and abandoned the conversation. This was a repeat of the discussion they'd had about S'n'c'r'ty's dad. Nathan Porter would have married Tawatha if she hadn't pressured him. When she wasn't stalking him at his job when he did work and wasn't writing poems, she was sitting outside his driveway, children in tow, waiting for him to come home. Never mind the fact he always refused to give her a spare key to his place. Lasheera thought of the time Tawatha crawled through Nathan's window to prepare dinner because she wanted him to have a hot meal when he arrived from work. She nearly caused the man cardiac arrest when he got home. Who could forget the way she called his mother every hour on the hour to assure her she'd be the best daughter-in-law in the world? Or the way she applied for a credit card in Roberta's name and redecorated Nathan's house, so they'd all be one big happy family. Tawatha had heard through the grapevine how appreciative Nathan's wife was to come into her husband's home so immaculately designed. No, Lasheera would seal her lips this time and pray her friend would finally see the light.

"I have a confession to make," Tawatha said.

"Are you pregnant?"

"*Hello*, my tubes are tied."

"Whew. Girl, I would have smacked you…in love."

"I'm a little jealous of your relationship with Lake."

"You lie."

"I am. He goes places with you, he's supportive, he treats you with respect. I wish I had that in a man."

"Tawatha, look at what I had to go through to get to this relationship. I've learned so much from the choices I made in the past. Perhaps…"

"I know. I keep making the same mistakes over and over again."

"That's not what I was going to say. Perhaps you should pray about the situation." Lasheera sensed Tawatha tensing up. "I've been a tad reluctant to share my faith with you and Jamilah because I didn't want to come off as preachy. But the peace and comfort I experience is too good to keep to myself. There are days that I want a hit of crack so badly that I break out in a cold sweat. I call my prayer partner from church and we do battle with Satan until the urge passes."

"I'm too messed up to pray. Besides, these holy rollers would have you believe they're so sanctified and they do more dirt than I ever have."

"Everyone isn't in church for the Lord. That's why you pray for discernment. You also study to show thyself approved."

"You don't mind sharing your business with the prayer partner?"

"Sharing always involves risk. I asked the Lord to send someone to help me through this time and I know Marcia was sent by God."

"You've got to know the Bible from Genesis to maps to be a Christian. I don't have time for all that."

"You're farther along than you think. Most folks stop at Revelations."

They both chuckled over the memory of tracing maps in the back of Roberta's massive Bible as kids.

"All I'm saying is try it. The peace you'll come to know is powerful."

"I guess."

Lasheera pulled a prayer card from the sun visor and handed it to Tawatha. "I read this when I'm down or hopeless."

Tawatha read the caption, *God's Peace*, aloud and scanned the scripture beneath a beautiful orange and white hollyhock featured on the card. *You'll experience God's peace, which is far more wonderful than the human mind can understand. His peace will guard your hearts and minds. Philippians 4:7.* "I'll try this prayer thing, but only for you, Sheer."

"Don't do it for me. Do it for God and yourself."

[36]
We're Gonna Have a Funky Good Time

Lasheera parked next to Bria's car. The original party schedule was six o'clock until nine; however, Bria explained Aruba's husband also had a surprise for her. Bria shortened the party to eight, so Aruba could join her husband. Lasheera still shook her head at the lie Bria had concocted to get Aruba to Bella Vita's. Poor Aruba thought she was coming to discuss Bria's exit from the company. Lasheera knew the night would be an unforgettable one for Aruba with all the people who were invited.

"I came here once with Mr. Hinton," said Tawatha. "There's nothing like the marina in the springtime."

Lasheera and Tawatha headed toward the entrance. They took in the sweet-salty scent of the air that wafted off the reservoir. The ambience of the restaurant was always vibrant and welcoming. They both enjoyed the sight of boats skidding on the water, a definite precursor to barbecues, road trips, and Indiana Black Expo. Twenty minutes remained before Aruba's anticipated arrival. They entered Bella Vita's and spotted Bria seated on a bench near the hostess station. She rose to greet them.

"Hey, ladies. I'm so glad you made it." Bria hugged Lasheera.

"Bria, this is my friend, Tawatha. Tawatha, this is Bria. She's one of our office managers."

"It's so nice to finally meet you. Lasheera talks about you and Jamilah so much we've named you the Three Musketeers."

"I hope the talk was all good."

"Absolutely."

"Is everyone here?" asked Lasheera. She set her gift bag on the floor. "Do you need help with anything?"

"I've taken care of everything. Dinner is on Sidney tonight, so order what you want. The gang's all here except Aruba's diva grandmother, Maxine. Maxi always has to make a grand entrance."

"I've wanted to meet her since Aruba told me she has the gift of foresight. Does she really?"

"I'll put it this way. Don't sit near her if you don't want the table to know your business. She can do a reading a mile away. The gift table is next to the table where we'll all be dining. You can join everyone else. Our table is situated so Aruba won't see you when she comes in. Go mix and mingle, ladies."

The sound of smooth jazz, clinking silverware, and light banter surrounded them. Tawatha eyed the women seated at party central, then quickened her pace.

"Is that who I think it is?" asked Tawatha.

"Who are you talking about?" whispered Lasheera.

"Dayton Abernathy. Is that her? The relationship guru on *Oprah* who's always giving relationship advice?"

"Yep...that's her. As a matter of fact...Watha, just wait 'til we sit down. I'll fill you in."

Lasheera placed her gift on the table. She marveled at the intricate designs on the Chanel purse birthday cake. She greeted the ladies. Some stood to greet her while a few others ended calls or texts they were in the middle of typing.

"Hi, Victoria. I was hoping you'd make it." Lasheera was excited to see one of Aruba's friends who'd been visiting the office lately.

"It's good to see you again, Lasheera."

"Victoria, this is my friend, Tawatha. Tawatha, this is Victoria Faulk."

"Weren't you on the cover of *Indianapolis Woman* last year? You're married to the doctor who performs all the heart surgeries, right?"

"Guilty as charged."

"It's so good to meet you."

Tawatha had no idea who this Aruba was, but to have this circle of friends said a lot about her. She couldn't wait to meet her. The night was turning out to be better than she'd imagined. As she sat next to Lasheera, she made a silent vow to block James from her mind. She wasn't totally convinced prayer was the answer to her problems, but the company of these women might be the ticket to ease her aching heart.

"Lasheera, how are things at the office?" asked Victoria.

"They're going well, Victoria. How's your daughter?"

"She's growing like a weed and is begging to go to Disneyland this summer. July's not getting here soon enough."

"I've wanted to take my kids to Disney forever," said Tawatha. She squeezed a lemon into the glass of water before her.

"Disney has great family packages. Our travel agent handles most of our arrangements."

Travel agent. I'll find a good one to help me plan the second leg of the honeymoon. Tawatha's mind wandered, fantasized about all the trips she and the children would take once the wedding was over. She'd pinched so many pennies in excitement of the wedding that she'd almost forgotten what it meant to have fun. She had established an account at Key Bank which now totaled four thousand dollars. The funds were earmarked for the wedding and honeymoon. James would be thrilled to have quiet time on the beach in Ocho Rios. The cashmere robe and slippers would suit his tall frame as they lounged in their honeymoon suite. He would need time to relax from his wife's death. Tawatha moistened when she visualized oiling him down, massaging his back, cracking his toes, then making love to him until he couldn't get enough. She'd erase all traces of his wife with a better life, better loving, and better moments.

"...there is no competition. Tyler is Tyler and I'm me. There's room at the table for anyone willing to work hard and get used to the word 'no.' I've had more nos than yeses," said Maria Jones, interrupting Tawatha's train of thought.

"But how many black women in Hollywood are on your level? Your name carries the box office. Your last film grossed one hundred million dollars the first weekend," said Barbara.

That's where Tawatha remembered her face. Maria was equally elusive and generous. She was short on words, but long on giving, rarely giving interviews, but always lending a helping hand to those in need. A number of soup kitchens, shelters, and youth organizations received support from her foundation. The most consistent bit of information tabloids reported about her was child-hood abandonment.

"Not many have my bankability. I still say, though, there's room at the table."

"You can say that again," Dayton chimed in. "The rule of thumb applies in every aspect of our lives. So many people don't have what they want because they harbor a lack mentality."

"Lack mentality?" asked Zenobia Wells.

"Thinking that everything is on the verge of running out. Jobs, men, houses. I think if people were clear about their purpose and desires, they would have the life they dream of."

"That's easy for you to say. Everyone doesn't have a Mr. Abernathy like you," Tawatha whispered to Lasheera.

Lasheera kicked Tawatha's leg under the table. "Stop whispering," she said through clenched teeth.

Tawatha swigged her lemon water. It amazed Tawatha how much women like Dayton took their abundance lightly. Mr. Harold Abernathy was a man touted in the media for his solo feat of turning around the failing Dressed to the Nines clothing company. His background in finance and public relations was the reason the CEO of Dressed wooed him. Add that to the fact their daughter, Lotus, a Brown alum, recently had joined the *Today Show*, broadcasting special reports. Hell yes, she could chide others about having a lack mentality because she had so much. Tawatha wondered what kind of influence these women were having on Sheer. It began with this new circle of women. Then it escalated to that Jesus business. There was a time when they chatted nonstop at dinner, even when others were present. What was happening to her friend?

Dayton caught the attention of the waitress. "Naomi, I'm ready to place my drink order. The drinks are on me tonight."

"The first round, or all night?"

"All night. Please run a tab for me."

"Certainly, Dr. Abernathy."

"Call me 'Day.'"

"What are you drinking, Day?"

"I'll have a Waiting to Exhale."

"We don't serve that one."

"I know." Dayton pulled a *New York Times* clipping from her purse containing the drink recipe and handed it to Naomi. "This is served at Sylvia's. It really is a sneak attack. Two or three of these and I'm out for the night. When Maxine gets here, I'll make her the designated driver."

Everyone placed their drink orders. Lasheera's phone vibrated and she read Bria's text: *SHE'S HERE!!!!*

"Everyone, Aruba's here. Let's stand so we can greet her when she snakes her way back here."

Bria jabbered a mile a minute with Aruba. Aruba hung on her every word, not paying attention to the crowd.

"Surprise!"

"Gotcha," said Bria.

"Bria, how could you?" Aruba playfully jabbed Bria's shoulder. She scanned the faces of the women before her and was beyond excited. "How did you pull this off?" Aruba managed before a few tears fell from her eyes.

"I had a little help from your ace."

"Lasheera, you kept this secret from me? You wait 'til we get back to the office."

Aruba walked around the table to greet everyone. Amidst hugs and "happy birthday" wishes, she noticed everyone seemed genuinely happy to be there except the woman standing next to Lasheera. The crowd may have been out of her element. She wondered if Dayton and Maria had overwhelmed everyone with their sage wisdom and success stories. Aruba assumed Shock Face was Tawatha. Lasheera had shown her photos of Jamilah a couple of weeks ago. She was pulled into a meeting just before Tawatha's image flashed during the digital camera slide show.

"Aruba, you look wonderful! Happy Birthday!" said Victoria. They hugged and kissed each other on the cheek.

It can't be. The world isn't that small and my luck can't be that bad. Tawatha gave Lasheera the stank eye, but quickly fixed her face. How could Lasheera have known this was James's wife? This was the woman who'd been in her home, taken her kids out to dinner, and according to Lasheera, asked about purchasing artwork from Aunjanue. Could fate be that cruel? Tawatha looked at Aruba and was happy she'd found a nice wig. *For a cancer patient, she looks good. People say you have a glow during the last days.*

"Aruba, this is my girlfriend, Tawatha. Tawatha, this is Aruba."

"It's nice to meet you," said Tawatha. She shook Aruba's hand instead of hugging her. Memories of James making love to her caused her to snatch her hand from Aruba's. Everyone watched the exchange with raised eyebrows.

"Your hand shocked me. Sorry."

"It must be static from my outfit. Please forgive me. By the way, your daughter Aunjanue is such a talented artist. Art is her calling. I think she'll go far."

"Thanks for the compliment. I'm so proud of her."

They eyed each other, both unsure of what to say next. Maxine sliced through the moment of awkward silence.

"I know my granddaughter didn't beat me to the party!"

"Grandma Maxie, where have you been?"

Maxine hugged Aruba, passed her gargantuan gift bag to Bria, and blew air kisses to all the ladies before commanding everyone to take a seat.

"Sugar, is this seat taken?"

"No, ma'am," said Tawatha.

"Don't 'ma'am' me, honey. I'm old enough to be your big sister, but that's about it. Call me 'Maxie.'"

"Have a seat, Maxie."

Maxine *had* to take a seat next to her childhood friend, Dayton, before answering Aruba's question.

"You know your momma and daddy are practically joined at the hip. Lance is still hobbling around after his foot surgery, so Darnella stayed behind to help him. I spent the last thirty odd minutes in the parking lot, talking my daughter through changing gauzes and treating infection. Your daddy should be up and about soon enough, thanks to me!"

"I spoke with them earlier today. They said you were bringing their gift. I kinda hoped they were joking with me."

"I got that gift. It's in my bag over there."

"I told them it wasn't necessary, but you know how they are."

"They probably want to make sure she's comfortable her last days," Tawatha whispered to Lasheera.

"What are you talking about now?" Lasheera hissed through clenched teeth. "I'm not telling you to be quiet again!"

"Come with me to the bathroom—now!" Tawatha shot back. "That water went straight through me." Tawatha stood and announced this news to no one in particular. "Lasheera, come with me to the restroom a minute."

"If the water went through you, I don't know what you'll do when you get a real drink later," said Dayton.

Tawatha shrugged her shoulders, smiled at Dayton, and grabbed her purse, Lasheera in tow.

"This better be good. You know I won't be here long and you're creating drama. Was I wrong for inviting you? I know this isn't our normal crew, but these are really nice ladies. I just wanted to get you out—"

Tawatha pulled Lasheera into one of the stalls. "Aruba is James's wife, Sheer. The man I'm in love with and plan to marry, that's his wife. Did you know that? Have you been playing both sides of the fence with us?"

Lasheera touched Tawatha's forehead. "Watha, are you okay? I thought you were just drinking water."

"Don't patronize me. What have you said to her about me?"

"Calm down. You're scaring me. What's going on?"

"Aruba. She has cancer. She isn't supposed to be alive. I thought she would have been dead by now with the way James described her illness."

"Tawatha, Aruba is fine. She's never had cancer as far as I know. She's healthy, fun-loving, and by the ton of roses she gets in her office, her husband seems to love her a great deal. Are you sure you're talking about the same woman?"

"Describe her husband to me, Sheer."

"From the photos in her office, he's tall, has dreads, could be a male model 'cause he's drop-dead gorgeous. You know I don't do light brights, but he's handsome. Really handsome."

"That's him! That's James."

"Sorry to burst your bubble, but you've been misled. She hasn't discussed getting a divorce, and she isn't sick. She hasn't even had a cold since I've been in the office. I'm sorry, honey." Lasheera hugged Tawatha, sad her girl had been bitten *again* by the love bug.

"You're mistaken. She probably didn't tell you because she didn't want office pity. But she has cancer. That night I was in their house—"

"Their house? You slept with him in their house?"

"There you go judging me again. I was with him the night of the accident. She had gone out with one of her friends to a support group meeting, then to shop for wigs. I bet that isn't even her real hair!"

"It is. I braided it for her a few months ago for girls' night out with Bria and some of their friends. Not a strand got wrapped underneath my nails," said Lasheera, flicking her hands front to back as proof.

Tawatha leaned against the stall, crestfallen, hopeless. How could she be duped so easily—*again*? She loved James with all that was within her. Perhaps Lasheera misunderstood. Perhaps James didn't want her to know how well Aruba responded to chemo. That's how noble he was. She'd even purchased the T-shirt she'd wear on their honeymoon, with the words, *MORE THAN JUST A GOOD D**K AND SOME MONEY*, rhinestoned across her chest with a finger pointed toward a photo of James to show the world she'd endured the storm with him and came out as Mrs. Dixon.

"Look, I can text Lake and tell him to cancel our date. I'm a little afraid of what might happen if I leave you here alone."

"Don't cancel your date. I can pull myself together. I can make it through this. What, you don't think I'm as refined as those hoity-toity broads out there?"

"Well, you *do* look like someone just stole your red Flyer. The one we used to haul dolls and comic books around in as kids," said Lasheera. Her heart warmed when Tawatha smiled.

"I'm going back in there and enjoy the night. Shoot, I might even order Pink Panties. I'll sort it all out tomorrow."

They performed the secret handshake they had invented as girls in Jamilah's backyard. As they stepped out the bathroom, Lake was waiting for Lasheera in the lobby and greeted her with a kiss.

"Here are the keys to my car. Call me if you need anything, Watha. Anything."

"I'll be fine. Trust me."

[37]
It's the Thought that Counts

"The tradition is we all read our cards, then the birthday girl opens the gift. Since we're a tad pressed for time because the birthday girl's *man* has a bigger surprise for her, we'll let Aruba open her gift from each of us as we read our cards. Instead of our personal dreams, Lasheera suggested we all tell Aruba what we dream or wish for her," said Bria.

Bria gathered the gifts together and whipped out her notepad to jot down the names of the givers. She prided herself on making sure the handwritten, thank-you notes were mailed out promptly after the party. She felt modern etiquette had gone to the dogs and she refused to be associated with email thank-yous.

"What happened to your friend?" Maxie asked Tawatha.

"Oh, her dude, I mean, her boyfriend, took her out for a night on the town. That's why she was drinking so light. I have the honor of reading her card," said Tawatha as she took a drag of the Pink Panties she had ordered.

"Do you have a designated driver for the night? I don't want anything to happen to you on the way home." Maxie was concerned about Tawatha's demeanor since her return from the restroom.

"I'm good. I've got too much on my mind to have messed-up vision."

Bria picked up Lasheera's gift first. "Tawatha, this is Lasheera's gift. Are you ready?"

Aruba delicately pulled tissue from the gift bag, honored that Lasheera had chosen such a thoughtful gift. Aruba displayed the ring, earrings, and necklace packaged together. Everyone *oohed* and *ahhed* at the intricate detail and crafty design of the set. As if on cue, Tawatha stood and read the words:

"Aruba, you're the best boss a girl could ever have. You're patient, kind, unafraid to share your knowledge with me, and you're so encouraging. You poked, prodded, and made me realize my lost love of making jewelry. My dream for you is to keep being an encourager to those of us who need to smile and remember why we're here."

Aruba blinked back tears, unaware that she'd influenced Lasheera in such a powerful way. She merely complimented her from time to time and told her to celebrate her sobriety and drug-free state.

"Thank you, Tawatha. Be sure to tell Lasheera she's forgiven for pulling this prank."

Tawatha smirked, took her seat.

"If you start that crying, we'll be here all night," said Maxie. "Dayton and I have more running around to do. Open my gift, honey."

Bria heaved Maxie's big bag near the center of the table. It contained a Burberry purse, Coach shades, a Teddy Pendergrass album, an envelope, and a glass beverage dispenser.

"I understand some of these gifts, but the Teddy Pendergrass album?" asked Aruba.

"Don't make me tell everybody at this party how Teddy Pendergrass, or as your paternal grandmother, Ella, called him, Teddy Pendergraff, was the first grown man you had a crush on."

"Please don't," said Aruba, blushing.

"Tell us," chimed Victoria. "I bet there's so much about Aruba we don't know."

"Honey, Aruba was always a drama queen. Aruba's aunts, Kinsey and Mayella, always found some men to take them to the Kool Jazz Festivals in Atlanta and the Teddy Pendergrass concerts back in the day. They'd always bring Aruba back program books, albums, souvenirs, anything they thought was appropriate for a six-year-old. Well, they caught her singing Teddy's songs more than any of the other songs they gave her. The night ABC announced Teddy had been stricken in that accident, Aruba took to her bed and never got over the fact that he'd been paralyzed. At first we thought she was joking, but she really wanted to go to Philly to look after him. That's right up there with her delusions that she was Flip Wilson's daughter, and was the stalking target of Spiro T. Agnew. I'm telling you, she's a dream girl."

"Thanks for spilling my secrets, Maxie. So what, I have an active imagination."

"Be grateful I didn't tell 'em about your staged sermons and funerals."

"Will you read your card, Grandma?"

"You know how much I hate the word 'grandma,' so here goes. Aruba, I dream the greatest latter years for you that only God can give. You deserve it!"

"All that tattling for latter years' wishes? Okay, I feel you," said Aruba. She blew Maxie a big kiss.

"We have a big envelope here from…" Bria turned the envelope over.

"That one's from me," said Dayton, smiling. "I hope you get a kick out of it. It's a little something from Harold, Lotus, and me."

Aruba opened the envelope. Aruba's eyes widened at the sight of the vacation package to Rio and Turks and Caicos. "Day!"

"I think you, James, and Jeremiah deserve some quiet time. Sun and sand always give the body a new perspective. My dream for you is that you have peace, life, and longevity. Cheers!" Dayton lifted her Exhale to Aruba.

"Thank you so much. I know we'll enjoy ourselves."

Bria was on to the next gift before Aruba could breathe. "Next, we have blue! Whose responsible for the Tiffany box?"

"That would be my gift," said Victoria. "Everything was selected with you in mind."

A twinge of guilt rose in Aruba as she opened the box. How had she allowed things to go so far? She'd served James with divorce papers, yet he insisted they meet tonight before he signed them. Victoria had been encouraging her to work things out with James, to see if counseling might mend their relationship. Aruba found it difficult to look in Victoria's eyes because she pretended she wanted counseling. Aruba opened the box and eyed the contents with confusion. Inside were three keys. "Keys? Are these to the cabin?"

"Aruba, those are the keys to my life. Since you want to live it so badly, I decided to bow out, let you take the reins." Victoria read from her card. *"My wish for you is that you make my husband happy, since you've been having an affair with him. The large key is to my house. Winston allows a generous decorating budget, so feel free to make it your own."* A collective gasp, then silence enveloped the table. *"The gold key is to my Mercedes, the car you and I rode around in sharing jokes, laughter. Wow, what a wonderful friend you are."*

"Victoria, can we step outside a minute?" Aruba stood, her hands trembling with the weight of being exposed.

Ignoring her, Victoria continued, *"The oval key is to Winston's practice. Up until I hired a private investigator a month ago to follow him going to your place, this is where I thought he was spending his time away from home."*

Tawatha perked up now, her second Pink Panties taking effect. *This is better than Venus and Serena at Wimbledon. I knew something would clear the way for me and James.*

"It's been nice meeting you, ladies, but I have to leave now. I have an early morning appointment with my divorce attorney," said Victoria. She snatched her purse and whizzed past Aruba who was fast on her heels. The women looked on in shock, neither daring to utter a word. Outside, Victoria struggled to open her door.

"Would you please just stop for a minute, so we can talk." Aruba's eyes pleaded with Victoria.

Victoria turned to face Aruba. "What's there to talk about? You won Winston fair and square. Would you please move, so I can leave?"

"I thought you were unhappy with him. All you ever did was complain about him, make light of his work, his accomplishments, his provisions. I just thought…"

"You 'just thought' what? That venting to someone I thought was a friend gave you license to slide on in and move me out of the way? How many other *friends'* husbands have you made a move on?"

"Victoria, I have never done anything like this before in my life."

Victoria applauded. "How lucky am I to have been the first backstabbing you've carried out. You're pretty damn good. I'm sure you can hone the craft with other men."

Aruba touched Victoria's arm. "Just let me ex—"

Victoria snatched her arm from Aruba's grasp. "*Don't touch me!* Don't ever touch me, come near me, or my child ever again! I'm trying to keep my cool, but you're testing my patience. Get away from me, so I can leave." Neither saw the security guard approach, or Bria, holding Aruba's purse, or Maxie, shame etching her face.

"Is everything all right here?" asked the muscular young man.

"Things will be fine if she moves out of my way, so I can leave," Victoria said to the man.

Aruba stepped aside so that Victoria could enter her car. She gave Aruba one last cryptic look before slamming her door. She backed out of her parking space, eyes straight ahead.

"Is it true? Please tell me it isn't true," said Bria.

Aruba's silence confirmed Bria's fears. Aruba sought an explanation, something to say to her friend, but she couldn't. Aruba's phone message indicator startled the three of them. She flipped open her phone and read James's text message.

WHERE ARE YOU? WE STILL NEED TO TALK.

"I'm sorry, Bria. I'm sorry, Maxie. I…I have to go. I have to get this over with James."

"Before you go, baby, tell me why? How could you do something like this?"

"You know I've been unhappy with James for so long."

"You had other options, honey."

"What about Mom and Dad? She's stuck by his side all these years. Remember Ms. Sheila?"

"Honey, I don't like secrets. Darling, Sheila confided in your father that your mother was cheating. She always had something tricky going on behind your father's back. He stayed with her because he loves her. I brag on my son-in-law because he's been good to your mother. She doesn't deserve such a good man. Nothing is as it seems, Aruba. I was hoping you'd turn out different. You'll see that when you get with this new man. I'm not saying you should stay with James, but I fear you've opened yourself up for a world of hurt."

"I'm going to see what James wants, Maxie."

[38]
Have a Little Faith

Winston had called for the fifth time. Aruba couldn't bring herself to answer his call. Not after the fiasco, not after the embarrassment. What was there to say? Hi, it's your loving homewrecker! What's new, lover? If only Victoria had let her explain that they hadn't slept together, that they weren't officially lovers. That her judgment was clouded due to the problems she experienced with James. Aruba's mind raced, her heart pounded. She was so absorbed in thought that she almost missed her stop. She gazed at the building sideways, thinking maybe she'd gotten the address wrong. She eyed the paper again. *420 N. Illinois Street.* She was about to pull away when she noticed their Pilot two cars ahead. She eased out of her company vehicle and approached the front door with suspicion. She knocked twice, afraid of what monkey business James had orchestrated. The good thing about tonight was that she could end their marriage.

"So what took you so long?" asked James as he opened the door, a wide smile on his face.

Aruba froze. She was speechless. Her first impulse was to touch James's hair. The man before her resembled the adolescent in stellar photos lining the walls of his parents' mantel. Gone were his well-oiled dreads that cascaded down his back, making women swoon. She adored the mop of curls framing his handsome face. *Is this my husband?* "James, what are you doing here? Why did you cut your hair?" Before the shock of his Samson transformation could sink in, she noticed the suit and tie hanging from his well-chiseled frame. She melted as she took in the smell of the cologne he wore.

"Come in, Mrs. Dixon. I don't have all night. I have a marriage to save."

The smooth sounds of Maxwell ushered her into a candlelit atmosphere. A table draped in white linen sat in the middle of the floor. Although the room was dim, she could tell that decorative, funky designs lined the walls. She also smelled James's signature steak, vegetable stir fry, and parsley potatoes. He handed her a single rose.

"Would you like dinner now, or after our chitchat?"

"James, we have a lot to talk about."

"I agree. Will you hear me out tonight?"

"Yes. I'll listen."

James escorted her to the table, pulled her seat out, and waited until she was comfortable. He'd taken care to set the table as she liked it. She noticed the wine chilling in the golden ice bucket.

"I miss you, Aruba. I miss Jerry. I miss us. I know I've messed up a lot in the past. You've put up with a lot of my shit over the years and I don't see how you've done it. A lesser woman would have left me years ago. I didn't think you were serious about leaving me until you moved out and I got served."

"James."

"You said you'd listen."

"I promised you a lot in the beginning and I haven't made good on those promises. I've really been trying though, baby. That's why I called you here tonight."

James slid her birthday gifts toward her. She hoped this wouldn't be déjà vu. The last thing she needed was another surprise like the one Victoria had given her.

"Why are you trembling, baby?"

Aruba shrugged her shoulders. If only he'd said those words a year ago. Or even six months ago. For the first time since their journey had begun, she felt his sincerity, his love.

She opened the first gift and gasped with delight. "James. The ladybug. You remembered after all these years?"

"How could I forget? I've never seen a woman so excited over a pin. Most women ask for a ring upgrade, but you always admired that ladybug. I hope you like it."

Aruba stopped short of asking how he had paid for the pendant. His thoughtfulness had floored her, filled her with more guilt.

He slid the envelope her way. "This is for you, too."

Aruba opened the envelope, then did a double-take. She looked at James. "I guess I'm not sure I get this one."

"That's the lease to this building. Our building. You're sitting inside Dixon's Hair Affair, Aruba. I own this shop."

"James, stop. How? When?"

"Close your mouth," James said. "I got a few investors behind me. Worked on the business plan you and I started together. When you left, I temped at Franzen Industrial Staffing. I don't believe in coincidences, you know. I met Katrina Benford, Isaak Benford's wife."

"The developer?"

"The one and only. Her cousin owns Divas in Training. The same lead you gave me last year. One thing led to another, and we hooked up. They've really helped me get myself on track. I was temping during the day and doing hair in our basement at night and on the weekends. Before you even ask, Victoria stopped by one day while I was doing our neighbor Paris's hair. I think she thought I had something going on."

"Yeah, she mentioned it. I didn't know what to think. James, I'm so proud of you. I knew you could do it."

"We did it. It took you leaving me to recognize what a good wife I have. I don't want a divorce. Can we try to work things out? I don't expect you to come running back into my arms like nothing happened. Will you give us one more chance?"

"James."

"You told me to walk the walk and not talk the talk. That's what I'm trying to do now."

Aruba sighed. Tonight cemented the uneasiness she felt about being with Winston. How could she be with him and have an honest relationship? She looked at James, really saw his genuineness, his desire to please her. She couldn't deny that she still loved him. He was the only man she'd ever loved. How could she start anew with all she'd done? She took his hands into hers and smiled.

"You haven't mentioned it, but I'm sorry I hit you. I will go to anger management if necessary, but I promise I'll never put my hands on you again. There's no excuse for me touching you."

The words "I still love you" danced on the tip of her tongue. She wanted to believe James, to imagine they could start anew. She looked deep into his eyes. She ran her fingers through his hair and formed the words "I'll try" just as a brick sailed past her, the storefront glass drowning out Maxwell.

Tawatha wasted no time disturbing the tranquil atmosphere. Aruba recognized her from the party, wondered why she was there.

"Oh, so this is loving me, James?"

"Tawatha, what is wrong with you? I know damn well you didn't crash this glass and walk in my business like you've lost your mind!"

Seeing James caused a new wave of emotions to flood Tawatha's senses. She looked at James and repeated the words he spoke during their time alone. "My wife doesn't appreciate me, Tawatha." "I want to be with you, Tawatha." "My wife has cancer, Tawatha." She yelled, "She doesn't even want you, James! She's seeing someone else!"

"James, who is this and why is she here?"

Tawatha stepped in Aruba's face, the Pink Panties bolstering her confidence. "I am the woman your husband has been sleeping with the past year. I am the woman who has been in your house, held your son, and would be sitting here with James if you would leave him alone."

James, nervous with Aruba's nonplussed stance, stood between the women. "Tawatha, I told you I don't want you. I love my wife, and I want to keep my family together."

"I'm not leaving until you tell her everything about us."

"There's nothing to tell. I made a stupid mistake sleeping with you and I regret it. I never told you I loved you, I never promised you anything. Don't you get it? I don't want to be with you!"

"While you've been lying to me, pretending Miss America here has cancer, she's been creeping with her friend Victoria's husband."

"I *know* that's a lie because Winston fronted me the funds for my business. No way would he be that kind of snake."

Aruba tried to process the information she'd been given. She couldn't imagine James being courageous enough to approach Winston for anything. Yet, they stood in a space a few days away from a magnificent grand opening. She refused to acknowledge Tawatha. She had to be the one to tell James about Winston. There was no turning back now. He had to hear the truth from her point of view.

"Tawatha, I know you hear the sirens nearing. You've set off the alarm system with all this high drama. My husband asked you to leave, so I suggest you exit the premises before you're arrested."

"Fine! To hell with both of you! You're a match made in hell. Playing games with people's feelings."

"Tawatha, just go. Please," said James.

"If you call me again…" Tawatha paused. She clutched her stomach, tried to hold the vomit rising to her throat. She ran out the front door of the shop, humiliated once again. She threw up on the corner of Illinois and St. Clair. She needed familiarity, something to calm her nerves. She jumped in Lasheera's car and sped away, cursing at her miserable luck.

Inside, James paced back and forth. He finally got the nerve to address Aruba. "Do I want to know what she's talking about?"

"Do I want to know why you were with her?" She shook her head. "At least I know who Miss T. is."

James leaned against the wall, then dropped to the floor. "How long have you been seeing Winston?"

"Probably as long as you've been seeing Tawatha."

"Did you sleep with him?"

"No, James. I can honestly say I haven't. Of course, you can't say the same thing about Tawatha."

"Did I hurt you that much that you had to turn to him? Hell, any other man for that matter."

"Yes, you did."

"Do you love him?"

"I don't know that I'd call it love. Fondness. Admiration, perhaps."

"Translation, money. Right?"

"No. It's not just that. Listen, I'm so confused right now, I don't know what to do or say. I want you to know how proud I am of you, James. Standing here takes me back to the beginning of our marriage. You're exhibiting what I knew you could do all along. I just hate that it took so long for this to happen."

James thought back on his mother's mandate. *It takes two people to make a marriage go bad.*

"Aruba, I love you. For the sake of our son and our vows, please, let's start over again. Let's leave the past behind us and start fresh. I know I've let you down in the past and I've hurt you, but I can't lose you. I don't want to be without you."

"James, let me think about it."

"Take all the time you need. I'm not going anywhere."

James scanned his hard work, his effort. He estimated the window repair would be at least twelve hundred dollars. *A small price to pay for the mess I've made.*

[39]
Wit's End

Tawatha staggered in the house as Aunjanue read to S'n'c'r'ty on the sofa. She kicked off her shoes at the front door, neglecting to place them on the shoe rack. She didn't care about order tonight. The most important thing was getting James out of her system. What would it take for her to find someone that would be hers exclusively? She couldn't stomach pursuing another man. Not after all the pain she'd endured.

"Momma, are you okay?" asked Aunjanue. "You look like you've been crying."

"What's it to you? Can't I cry or be down without the four of you in my business?" Tawatha snapped.

"I was just concerned." Aunjanue paused. "I…I wanted to know if I could still go to Tarsha's for the sleepover tonight. She's a few doors down and I'm close enough to come back home if you need me."

"I wanna come," S'n'c'r'ty piped in.

"It's a big girl party, remember?"

"Onnie, you're always leaving me!"

"I'll be back Sunday. We'll play Connect Four when I come back."

"You promise?"

"Yes, I promise. Now let me pack the rest of my things."

"Mind your manners at the Mosleys' house," Tawatha said.

She tried to hide the irritation in her voice, but the night's events made it hard.

"Yes, ma'am."

Aunjanue headed to her room, grateful that tonight would be one spent away from babysitting, cooking, and cleaning. She didn't mind helping out with her siblings, but she felt Tawatha was taking her presence for granted more and more. She could count on both hands and feet the number of girls at school who experimented with sex, talked back to their parents, or had been sent to alternative schools throughout the city because they'd gotten pregnant. Where was her reward for being diligent, for forgoing the things girls her age did? She wasn't sure how to broach the subject with Tawatha, but when she returned on Sunday, she would ask Tawatha about the possibility of having a closer relationship with her biological father. Was he married now? Did he have other children?

Spending time at the Mosleys' home had begun taking its toll on her psyche.

Tarsha's father, Jayson, came home like clockwork from his job at Merck each night. Aunjanue witnessed him walk through the door, give Tarsha's mother a kiss, ask her about her day, and sit down to dinner all ready on the table for him. Sometimes their conversations were about the news or other mundane details; other times he rooted for his wife in regard to her decorating business. Aunjanue had always heard marriage wasn't easy, but theirs was the one union that made her reconsider her stance to never jump the broom. At least that's what they were doing on a photo in the living room.

Aunjanue rifled through her closet in preparation for the weekend. The Mosleys had planned a packed weekend for her, Tarsha,

Johanna Patino, Jennifer Wilson, and Carmen Lawrence. Their reward for having all A's on their report cards was a slumber party, breakfast at LePeep on Saturday morning followed by full spa services at Divas in Training. Mrs. Mosley planned a backyard barbecue after the spa visit. The weekend would end with church on Sunday and a visit later that evening to Caribbean Cove. The most Tawatha gave Aunjanue for getting good grades was a weak "I'm proud of you, baby" or "Keep up the good work."

Aunjanue was smitten by the Mosleys; they were her first couple crush. She looked at them and wondered if her brothers and sister would be happier, have more opportunities if they had a man like Jayson around. She even loved Jayson's corny sayings. Like the time he put a spin on a familiar phrase by saying, "When life gives you eggs, you'd better make a darn good omelet. Just make sure the chickens are free range, though."

S'n'c'r'ty sat on the bed as Aunjanue packed her clothes.

"What are you doing in here, lil' bit?"

"I came to help you pack. Plus, Momma's got a funky attitude. What's she crying about?"

Aunjanue packed jeans and two blouses in her suitcase. "I don't know. Just stay out of her way while I'm gone, okay."

"Can I help you pack?"

"*May* I help you pack? I know you remember that."

"May I help you?"

"Look in my top drawer and get my travel bag. I have my toothpaste, toothbrush, and deodorant in it. The pink one."

S'n'c'r'ty bounced off the bed and retrieved the bag. She gingerly placed it in Aunjanue's suitcase and hugged her from behind. She peered over into the suitcase, and exclaimed, "I'm telling Momma you've got a grown-lady gown."

"What are you talking about?"

S'n'c'r'ty lifted the pink Candies baby doll nightgown and match-ing panties and twirled like a ballerina.

"That's one of the sets Auntie Sheer bought me. Actually, Auntie Sheer and her boss, Miss Aruba, bought me some clothes and lingerie from Victoria's Secret. They said a growing girl needs feminine underwear. They really bought me some nice things."

"I hope someone buys me some nice things like that when I get bigger."

"I'll buy you nice things when you get bigger. I plan on finding a part-time job in three years. I can't work until I'm sixteen."

Aunjanue recognized S'n'c'r'ty's ploy. Whenever she had some-where to go, S'n'c'r'ty made idle chitchat, hoping to keep her home. As much as she enjoyed her sister's company, she was ready to breathe, laugh, giggle with the girls, catch up on gossip, and for a brief time, settle in to normalcy with a real family.

"Zip up my suitcase for me, lil' bit."

S'n'c'r'ty obliged. They gathered Aunjanue's suitcase, setting it by the front door. The television blared gospel programming, but it was obvious Tawatha was in another galaxy. She stared past the TV, her dejected expression not lost on the girls.

"Let's check on Sims and Grant."

Aunjanue peeked in on the boys, both in a serious Xbox battle. "Don't forget to—"

"Take out the trash and clean the tub," Grant called over his shoulders.

"And I'm supposed to do waffles and bacon in the morning. I remember," said Sims.

"Stay out of Momma's way, okay, Grant and Sims." She waited for a response from them. "I can't get a hug before I leave?" she asked.

They threw down their joysticks, gave her a quick hug, and mumbled, "I love you," before getting back to their game. S'n'c'r'ty trailed her back to the living room.

"Momma, I'm leaving now."

Aunjanue sat next to Tawatha, hoping to get her attention.

"Don't go down to the Mosleys acting crazy. Do what they tell you to do and mind your business, okay."

Her words were distant. She stared at the charismatic preacher on the screen, speaking more to him than Aunjanue. Aunjanue kissed Tawatha's cheek, hugged S'n'c'r'ty, then dragged her roll-away suitcase out the door. She couldn't wait to spend time with the girls.

[40]
Let's Help Her Together

Sims had almost forgotten the soccer application. Coach Ford reminded him twice to make sure his mother filled out the paperwork and supplied the registration fee. Now was a good time to approach her for the money. He'd rehearsed his speech several times, remembering to impart the importance of sports as a means of socialization. That's what Coach Ford swore by when he encouraged the boys to participate in soccer. Sims thought of Aunjanue's words, to leave Tawatha alone because she was in one of her moods. He needed the money, needed his classmates to know he was just as worthy as they were to participate in fun and games. He'd approach Tawatha boldly with the application because soccer was the first thing that stirred his passion. Not only was it fulfilling, but Coach Ford beamed when he made a goal or gave it his all. As he stepped from his bedroom, Sims thought he heard someone call his name. He shook off the notion, attributed it to playing Xbox too long.

"Sims, come here!" demanded the whisper.

Sims looked around the corner and saw S'n'c'r'ty peeking through her bedroom door. She beckoned him in a come-here-or-else motion.

"What is it?" he asked, matching his sister's low tone.

"It's Momma," S'n'c'r'ty said as she pulled Sims into her bedroom. "She's acting funny and she's scaring me. She's in her room talking to herself and cutting up stuff. What are we going to do?"

Sims wished Aunjanue hadn't gone to the Mosleys. They needed her. They couldn't handle Tawatha like Aunjanue could. "Let's call down to the Mosleys. Onnie can tell us what to do."

"You know she said not to disturb her. I don't want her mad at me, Sims."

Sims held S'n'c'r'ty's hand. They crept downstairs to Tawatha's main-floor bedroom. Her door was cracked. A wedding gown, silk flowers, and wedding invitations were sliced and shredded by a large pair of scissors Tawatha wielded. She sat on the floor, hair disheveled, her left breast spilling from the Victoria's Secret teddy she'd purchased for the honeymoon. Tears streamed down her face.

"What will it take for me to find a good man? What do I keep doing wrong? Even a crackhead like Sheer can find a good man," Tawatha said to the ruin around her. "I'm sick of this shit! Sick of it!"

"Sims, do something! Momma's gonna cut herself." S'n'c'r'ty held Sims's leg. She stifled the urge to pee, knowing if she did, Aunjanue would make her clean the spot up herself and shampoo the carpet.

"Go upstairs and get Grant. We can talk to Momma together."

S'n'c'r'ty trudged up the stairs, feeling abandoned by her big sister. Aunjanue felt more like her mother than Tawatha. They couldn't call Grandma Bert because Mr. J.B. had taken her on an Alaskan cruise. They were always doing things together. Maybe the man her mother wished for would be good to her like Mr. J.B. was to Grandma Bert. Or good to her like Auntie Sheer's new boyfriend, Mr. Lake. S'n'c'r'ty snuck in her room to call Aunjanue. Maybe Grandma Bert would buy her a cell phone when she turned thirteen just like the one she'd bought Aunjanue.

She dialed Aunjanue and was disappointed that her phone went straight to voicemail. When prompted to leave a message, S'n'c'r'ty said, "Onnie, Momma's not doing too good. She has scissors and I think she's gonna hurt somebody. Call us when you get a minute. I can't wait 'til you come back home. I love you."

Sims and S'n'c'r'ty approached Grant. "Grant, we need you. Come downstairs with us," S'n'c'r'ty said, prying Grant from his game. They went downstairs and stood outside their mother's door.

"On the count of three we'll go in together and try to help," said Sims. He tried imitating Aunjanue's bossiness, but he knew he fell short as Grant and S'n'c'r'ty froze. S'n'c'r'ty's eyes filled with fresh tears. "You gotta be a big girl, lil' bit. Isn't that what Onnie tells you?"

"Yes," she said as she nodded and wiped her face.

They counted in unison. "One, two, three." Sims opened the door, startling Tawatha.

"What the hell do you want?" Tawatha hissed. She was in no mood to be bothered. Aunjanue had cooked dinner before leaving, so she wasn't sure why they felt the need to approach her.

Sims took the lead. "You were crying and we were worried about you. You're gonna cut yourself, Momma. Let me take these scissors back to the kitchen and put them with the knives in the cutlery set."

"Get the hell away from me! All of you are nothing but a bunch of selfish bastards and I can't stand the sight of you!"

S'n'c'r'ty burst into tears. She hated to hear anyone curse, but profanity hurled at her felt like shards of glass ripping through her insides.

Tawatha stood. "What the fuck are you crying about? First of all you come in here unannounced; now you're trying to force me to tell you what's wrong." She snatched S'n'c'r'ty's arm. "Why you bawling like a damn newborn? You're five years old. All of you go to the basement and don't come out 'til I tell you." She released S'n'c'r'ty, then slammed her door.

Without protest, they filed out the bedroom and went to the basement.

"Momma's gonna calm down and apologize later," Sims assured them. He held S'n'c'r'ty's hand, guiding her down the steps.

Sims instructed S'n'c'r'ty to pick out a movie as he plopped a bag of popcorn in the microwave. They'd wait it out like they always did. They'd wait until the monster inside their mother fled.

Tawatha stood, surveyed the sliced invitations, wedding gown, and gifts she'd purchased for James. This was the last time she'd allow herself to be taken. How many times had she believed the words of some sexy man telling her how fine she was, how much he wanted to be with her. All that talk with no action had gotten the best of her. She looked in the mirror at her tear-streaked face, the smeared makeup that gave her a clown-like appearance. She swiped Kleenex from a box on her dresser and wiped her face.

"No more. This will never happen to me again."

Tawatha threw on a pair of sweats, trekked to the kitchen for the huge garbage can, then returned to her room.

"Muthafucka never had any intention of leaving his wife," she said, tossing the gown and wedding remnants in the trash. Still, his hold on her was so strong. *I can't live without that man.* "I'm gonna be with James Dixon if it's the last thing I do."

Her intent was to return the can to the garage, to take a walk, clear her head. The kids' laughter rose from the basement, irritating her all the more. "Shut up! I don't wanna hear that noise tonight!"

Day in, day out, they were always asking for something. Needing something. Lately, she'd wondered what life would have been like if she'd never had them. Doctors' visits. Homework. Field trips. "Momma, help me do this." "Momma, do that." She rued the day she made the first child and hated that she didn't have sense enough to stop having babies. The kids laughed again. Tawatha went to the garage, found the mower gasoline can, snatched the keys from the key holder, and rifled through them until she found the basement door key. She locked the door, positive this was the only way to start anew. She poured gasoline throughout the living room, kitchen, and garage.

"A man will find me attractive without the burden of these fucking kids," she reasoned, pouring more gasoline just outside the area near the basement door. "Shouldn't have laid down that many times anyway."

Tawatha gathered a few personal items, matches, and the grade-school photo of her nestled between Jamilah and Lasheera. She held her breath, overpowered by the gasoline fumes. She walked out the front door, removed the matches from her pocket, and tossed a match into the living room, quickly shutting the front door. She wandered into the neighborhood, talking to herself, thinking how proud James would be that she'd gotten rid of the hindrance keeping them apart.

"You smell that?" Sims asked.

"Something's burning!" Grant shouted.

S'n'c'r'ty walked up the stairs, pulled on the door, and jerked her hand back from the heat. She retreated back down the stairs with her brothers. Sims picked up the phone, tried calling out, but couldn't get a dial tone. Aunjanue would know what to do. If he could just get her on the phone.

"Let's break out the window," said Sims.

"We can't. The burglar bars'll block us," said Grant.

Smoke filled the basement, overpowering them. S'n'c'r'ty remembered the game she played with Aunjanue when they hid from the boogeyman. She still heard Sims's and Grant's voices. "Let's crawl in the corner. Somebody's gonna get us. Aunjanue always promised someone would get us from the boogeyman." S'n'c'r'ty coughed the words out, praying Aunjanue would get the message she'd left earlier.

[41]
Ashes to Ashes, Dust to Dust

Johnny did his best to console Roberta, to tell her that it wasn't her fault the house burned down. "It's just a house, love," he said, guiding her into the limousine that waited outside her home. "I'm here for you and I'm not leaving you or Onnie."

All week long she'd been apologizing, replaying the past month in her mind, wondering what she could have done differently to help Tawatha. Aunjanue squeezed in next to her grandmother, Lasheera, and Jamilah. She wanted to protect her grandmother, to shield her from the nasty things that had been said the past week about Tawatha, about her, about their circumstances.

"Grandma Bert, we'll be okay."

Johnny slid in the car as well. Behind them, cars lined up and followed suit to New Beginnings Fellowship Church. The what-ifs rattled around in each one's head, neither drawing any conclusions.

What if I'd been a better friend and taken the keys? What if I'd just cancelled my date with Lake, pulled Tawatha aside for good old-fashioned girl talk, then took her home and sobered her up? What if I'd insisted she break things off with James when we were walking at the mall?

What if I'd told J.B. the Alaskan cruise could wait?

What if I'd answered S'n'c'r'ty's call instead of polishing my nails and toes and giggling about some random boys?

What if I'd visited Indy more instead of staying in Bloomington?

Roberta broke the strings of what-ifs with, "Is there enough room in the church for all these people?" She'd turned to see the funeral procession behind her and wondered how many people were genuinely concerned, or mere spectators, trying to get the goods on the event.

Roberta and Aunjanue were overwhelmed by the love showered on them by the City of Indianapolis. They'd both experienced a whirlwind week since the fire. Calls, visits, food, and prayers became the backdrop of their mourning. They planned the funeral together, picking out key elements that would make the homegoing one the children would be proud of. At Aunjanue's request, the remains of Sims, Grant, and S'n'c'r'ty were cremated and placed in a single urn. It was only fair that they'd rest in peace as they'd all lived and grown—together.

Roberta didn't know the monster featured in the headlines and news captions: *Scorned Woman Kills Three Children*; *Affair Ends Tragically for Indianapolis Mother*; *Students Perish at Mother's Hands*. Roberta was always leery of the media; the stories about Tawatha confirmed her dislike for the news. Roberta asked that no cameras enter the sanctuary, but if they wanted, they could film the procession. Stations near and far had contacted Roberta for an interview regarding the fire. She released a statement to CNN when asked if she felt she'd failed Tawatha as a mother:

"We, the Gipson Family, ask for your thoughts, prayers, and privacy during this very difficult time. I have lost a daughter to the correctional system, but my granddaughter is motherless and will never be able to see her siblings again. Please reach out to those dear to you, to those you love or haven't seen in a long time. Express your feelings. Bless them with kindness. Give them a hug. You will honor us by doing so."

"There's plenty of room for everyone. I took care of catering for two hundred fifty people at the community center, and the sanctuary will hold the people," said Johnny. He rubbed her hands again in the reassuring manner that soothed her.

"Johnny, I wouldn't have made it through the—"

"Shhhh, sweets. Just relax, baby," said Johnny, placing a finger over Roberta's lips. "There's nothing to make up. We'll have this discussion later."

"Onnie, how you holding up?" asked Lasheera.

"I don't know. I cry sometimes, then I laugh. I keep thinking of S'n'c'r'ty begging me to stay home with her. I feel like it's my fault."

"Don't blame yourself. Your mom's emotions were out of control. It's not your fault. There was nothing any of us could have done to stop her." Lasheera embraced Aunjanue, encouraged her to put her head on her shoulders.

The silence bothered Roberta. She took Ernest Pugh's *Live: Rain on Us* CD from her purse and passed it to the limo driver. "Track four, please."

With the choir as the backdrop, Roberta reflected on her grandchildren. How Sims's soccer obsession pleased her because he was growing tall and strong and needed physical activity. She thought of Grant's penchant for Oreos. S'n'c'r'ty as Aunjanue's shadow. She also thought of Tawatha. She knew she'd fall apart at the service if asked to speak, but she'd be strong for Aunjanue. When she tried practicing the tribute she'd written for the children, fresh tears fell at the realization she'd never see them again.

"Who are they?" asked Jamilah. She leaned forward and eyed the long row of people lining German Church Road. Dressed in white T-shirts with block CFC royal blue letters and jeans, they held up signs that said, *Our Prayers Are with You* and *We Love You, Aunjanue.*

"What is CFC?" asked Roberta.

Lasheera snapped her finger as she thought of last night's broadcast. "Citizens for Children. They're supporting the family at the funeral and trying to raise awareness about child abuse. The story has made national news, so lots of advocacy groups are speaking out."

"Anything else from Watha?" Jamilah asked Roberta.

"Well, I knew they wouldn't let her out, but she kept calling me about attending the funeral. The State of Indiana doesn't play with offenders. You have to practically be on work release, close to parole, or a model inmate to attend a funeral. Then you have to pay a fee. I feel for her, but what can I do?"

"I heard she's been beaten up twice and had to be put in isolation. I didn't know prisoners had limits to what they found offensive," said Lasheera.

"Yes, children are off-limits. I guess because they're so precious," said Roberta.

As they pulled into the church parking lot, the sickness within Roberta welled up again. The parking lot was packed from end to end, save the spaces reserved for the family.

"I can't do this," said Roberta.

"I'm here. I'll get you through this," said Johnny.

"Grandma Bert, I thought you said Momma couldn't come," said Aunjanue. She pointed to Tawatha standing near the front door.

"Honey, she can't—" Roberta paused.

She did a double-take at the four people standing at the entryway of the church. Shirley Gipson stood ramrod straight in a black three-piece suit, his hair slicked back and curly like she remembered it. He was as handsome as the day she'd met him thirty-one years ago, but his butterscotch skin was weathered, his countenance low. Next to him were the triplets—Connie, Candace, and Carson. She remembered them from the photos Carol showed her at the apartment. Candace was the spitting image of Tawatha. Same build, same beauty. The only difference was Candace's natural hairdo. Connie looked as if she'd stepped off a runway with a purple wrap dress, gold jewelry ensemble, and a head of bouncy curls. Carson was Shirley thirty-one years ago. She figured they were thirty-four now. *Nothing like a funeral to bring out strangers.*

"Onnie, that's not your mother. That's your aunt. Well, your aunts and uncle. The older man standing next to them is your grandfather. Shirley Gipson."

"A man named Shirley?"

"Yeah, baby, a man named Shirley."

The limo driver opened the door. Aunjanue exited the limousine first, clutching the urn that held her siblings' remains. She scanned the many faces watching her and spotted the Mosleys near the entryway. She motioned for Tarsha to join her. Slowly, with Tarsha's arm wrapped around her, she entered the sanctuary to say her last good-byes to Sims, Grant, and S'n'c'r'ty.

[42]
Midnight Train to Georgia

"**L**ook at my gorgeous niece!" Marguerite squealed. She hugged Victoria and planted light kisses on Nicolette's face. "It's about time you all got here. I was wondering if some terrorists had high-jacked you for all that money you got in the divorce settlement."

Victoria shook her head and held on to the laughter welling up inside her. Victoria knew that fuchsia top anywhere. Missing were the fuchsia bell bottoms with fringe lining both sides. At least Marguerite wore skinny jeans and stilettos with the top. She must have been reflecting on the good old days. The fuchsia outfit was a throwback to the Isley Brothers 1993 concert. Marguerite wore the outfit at the end of the show as Ronald Isley belted out, "Fight the Power." Victoria stood backstage as "Petite Marguerite" whirled around to the drum beat, shimmying her hips to the rhythm, gyrating on Ernie as he played the guitar. She wasn't tall enough to be that lady during the "Who's That Lady" vignette, but Marguerite brought the house down with her show girl moves.

"*Time is truly wastin', there's no guarantee, smile's in the makin', we gotta fight the powers that be,*" sang Victoria, remembering the simpler times with her aunt.

"After all these years, you remembered. You know I was the baddest chick on the tour, hands down."

"Hey, since you're playing hostess, I'll go along with anything you say."

"Since you're curious about the settlement, here's the scoop. If I learned anything from Winston, it was how to hide money," joked Victoria.

"Y'all can't hide money like I can."

"What's with this, 'y'all'? Soon it's gonna be 'honey chile.' Then shut your rubber lips. I know you're not letting the South get into you, Marguerite Mason."

Victoria loved the hustle and bustle of Jackson-Hartsfield Airport. She was exhausted from the divorce proceedings and felt awash in relief when Marguerite suggested she relocate to Atlanta. Indiana had taken its toll on her, and the thought of running into Aruba, or Aruba with Winston, sickened her. As she watched the carousel of luggage, she looked down at Nicolette and wondered how she'd raise her child alone.

"Did you hear me, Tori? Do you want to eat now or later?"

"I'm starving. I could eat a horse and two pigs right now."

"Mommy, I'm hungry, too," said Nicolette.

"Let's slide into Blues and Brews, so we can catch up. I've got so much to talk to you about. Don't forget, we're due in Riverdale at Annie Laura's at four this afternoon."

"That's right. To meet Momma. Have we found a caretaker for her yet?"

"You know my sister Lillith isn't going down without a fight. Or a fifth of gin. She swears the doctors are wrong and she doesn't need anyone to help her. She still has partial paralysis on her right side. All we'll need is a personal care aide to come in and bathe her, feed her, and massage her right side. She's not hearing it. Can you believe she's pretending the slight twist in her mouth from the stroke is due to a Botox procedure gone wrong?"

"Of course I can. Momma was always vain. And dependent on the love of a man. You know that runs in our family."

"Tell me again what that grimy-ass nephew of mine did to you. I can still put a hit out on him if necessary. I know low people in high places."

Marguerite held her hand to stop Victoria from speaking and motioned to the waitress. She didn't want to miss a tidbit about the breakup. Never mind that they were her superstar role models. It was rare to see a man genuinely interested in taking care of his family, loving his wife, and sacrificing the way Winston did. She couldn't imagine how another woman took him away.

"I'll have the beef brisket sandwich," Marguerite said to the waitress.

"I'll have the pulled pork barbecue sandwich, coleslaw, fries, and sweet tea. I'd also like a hot dog, fries, and Coke for my daughter."

"Whoa, did you just order meat? Pork? The almighty pig? The South may have gotten into me, but what's gotten into you, 'Miss I've Gotta Watch my Figure'?"

"Little pitchers have big ears, so I'll tell you later."

"Back to the grime. I mean, Winston. You've been tight-lipped for seven months. What gives?"

"Well, my saving grace was a pre-nup with an infidelity clause. Winston didn't have a fighting chance with the evidence I'd gathered on him. I got property and money, but I still don't get the twisted way he funded his lover's husband's salon."

"I can believe that because Winston was always a generous man. What happened between you two?"

"Let's just say I let my lips talk my husband out of my life."

"So you're telling me you violated the carnal rule I taught you as a child? That women are to be tolerated, not trusted?"

"I didn't agree with you then, and I don't agree with you now.

Experience is a rough teacher. You get the test first and the lesson later. What you *should have* taught me was the importance of genuineness. To have a friend, you have to be a friend, and I admit I wasn't a very good friend to Aruba."

"Bullshit. Don't you sit here and blame yourself for that sneaky tramp walking away with your *good* husband." Marguerite pursed her lips.

"Don't say 'bullshit,' Aunt Marguerite," said Nicolette, blushing. "Daddy said people curse when they have a limited vocabulary and can't express themselves."

"Grownups are talking. Don't interrupt, Nicolette. Get your crossword puzzles out of your bag." Victoria looked at Marguerite and said through clenched teeth, "I told you little pitchers have big ears."

"I'm sorry. It's just…I admired you guys so much."

"At my last court date, a memory came back. Do you remember when Momma and Daddy were still married?"

"I do. But I know you don't. You were so young."

"That's the thing. Court triggered a memory for me. I remembered the new anniversary ring Daddy bought Momma for the B.B. King concert. She was so happy to get that ring. He worked so hard to keep her and he wanted to make her happy. They were going to Chicago to the show, and Momma bragged that whole week to Miss Julie Adams about Daddy buying her the ring. "Leland did this, and Leland did that. Don't you wish Hank could…" She knew Miss Julie and her husband were struggling, but every chance she got, she threw up in her face what Daddy did for her. She sounded like a yapping dog."

"Lillith did that?"

"Sure did. Remember what happened that Thursday?"

"Family lore, girl. Lillith walked in on Miss Julie and Leland in the bedroom making love. Miss Julie was standing up near the window, wearing Momma's ring since it was to be cleaned that day. Miss Julie giving it to Leland like that was her last rodeo ride."

Marguerite mused over Victoria's words. "Are you telling me you deliberately tortured another woman with your blessings?"

"Guilty. I didn't even realize I was doing it until it was too late."

The food arrived. Marguerite, normally chatty and full of sage wisdom, ate in silence. What was wrong with the women in their family? Even her mother had issues maintaining friendships with women. One minute, she'd fall in with a new crew of ladies. Then someone would say something to offend her, and she'd stew and withdraw herself from the ladies. Lillith and Marguerite listened to their mother rant about how untrustworthy and catty women were. They never heard her say negative things about men, though. After their father died, their mother, Tessa Mason, flitted around men, laughing, flirting, trying to upgrade her widow status. Maybe their bloodline was the problem. Marguerite was tired of being reserved around women. She craved fellowship, laughter, the kind she saw in her old neighborhood in L.A. and on television. Atlanta had opened up new possibilities and challenged her old way of thinking.

"If you had to pinpoint a specific cause of your breakup, what would it be?"

"Chronic bellyaching. That and no sex."

"Don't tell me you shut the garage down!"

"Winston was so sweet and accommodating. I thought he'd always be there while I did what I wanted. I claimed to have more headaches than Tylenol could cure, but the real issue was punishment. I resented him so much for being away from home. I thought if I punished him for working, he'd give in and cut back some."

"Tori, a man that successful *has* to put in work. For chrissake,

Winston's visibility and solid work ethic made the life you lived possible. He was so modest about his abilities. You don't find that every day."

"I know that now."

"Mommy, is Daddy coming to Atlanta to see us?"

"I'm sure he will, sweetheart."

"I miss him so much."

"How much?" asked Victoria.

Nicolette opened her arms wide, smiling as she did so.

"He'll visit us soon. I promise. One thing about your daddy is that he keeps his word."

Marguerite gave Victoria the thumbs-up. Of all the advice she'd given her over the years, she still believed a wife shouldn't bad-mouth her husband in front of his children. She was proud Victoria didn't take the opportunity to bash Winston in Nicolette's presence.

"Do you think Momma is ready to see me? It's been so long. I hope she's open to reuniting. After all, she's got a beautiful grand-daughter to spoil."

"Of all the things Lillith regrets is never having a stable marriage after Leland died. Your father was the closest thing she had to stability. She couldn't bring herself to forgive him for his indis-cretion with Julie. He was so remorseful, but that stout-hearted sister of mine told him where to get off."

"I know. I still believe he died of a broken heart. He loved her so much."

"She lived vicariously through you and Winston. She was so proud of you for having married a successful man."

"Guess I messed that up, huh?"

"Just take to heart the lesson, so you won't repeat the same thing twice."

"Twice? Oh no, I'm never getting married again."

"Eat your food, Halle Berry. We have to get to Lillith before she accuses us of neglecting her."

"Enough about my sad little soap opera. California was your life, Marguerite. Why Atlanta?"

"Pick a reason. High property taxes. Decreasing property values. Cost of living. Earthquakes. Plastic women. Plastic men. I'd just had enough. I sold my theater arts school and decided to give Atlanta a shot. Everybody in the business is moving here and it's cheaper. I paid four hundred thousand for my mini-mansion in Alpharetta. I couldn't have gotten that in Cali for less than one point seven million."

"Things really changed since we were there. I'm not in the market for buying a home. Sounds promising here, though."

Marguerite exhaled. "Well, that and this." Marguerite extended her left hand to Victoria, flicking her princess-cut diamond ring back and forth. "I got engaged to Foster Richardson two months ago."

"You dog! Why didn't you tell me?"

"Honey, you were going through what looked like the makings of your own reality series pilot. I didn't want to flaunt it."

"It's possible to go through turmoil and still wish the best for someone else."

"Girl, that divorce has growed you up!"

Victoria playfully punched Marguerite's arm. "See, the South is getting into you. Tell me about Mr. Richardson, or should I call him Uncle Foster."

Marguerite flashed a schoolgirl-crush smile. "He's a youth pastor at a small congregation in Decatur. By day he works at Lithonia Lighting as a supervisor, and he's such a natural with children. He was visiting his sister in L.A. and was a potential buyer for my school. He invited me out for dinner, then an art show, and one thing led to another. We've been together over a year-and-a-half.

"I've spent so much time keeping people at bay. I woke up three years ago at the age of forty and decided we'd been passed on a bunch of crap in our family. I want to love and be loved. And I'm tired of wearing this forty-two-percenter tiara."

"'Forty-two-percenter tiara'?"

"Like you don't know that forty-two percent of black women will never get married. You really were sheltered, weren't you? It's rough out here. I'm just glad I met Foster. He found me; I didn't go looking for him."

"I'm so happy for you. That's the best news I've heard in a long time."

Victoria swigged the last of her tea. Thought about the magnitude of dating again. Thought of how ugly the last days of her marriage were. She heard Lillith's words: "You can't break the chains of love, but the links can come loose." *I loosened a damn good thing.*

[43]
Taking My Time

Shandy Fulton was crushed. She'd taken it slow. Kept things professional. She only talked shop with James each time she visited Dixon's Hair Affair. As owner of the salon supply business, Fulton and Company, she hoped James would be the kind of man with whom she could build a beauty supply dynasty. In less than a month, he had purchased two dryer chairs, a pedicure chair, and a facial and massage bed. Usually men threw themselves at her, asking for her number, offering to take her out. James Dixon was a tough nut to crack. After he signed the checks for his equipment, he was back on his cell phone talking to customers or vendors. Where was he when he wasn't in his office crunching numbers and running his fingers through that curly hair of his? Did he play basketball with his boys? Or was he a workaholic that needed her special touch to help him unwind? When she asked around about his status, the most she'd get was, "He's off the market." No one explained what "off the market" meant, but she hoped she'd find out tonight. That's why she waited outside the salon until he finished his last customer. She took care to look extra special tonight, treating herself to a manicure, pedicure, and magic mud facial. She selected a free-flowing dress that accented her slender frame. She ditched her normal cream-colored attire in favor of something red. Red said confidence. She wanted to radiate confidence in his presence tonight.

Shandy watched from her car as James removed the decorative smock from his last client, took her payment, and made light conversation. She walked toward the door as the young lady stopped to peruse the wall of beauty supply products. She waltzed into the shop before her confidence waned.

"Miss, I'm done for the night." James did a double-take and recognized her. "Shandy, I knew you'd come back. I just thought it would be next week."

"Back?"

"You're a workaholic, too, right? You're so busy, you forgot you left your appointment book and some orders. I thought I had your number stored in my cell, but I don't. I planned to call you, but I was swamped today." James went to his office, retrieved her items, and handed them over. "You flew outta here yesterday like your house was on fire."

"I had to meet with a warehouse rep. I'm all about the business."

"I'm locking up before someone else tries to sneak in."

James locked the door and offered Shandy a seat. She looked stunning in red and he wanted to tell her. He wanted to tell her how much he admired her work ethic, her drive, and commitment to growing Fulton and Company. Lately, he was deadlocked when it came to women. Dixon's Hair Affair became the go-to beauty shop overnight. It was nothing for women to slip him their numbers, invite him out for a drink and more. Shandy never approached him in a seductive manner. She came to the shop in uniform most days. He thought it odd that a business owner with an expansive client base would still make cold calls to shops. Shandy told him the way to grow a business was hands-on involvement. She wanted to be the face of Fulton and Company and networked whenever the opportunity presented itself. She was different than any other woman he'd met, including Aruba.

The death of Tawatha's children and the divorce had taken its toll on James. He withdrew himself from the dating world altogether. Unbeknownst to her, Shandy planted a grow-the-business seed in his head as he launched an aggressive marketing campaign. In seven months since he'd met Shandy, he'd drummed up more business than he could handle. His biggest regret was that Aruba didn't enjoy the fruits of his labor, the realization of his goals. He looked at Shandy now, surprised that he was attracted to her. She was the opposite of everything that turned him on about women. He liked thick, voluptuous women; Shandy was at least six-one, thin, but had enough meat on her bones to know she was a sista. He liked his berries dark brown to deep chocolate. Shandy was golden and glowing. She was quick to smile, slow to get frustrated when she negotiated prices. Still, he'd had enough of dealing with women. The break had allowed him to dig his heels into the salon and nix the negative things said of him over the years.

"I didn't realize I'd left my things here. I'm slipping fast in my old age. Thanks for keeping them for me."

"Old age. What are you? Twelve?"

"Plus fifteen. I'm an old twenty-seven. I'd love to retire by thirty-five."

"You're definitely on track with the way you work. By the way, if you didn't come for your things, why are you here?"

"Friday night is Shandy night. Kinda my way of unwinding from a long work week. I'm eating close to the shop and thought I'd stop by to see if you were pleased with the products I sold you last week. I'm still twisting your arm about the manicure station, so let's say I'm getting a jumpstart on the next twist."

"Me night, huh? I like the sound of that."

"It's good to spend time alone. No one bothering you or invading your privacy."

"What does your man think of that concept?"

"If I *had* one, he'd probably be disappointed. Or swear I was out cheating. I value being alone because I get in touch with myself. I meditate, do yoga, and treat my body as a temple. I gave up meat about five years ago. Since you're curious about my status, there are too many men playing games, so I'm single and satisfied."

"Good for you. You seem like a nice young lady. You deserve someone who'll be good to you."

"Since you're all up in my peach nectar, what's James Dixon's status?"

"I'm newly divorced and have a five-year-old son named Jeremiah. He means the world to me."

"I didn't realize you were divorced. I've been told divorce is like death." Shandy paused, hoping he'd divulge what happened to the union.

"It is. A lot of things die and you lose things you didn't realize you had."

"I know how private I am, so I'll change the subject. We don't know each other well enough to discuss such things."

She did it again. Why didn't other women who crossed his path take the hint and accept some subjects were off-limits? Shandy's stock was rising more and more by the minute. He had to get her out of the shop before he followed her to dinner.

"My dinner reservation is good 'til nine. I've got to get going. Thanks for keeping my things." Shandy stood to leave. "By the way, call me Shan. You started out with Miss Fulton, then Shandy. Everyone, family and associates, calls me Shan."

"Shan, have a nice evening."

James watched Shandy drive away in a Toyota Prius Hybrid. He knew the type of car she drove because she went on and on about emissions and protecting the environment. He loved how natural she was. Someday, when the time was right, he wanted to find someone like Shandy to rebuild his life.

James checked the last of the bills, counted the night's till and prepared the bank deposit slip, taking care to place the bills in order by denomination. Another Shandyism. She swore that money grew when you honored it. Just as he locked the safe containing the shop's money bag, he saw the letter. He should have thrown it away, but it served as a reminder of why his life was in shambles. He turned it over and saw her name in the upper left-hand corner. The letter had arrived at the house a month after her incarceration. Tawatha, housed at the Indiana Women's Prison, awaited sentencing for the murder of her children. He hoped her time away from others would provide some semblance of mental stability, but she seemed worse. His saving grace was only he, Aruba, Lasheera, and Roberta knew he was the reason she had killed the children. When prodded by the media as to why she did it, she said it was for Magic. He opened it, read the words again:

Dear James:

I tried to give you a little time to come visit me. I put you on the visitor's list at the facility and hope to see you soon. I miss you and love you now more than ever. I think back on the night at your shop and I apologize for barging in like I did. I understand that you lied to me because you needed more time to break things off with your wife. I guess saying she had cancer was the best way for you to work things out. I should have been more patient. I dream about you every night. About the love we made. The time we spent together. All the plans we had together. I pray you know I did what I did for you. For us. I don't think you liked the idea of me having different children by different men. They are no longer in our way.

S'n'c'r'ty came to me in a dream and said she forgives me. Grant and Sims don't talk to me, though. I want to take this time to apologize to you as well. Actually, you and Lasheera. The night I went to your wife's party, I wanted so badly to share my secret with Sheer. Or you. I know you were as weak for me as I was for you about two weeks before the party. The night you stopped by to tell me to stop calling and texting. We wound up making love like never before. I didn't really tie my tubes. I actually was taking Depo-Provera, but stopped it shortly after I met you. You deserve a daughter, and I'm giving you one the first of next year. I plan to name her Jameshia Dixon. I know she'll have your eyes, your curly hair, your devilish grin. I want Aunjanue to embrace her, but my mother won't allow her to visit me. Please don't leave me or our child this way. I long to see you and have things the way they used to be. I love you.

With My Deepest Affection,
Mrs. Tawatha Dixon

James sealed the letter, grabbed the bank bag, and headed to Chase Bank. *Lips, hips, and fingertips have cost me the best thing that ever happened to me.*

[44]
The Real Housewife of L.A.

Aruba twiddled her thumbs, eavesdropped on diners, and sighed. Two hours had passed and Winston still hadn't arrived at Spago for their dinner reservation. She avoided firing off another text since he hadn't responded to the last three she'd sent. His late dinner arrival was a tiny infraction compared to the new life she enjoyed. *Sacrifice and a no-whining spirit will keep me living this fabulous life.* Aruba drained the last of her Napa Valley Cabernet Sauvignon from a sparkling flute and reflected on her life. The salon incident and the fire were the last straws in her decision to divorce James. She'd planned to move on with her life, but James's refusal to acknowledge Tawatha Gipson's craziness was an indication he'd lost *his* grip on reality. He compared his infidelity to her affair with Winston. He begged her to stay with him, to start anew, but she couldn't. *At least I didn't sleep with Winston.*

Bria was slowly coming around and attempting to forgive her. Bria's question rattled around in her brain again at Spago. "How can you sleep at night knowing you took your friend's husband?" *Very well on thousand thread-count sheets, thank you.* How could she explain to Bria how miserable she was in her marriage, how irresponsible James was during their union? Everyone didn't have a solid relationship like hers and Sidney's. Women like Bria annoyed her sometimes, throwing euphemisms and scriptures her way like snake oil as a form of inspiration. Sure, James was doing well with his business *now*, but look at all the years she supported him with nothing to show for it. Winston had elevated her status a hundred-fold, and she'd forever be grateful for all he'd done. She and Jeremiah were enjoying creature comforts she thought only certain women obtained.

His proposal came as a pleasant surprise five months ago. He stopped by to check on her two weeks before she tendered her letter of resignation at State Farm. In the midst of a conference call with a district manager, Winston released the call, pulled out a Harry Winston box, and proposed. The ink was barely dry on her decree, but she said yes, stifling the glee behind her closed office door and planting a passionate kiss on his lips. Aruba locked the door after he entered her office, lest Bria came charging in, giving her that judgmental look she'd perfected since the divorce was finalized. They both needed comfort after their respective divorces. Victoria received a $3 million settlement; James received the house and everything else Winston convinced her to sign over. He promised they'd start life fresh.

Fresh was an understatement. When he accepted a position at Cedars-Sinai, he told her she had to get in gear as Mrs. Faulk and make the transition from Indianapolis to Los Angeles a reality. Winston handed over his checkbook and told her not to break the Faulk bank. Aruba knew she wanted to settle in Beverly Hills. After a short search, she settled on a beautiful Georgian estate that sat on nine acres. The ivy-covered porch beckoned her when she visited the property with the realtor. The seven-bedroom home would be a challenge for Aruba to clean, even with a live-in nanny. She would seek out neighbors' help for a good cleaning team, landscaper, and decorator. The walnut floors, crown molding, and the privacy offered by the cul-de-sac were no match for what sold her on the property—the screening room that was once a guest-house. With only a month to pull things together, Aruba went into overdrive outfitting the property fit for a king, her king Winston. She was proudest of the one-of-a-kind pieces she acquired: crème chenille sofas reproduced from similar pieces in Coco Chanel's Paris apartment; a baby-grand piano from Liberace's estate; the Irish mahogany console and hand-blown glass chandelier once owned by Hattie McDaniel. She couldn't wait to invite Bria, Day-ton, Maxie, her mom and dad, and any other relatives willing to see how well she'd done for herself. She imagined parties near the pool house and all the children swimming in the lush pool recently refurbished in iridescent blue ceramic tile. She pictured Day and Maxie lounging in the sun and on the dark chocolate couches with monogrammed cushions and wicker tables on the upper deck of the pool house. She thought of children laughing and darting under the trellis covered with bougainvillea on the lower deck while she made lemonade, cookies, and sticky ribs. If Winston happened to arrive after three hours of doing what he needed to do, she wouldn't complain. Aruba perused the menu again, certain it was time to order for Winston. For starters, she'd order the sautéed Maryland crab cake for him, the endive and spring veg-etable salad for herself. She called a waiter over to the table, but felt relieved when Winston approached her with a nervous smile and outstretched arms. She stood to give him a passionate kiss, a promise of more to come for the night. He kissed her, but it felt restrained, guarded.

"Babe, I was so worried about you. Is everything okay?" To the waiter she said, "Please give us a few more minutes."

Aruba noticed Winston for the first time since his arrival. She grabbed a napkin from the table to wipe his forehead. He must have swung by the house before coming to Spago, but he didn't dress in a signature dapper suit as he'd done for past dinners. He was dressed down in a simple white cotton dress shirt, khakis, and shiny loafers. She recalled when he was married to Victoria, she called his current attire the get-ready-for-a-big-announcement out-fit. She took in a few breaths and interrupted his announcement.

"Babe, I got a little something for you today. You've been put-ting in long hours at Cedars and as much as Jeremiah and I miss you, this token is just my way of saying how much we honor what you do. I love you."

Aruba slid the box toward Winston. He tinkered with the wrapping paper and opened it, hoping it wasn't another expen-sive trinket like the ones she'd been purchasing for him lately. He appreciated her devotion to him, her desire to please him, but he wanted her, not expensive toys.

"You shouldn't have done this, sweets. You're too good to me as it is."

Winston sighed when he opened the box and saw the Cartier fountain pen. "Can't be too stylish writing prescriptions?"

"Never."

"Baby, we have to talk. I was hit with news today that I have to share immediately. I'd rather this discussion be in our home."

"Winston, how serious we talking? My mouth is all ready for the steamed red snapper, Hong Kong style."

"I'll make it up to you. I promise."

As they left the restaurant, Aruba stymied the déjà vu feeling coursing through her veins. Winston was always loving and complimentary. Tonight he didn't notice the care she'd taken to dress in his favorite outfit. Nor did he say how beautiful she was, how his day was incomplete without her presence.

"Sweets, will you drive? I'm not up to it right now."

"Yes. Babe, you sure this has to wait 'til we get home? You're scaring me."

"Could you just do as I asked?" Winston snapped, snatching his arm from Aruba's embrace and quickening his pace to the valet. She tried keeping step with him, but she was no match for his swift footfalls. He handed the valet his ticket and looked away from Aruba. Once they entered the car, Aruba drove home quietly. Something had gone down at Cedars. How would she support him? What would she say? The last thing she wanted to do was react in a way characteristic of Victoria. She meant it when she told him she would be with him through thick and thin.

"Baby, I'm sorry I yelled at you. I'm not myself right now."

"Winston, it's okay. I knew it would be an adjustment relocating, getting used to your new job. I knew what I was signing up for when I married you. I'm with you always, Winston. I love you."

Winston had heard those words from Victoria years ago. When things were fresh and new in their marriage, Victoria made a point of massaging his feet each night with a homeopathic balm mixed with lavender, vanilla, and tea tree oil. She said it was whipped with love because she knew how hectic his long days and nights were. He remembered the early years, before Nicolette's arrival, when Victoria would wait up and quiz him about the day's events. She listened with wide-eyed intensity as he talked about his patients, his hopes, and his fears. Those and many memories from the good old days prompted him to share the news with Victoria first. She had been his rock and he felt stupid for allowing his ego to ignore the changes he caused in her. Her quiet support during the times he doubted himself meant everything to him. He had called her earlier in the day as soon as the double whammy hit him. He waited for her to release curses and say good riddance.

Instead, she had wept. She'd told him she would always love him and still wanted the best for him in spite of everything that had happened. Those words made him feel worse than he'd felt since the divorce. *Why didn't I try harder to make my marriage work?* After Nicolette's revelation in the cabin, Victoria refused to talk to him and filed for divorce immediately. The few times they'd spoken after the divorce were about Nicolette, Victoria's relocation, and the pending sale of their home. Only now did he realize he'd given up too soon.

"Are you still waiting until we get home to talk?" asked Aruba, bringing Winston back to the quiet ride home.

"Huh?"

"You look worn-out. Like you've seen a ghost."

Winston clenched and unclenched his fist. "Aruba, please. Let's get home first."

"I'm sorry for being so impatient. I'm concerned about your well-being. I know our marriage is new, but I need you to believe I'm here for you."

Hope you know what you're saying. "I know, sweets."

Aruba pulled into the garage, held Winston's hand, and waited for his cue.

"Inside or here, Winston?"

"I don't know if I can make it inside," said Winston. He held Aruba's face in his hands. "Bad or worse news first?"

"Bad."

"I've been hit with a malpractice suit. Lori Hunden's family is alleging I misdiagnosed her condition. She suffered a massive heart attack two months ago."

"The seventeen-year-old?"

"Yes. She was a patient of mine since she was eight. We attended the funeral, remember?"

"I'm sure it's a mistake. We can fight this case and win."

"Most malpractice suits don't make it to court. Families usually settle out of court. I pay a hefty price for malpractice insurance, but if they win, our finances will be hit."

"Trust me, things will be fine. We'll come out swinging and get the victory."

"What if you have to fight for me alone?"

"We're in this together, remember?"

"What if my Lou Gehrig's kicks in hard before the proceedings?"

Aruba thought she heard him say Lou Gehrig's, but he was mistaken. Prostate cancer, she could believe. Two of her uncles and a high school coach battled prostate cancer and won. But how could a man as vibrant and lively as Winston have been diagnosed with Lou Gehrig's? Lately, she'd seen news stories of mostly men and some women affected by the disease, but she couldn't imagine the beautiful man before her being ravaged by ALS. The disclosure left her speechless.

"Aruba, talk to me." Winston waited for Aruba to respond, but she continued to gaze in his eyes. "I was served with papers about the suit this morning. I wanted to call you once I received the news, but I had to let it sink in. Lori was like a member of the family. Victoria used to bake her cookies when she was younger. She even spent the night at our house a time or two. I decided to keep my doctor's appointment, and that's when I got the news."

"You couldn't call me?"

"I didn't know how to tell you. We just started on this journey, and you've been hit with some tremendous blows. You deserve better than this."

Aruba held his hands tighter. "What will this mean for us?"

"I'm so proud of the job you've done with the house. You stepped in and made the house spectacular. Sadly, we'll have to downsize.

I don't know that I'll need a significant amount of funds for the lawsuit, but we'll have to find a home that's handicap accessible for when my muscles weaken. Our current home is over ten-thousand square feet and that's a tad much."

Aruba gulped. She'd just completed designing the home of her dreams, and now it was being snatched from her.

"I'm still paying the mortgage on the Carmel house until it's sold. Victoria didn't want it anymore and I'll probably have to reduce the selling price to get it off my hands."

I didn't sign on for this. Aruba tried, but she couldn't hold back the tears. The struggles she had with James paled in comparison to what she faced now. How could she have been so greedy, so hasty?

"Let me hold you, Mrs. Faulk. It's going to be fine. Just trust me."

Aruba Aneece Faulk. In Winston's arms, the name had lost its luster.

About the Author

Stacy Campbell was born and raised in Sparta, Georgia, where she spent summers on her family's front porch listening to the animated tales of her older relatives. She lives with her family in Indianapolis, Indiana. *Dream Girl Awakened* is her first novel. You may visit the author on Facebook.

You may also email Stacy at georgiapeach2814@aol.com or visit her website at www.stacyloveswriting.com.

Reader Discussion Guide

1. What other avenues beyond infidelity should Aruba have explored to improve her marriage, or should she have sought a divorce?

2. Do you think Victoria made it easy for Aruba to pursue Winston?

3. Throughout the book, many characters expressed mistrust amongst other women. Why do you think this is the case?

4. Should Maxine have intervened at the cookout during her reading?

5. James was the husband women love to hate. Do you think Hinton and Conyers should have hired him given his sketchy work history? Do you think he would have crossed paths with Tawatha otherwise? What do you think about the turnaround he made?

6. Tawatha was all too happy to be with James at any cost. Could Lasheera and Jamilah have helped her, or was it impossible to talk any sense to her?

7. Which character did you relate to most?

8. What do you think the fallout of Tawatha's actions will be for Aunjanue in the future?

9. Do you think Aruba got what she deserved in the end?

Forgive Me

BY STACY CAMPBELL

COMING SOON FROM STREBOR BOOKS

[1]

Today is a good day to be released from prison, Tawatha thought. She gathered her duffle bag and wondered what was taking Royce so long to pick her up. She glanced backward at the Indiana Women's Prison, her home for the past five years. She would miss the few friends she'd made, the Wednesday evening Bible study sessions, and the exchanges amongst the others who were also confined because of bad love choices.

She still wasn't convinced about spirituality and all the things she'd learned behind bars, but she was sure of one thing: her girlfriend, Jamilah, pulled a ram out of a bush and set her free. Not only was she free, but she'd gained a certain measure of respect from the other prisoners. Even after killing three of her four children in a house fire.

"Tawatha," a voice called out behind her.

Tawatha turned to see Faithia Perkins, a trustee and mother of the group. She'd embraced Tawatha from the beginning of her stint and kept the wolves at bay after Tawatha's first beating by the other inmates.

"I almost missed you. CO Morris told me you were leaving. I hopped all the way from the infirmary just to say good-bye."

"I was hoping I'd see you," said Tawatha.

"I just wanted to give you a hug and tell you to keep your head up. I don't want to see you back in this place. You've got a second chance to get it right and I want you to make good on it."

I will not cry, I will not cry. Tawatha opened her arms and let Faithia's embrace soothe her. She would miss the earthy smell of Faithia's skin, the gentleness of her hands when she braided her hair, and all the long talks they'd had about Faithia's sentence. "I knew saying good-bye to you would be hard. That's why I snuck out."

"No matter what happens, you have to move on. Don't look back; move forward, Tawatha."

Before she could shed a tear, Royce's Mercedes appeared. He smiled when he saw her, then dimmed his wattage at the sight of Faithia. He pulled alongside the curb.

Faithia watched the handsome, salt-and-pepper-haired gentleman alight from the stylish car. Tawatha had mentioned her former boss would pick her up, but from the look in his eyes, Faithia picked up on more than an employee/employer vibe.

"Mr. Hinton, I'm so happy you're here," said Tawatha. "This is Ms. Faithia Perkins, prison trustee and the only reason I survived in this place."

Royce folded his arms, raised an eyebrow, and gave Tawatha a look.

"*Royce*, this is Ms. Faithia Perkins," Tawatha corrected her formal introduction of Royce's name.

"That's better," said Royce, extending his hand to Faithia.

"I trust you'll take good care of Tawatha. She's special to me. She's come to be like a second daughter."

"I plan to take the very best care of her," said Royce. He took Tawatha's bag, popped the trunk, and placed it among the surprises he'd planted for her. He opened the passenger door and Tawatha eased into the seat, unsure of where they were heading.

She waved to Faithia one last time and looked ahead as Royce drove away from the prison. There was no need to look back. Only forward.

"So where are we going?" asked Tawatha.

"Well, I figured you'd want to take a shower and perhaps go out to dinner. I remember you loved Olive Garden. I just want you to unwind tonight."

"Did my mother return your calls?"

"She did." Royce sighed. "She said she's not ready to welcome you into her home right now, and asked that you give her some time."

Tawatha's countenance deflated. "So where am I supposed to go? She didn't write me in prison and the few times she came to see, me she just stared at me like I was a monster."

"Calm down. I anticipated this before I picked you up."

"What about Lasheera?"

"Ditto. Since Lasheera and Lake adopted Aunjanue, they feel your presence will disrupt her life. This is Aunjanue's senior year, and well…" Royce's voice trailed off.

Tawatha sat back in her seat, unable to hide her hurt. She almost wanted him to turn the car around and take her back to prison. What kind of life would she have if the people she loved treated her like she didn't exist? Jamilah was the only crew member who still communicated with her and had her back. To everyone else, she was a child-murdering ogress who should have been given the death penalty.

"Is that okay with you?" Royce asked, interrupting her thoughts.

"What did you say?" she asked.

"I asked if you'd be all right staying at my place for a while. You won't actually be staying with me. There's a carriage house in back of my property and you're welcome to live there 'til you get back on your feet."

"What about Millicent?"

"Millie and I have been divorced for about two years now. After our daughter died, things never were the same between us. I filed. I don't think she wanted to admit we were through."

"I wish you'd told me that. Ms. Millicent was always nice to me when she came by the office. I envied your relationship. How long were you married?"

"Thirty-four years."

"That's a lifetime."

Royce drove past the main dwelling to the carriage house. His in-laws had passed on four years ago, leaving the house lifeless.

"Royce, this place is beautiful. Are you sure it's okay for me to stay?"

"Last time I checked, my name was on the deed to both places. Come on inside."

Royce removed her bag and gifts from the trunk. He gave her a set of keys to the house and stepped just inside the living room, giving her time and space to take in her surroundings.

"Get some rest and call me if you want to go out later tonight."

"Royce, I'm speechless. If it takes me forever, I promise I'll make this up to you." She hugged him and counted the ways she'd show him just how much she appreciated his kindness.

[2]

"Baby, don't fidget. Let me get this tie straight," said Shandy.

"How many times do I have to tell you I can knot my own tie, Shan?" James joked and swatted Shandy's hand.

"And have us looking crazy at this banquet? No way."

"Oh, I'm representing *you*, now, huh?"

"Don't you forget it, either." Shandy kissed James on the lips, grateful for an evening on the town. Maybe this kiss would be a precursor to a night of passion that kept eluding them.

"Slow your roll, Ms. Fulton. We've got all night to be together," James chided.

I won't start with him tonight. I'll let things unfold. "So how long do you think this shindig will last? When Isaak gets worked up, he can't stop. Even Katrina can't make him be quiet."

"If my mentor wants to talk all night, let him. Sitting at his feet made me the success I am, so you won't hear any complaints from me."

James raked his fingers through his curly mane as he eyed Shandy. His thoughts worked double-time to concoct another excuse to be intimate with her. They'd grown closer over the past four years of dating, but something was missing in their relationship and he couldn't put his finger on it. He knew any man would gladly trade places with him. Shandy had become his business partner first, then his lover. She'd moved in with him over a year ago and went to work making his house her own. She never uttered why, but he knew the renovation was to erase all traces of his ex-wife, Aruba.

Maybe Shan could erase traces of Aruba, but he couldn't. Of late, Aruba was all he thought about. Their divorce had ended bitterly after she pursued her friend's husband, Winston, and won hands down. Aruba waited for him to get his act together, encouraged him to work, and reassured him she'd always be there for him. She held out for ten years and then swiped back the promise of forever when she discovered he'd had an affair with Tawatha Gipson, a secretary at his former job. Tawatha's obsession graduated to insanity when she burned three of her children in a house fire to be with him. He marveled at Aruba's audacity, self-righteousness, and unwillingness to give their marriage a second chance since she crept with Winston just as he crept with Tawatha. Who was he kidding? It would have been chance number 300 after the way he'd treated her. If that wasn't enough, an out-of-wedlock daughter he produced with Tawatha, Jameshia, was still at the forefront of his mind. He always said if he had a child, he wanted to be a part of the child's life. This wasn't how it was supposed to be and he didn't know how to make things right. The few times he'd visited Aruba in Los Angeles, their son, Jeremiah, refused to talk to him. Little man had grown into a sharp, witty nine-year-old who needed him.

"So will I have to stage a mutiny for a vegetarian meal tonight?" Shandy asked, coaxing James from his thoughts of Jeremiah and past indiscretions.

"I got that taken care of already. I know how much you detest meat, Shan."

"Keep eating secretions if you like. I just want my man to be healthy."

"I'm pure meat and potatoes. Always have been, always will be."

"I'll wear you down eventually," said Shandy. *Literally and figuratively*. She wanted to know what he was thinking but was too afraid to ask. When she scooted closer to him at night in bed and rubbed his hair or his stomach, he'd turn to her, eyes still shut, and say, "I miss you, Aruba." The only thing she knew about their divorce was that Aruba cheated on him with her girlfriend's husband. She wondered why he'd miss a woman like Aruba and why, after all these years, he seemed filled with regret. The last time she broached the subject, an ugly shouting match ensued, James stormed out the house, and he spent two nights in a hotel. No way was she mentioning the subject again. She loved him so much and wanted to be the new Mrs. Dixon. This summer would be the mother of all tests because his son, Jeremiah, was coming to stay from late-May to August. Her exposure to children was babysitting her niece, Kathryn, whenever she visited Vegas and gave her twin brother, Simeon, a night on the town with his wife.

"And afterward, we can go dancing if you like," said James.

"What did you say?" asked Shandy.

"I said after the banquet, we can go dancing if you like."

"Or we can come home and make passionate love until the sun comes up."

"Is that all I am to you?" joked James.

"Of course not. That's one of many things I like about you, James Dixon."

Shandy twirled around in her teal and black floor-length dress. She'd had her shoulder-length hair pulled back in a bun and her makeup done at the same studio she'd frequented since meeting James. Maybe James would find the look appealing enough tonight. She always looked good on his arm; lately, she had found it hard to captivate him behind closed doors.

Tonight has to be different. I can't take this pain much longer.